POWER PLAY

L.A. PHANTOMS, BOOK ONE

KAT MIZERA

PROLOGUE

G *abe*

Bringing the tumbler of bourbon to my lips, I stared out at nothing. The rows of whiskey bottles on the mirrored shelves of the bar all blurred into one another as I downed my drink and motioned for the bartender to bring me another.

I was a moody bastard on the best of days, and this hadn't been a good day.

Thinking back, I hadn't had a good day in a long fucking time.

The meeting earlier today with my attorney and ex-wife number three had been a disaster, and it was probably going to take a lot more than bourbon to make me feel better. Hopefully, no one would recognize me as I attempted to drink myself into oblivion.

I felt the woman approaching before I saw or heard her, and I kept my head down, hoping she'd keep walking. I enjoyed the ladies, probably a little too much, but I wasn't in the mood tonight.

Stiletto-clad feet topped by shapely calves paused next to me and a familiar soft and well-modulated voice asked the bartender for Four Roses bourbon with one ice cube.

Oh, fuck no.

I couldn't deal with two ex-wives in one day.

Especially not this one.

"I know you see me, Gabe." Ex-wife number one sank onto the barstool next to mine.

What the hell was she doing in Fort Lauderdale?

"Not in the mood, Harper," I said gruffly, refusing to look at her.

"You're never in the mood," she said. "But you've been ignoring my messages, so I had to come find you."

"Well, you found me. Now get lost."

"Surlier than ever, I see." She nudged me, something she'd done a lot when we'd been married. But we weren't married anymore, and I didn't like being nudged.

"What do you want?" I asked, lifting my glass to take another sip.

"You."

I laughed, but it was without humor. "I doubt that's true. Once upon a time, you couldn't file those divorce papers fast enough."

"Our marriage was over," she said quietly. "But that was personal. This is business."

I finally looked up, meeting her gaze with a frown. "What business could we possibly have? If you're looking for some kind of delayed payout, you're going to have to get in line because I don't have anything left after today."

She looked genuinely confused, frowning back at me. "Why? What happened today?"

"Doesn't matter. Just tell me what you want and let me drink in peace."

"I wanted to give you a head's up about what's coming now that the season is over."

"What the hell are you talking about?"

"I'm taking over the team."

It took a few seconds for her words to sink in, and I had to admit, she'd momentarily shocked me. "What?"

"Edward left me the team in his will. The Phantoms. His sons are fighting me for it, but they're going to lose. After we see the judge next week, I'm taking over. Starting immediately."

"You're going to run a professional hockey team?" I stared at her for a beat. Then I burst out laughing.

"Stop it." She glared at me. "I know it's second nature to you, but could you at least *try* not to be an asshole?"

I downed the rest of my drink, motioned to the bartender to hit me with another, and then looked at her. "Fine. I'll do my best not to be an asshole. But seriously, how the fuck are you going to run a hockey team? When we were together you were just beginning to understand icing, much less the intricacies of the business end."

"I understand a lot more than you think these days. I've spent the last five years learning from Edward, even as those idiot sons of his tried to run it to the ground. But that's done now. I refuse to sit back and let them fuck it up any longer, so I'm stepping in. It'll be big sports news soon, which is why I thought I'd give you a head's up."

Edward was Edward Barrowman, her billionaire late husband and the owner of the L.A. Phantoms hockey team. He'd been a shrewd businessman before he'd succumbed to cancer.

I had so many questions, but now a lot of rumors I'd been hearing made sense. I usually ignored that kind of shit, and I still didn't know what any of this had to do with me, so I picked up my drink and took a slow, deliberate sip. I kept my eyes on hers over the rim of the tumbler I was drinking from. "What do you want from me? Advice?"

"Don't be ridiculous." She took a delicate, lady-like sip of her own drink.

I didn't miss the irony of the fact we were both drinking Four Roses bourbon. The only difference was I didn't take an ice cube in mine. I'd taught her to drink bourbon back when her twenty-one-year-old self had wrinkled her nose in distaste; that didn't seem to be the case anymore.

"I'm going to bring you in as our starting goalie, and I wanted to make sure you were on board," she said after a moment.

"Why the hell would I want to move to L.A.?" I asked. "It's expensive as fuck, and I'm broke."

She furrowed her brow. "That's the second time you've said that. Your salaries over the years are public record, so I know you've been making good money. You pick up a gambling habit or something?"

"No." I looked away, figuring there was no reason to hide anything. She had the money and resources to find out whatever she wanted to know. "There was a fucking loophole in the prenup I had Brittany sign, and instead of walking away with nothing but gifts and marital assets, she's trying to get half of everything that isn't in Brandy's name."

Her face momentarily tightened at the mention of my eight-year-old daughter. The emotion disappeared as quickly as it had come as she asked, "You can't fight it?"

"I've already wasted nearly ten grand fighting it. At this point, it's moot. So, if you're looking for some kind of payout, half of everything is probably going to Brittany, most of the rest goes to Brandy and her mom, which leaves me with just enough to survive."

"Trust me, I have plenty of money. That's not what I'm after."

"Then what?"

"I already told you—you."

I rolled my eyes. "Unless you'd like to go upstairs and suck my dick, I can't think of anything else you'd need me for."

"Business, Gabe," she continued, as if I hadn't just asked her to give me a blowjob. "Focus. In fact, I think I've come up with more than fair terms." She started to pull something out of her purse.

"I'm not interested in moving again, Harper," I said, pushing her hand and whatever was in it back into her bag. "I like it here. And I'm tired. I'm getting close to retirement."

"You don't really have a choice," she replied. "I came here as a courtesy. It's essentially a done deal. This was worked out ahead of time, before Edward passed."

I suddenly got a bad feeling in the pit of my stomach. "What are you talking about?"

"Remy Knight was a friend of Edward's," she said. "They came up with this plan before he died. I'm waiting for Remy to decide who he wants for you, and then we're making the trade."

I stared at her. "Are you fucking kidding me?"

"This is how it works. You know that."

I shook my head in frustration. "God dammit. You're trying to manipulate me. *Again.* You did it when we were married, and you're still at it now."

"I never manipulated you when we were married," she snapped, her eyes flashing angrily. "And like I keep saying—this is *business.*"

There she was.

Sexy, pissed-off Harper.

This was my favorite version of her.

Other than the version when she was on her knees with my dick in her mouth.

"Jesus fucking Christ. My life is already a shit show, and now you're going to flush me right down the God damn toilet." I downed my drink and motioned for another, making a mental note that I'd have to get an Uber since this was going to be drink number four.

"It'll be good for you," she said quietly. "Like I told you, I plan to be generous. Money won't be a problem."

"L.A. is ten times as expensive as Fort Lauderdale," I replied. "You planning to pay me twenty million?"

She didn't bat an eyelash. "No, but you can even live in my guest house if finances are an issue."

"Look, if this is already a done deal, you might as well do whatever you're going to do. I don't give a fuck. It's not like you ever gave a shit about anyone but yourself anyway."

"That's not fair," she said, her cheeks turning pink. "We were young when we were together. You were just as selfish as I was. Don't even pretend you tried to make our marriage work."

"At least I didn't walk away the second things got tough."

"You expected me to stay after the shit you did?" she demanded. "You treated me like a goddamn afterthought. And when I caught you—"

"That why you married a fucking grandpa?" I interrupted snidely. "Someone too old and tired to pay attention to anyone but you?"

"Edward was a wonderful man," she said under her breath. "And an even better husband. You don't know a damn thing about him. Or me anymore, for that matter."

"Don't want to, either." I made a shooing motion. "So now that you've said what you wanted to say, you should get going."

She sighed, blowing out an obviously exasperated breath. "Dammit, Gabe. Does it always have to be like this? I need you in L.A. This will be good for both of us."

"How, exactly, is me moving to yet another team after less than a year, good for me?"

"Money. The opportunity to make a difference in a very beaten-down locker room. A chance to be a contender once more before you retire."

"Please." I tipped my head back, letting a big gulp of bourbon burn its way down my throat. "If I was going to be a contender, it would be here in Florida. The Phantoms are years away from that, even if you start rebuilding right now."

"I *am* rebuilding, and we're going to get there within three years," she said firmly. "I have a plan. I'd like it if you were on board, but as I said, this is happening whether you are or not."

I shrugged. "Do what you have to do, Harper, but don't be surprised when I retire."

She downed the rest of her drink and set it on the bar with a thump. Then she got to her feet and glared at me, hands on her hips. "You know damn well you're not going anywhere. Especially not if you're as broke as you say you are."

Well, she had me there.

Not that I'd admit it.

I liked having this opportunity to look at her, though. I'd almost forgotten how pretty she was with her long-lashed, blue eyes and dimples. Her dark hair was sleek and straight now, not wild and curly like it had been when we'd been together, and I had to admit both looks suited her.

She still had a fantastic rack, the swell of the tops of her breasts peeking out from the somewhat demure tank top she wore beneath her blazer. Long legs were mostly covered by a knee-length skirt, but I knew exactly what those legs looked like. I distinctly remembered what they felt like wrapped around my head too.

Fuck.

"I don't want to move again." I made sure to avert my gaze. "If you force my hand, I'll retire."

"Gabe." She drummed her fingers on the bar.

"You can't manipulate people until they bend to your will," I said. "Your pretty face will only go so far in that regard. You're what, thirty-five now?"

"Why can't you ever be nice about anything?" she asked angrily. "I was planning to offer you a lot of money, and fringe benefits to—"

"Fringe benefits?" I arched my brows. "Like the kind you used to get your rich sugar daddy?"

I knew that was going to piss her off, but I didn't expect the slap that came out of nowhere.

Damn, she'd learned to pack a punch over the years. So to speak. It wasn't the first time she'd slapped me, but it was definitely the hardest.

I laughed, though. "That all you got?"

"Don't you dare," she said, her eyes blazing. "Don't you dare talk to me like one of your little puck bunnies."

"Truth hurts, don't it, sweetheart?"

"Fuck you."

"No thanks."

We glared at each other in silence.

"What do you want?" Her voice came out as a low, steely growl. "What?"

"What. Do. You. Want." Her chest seemed to be rising and

falling with the exertion of holding back since she probably wanted to smack me again.

"Lots of things." I decided to fuck with her.

It wasn't like I had anything to lose.

And it was kind of fun to get her all riled up.

"Just tell me what it's going to take to get you to L.A. And no, I can't pay you twenty million, so don't go there. Be reasonable."

I shrugged. "You serious? You'll do *anything* within reason?"

"Yes." She practically gritted her teeth as she waited, probably assuming I was going to say something crass. So, I went in a completely different direction.

"Get Brittany to back off."

"What?" I'd caught her off-guard with that one because she looked completely blank.

"Ex-wife number three, the one trying to take half of everything."

"I thought it was a done deal."

"Not yet, but very soon."

"And what do you want me to do about it?" she demanded.

I shrugged, pulling some cash out of my wallet and putting it on the bar. "Get her to back off. I'm sure you can afford a private detective or a fancy lawyer or whatever you billionaires do to figure shit out."

"You're serious."

"As a heart attack."

She glared at me. "You've been nothing but a pain in my ass since the day I laid eyes on you."

"Ditto, sweetheart."

"How the hell do you expect me to do that?"

"Not my problem. You want me to move to L.A. in the off-season? Make it happen."

Then I turned and walked out of the bar.

1

H*arper*

MOST OF OUR LIVES, we've always been warned to "be careful what you wish for." For the first time, I understood what that meant. All I'd wanted for over a year now was to take ownership of the L.A. Phantoms. Edward's sons had taken me to court, fighting the will and everything they could think of, and I'd remained steadfast in my determination to abide by Edward's wishes.

I'd finally won.

The judge had told Eddie and Tim to stop being pains in the asses and to take their billion-dollar inheritance and stop wasting the court's time.

The Phantoms were mine.

I owned a professional hockey team.

And the entire hockey world hated me.

Management. The players. Even the staff.

And they were going to hate me even more once the season officially came to an end, and I cleaned house.

This was not a job for the faint of heart.

But I'd been through enough in my almost thirty-six years on earth to be up to the challenge.

One divorce, three failed rounds of IVF, and my second husband's long battle with cancer had left me geared up and primed for the fight of my life.

"Are you sure you want to do this?" Sloane Hajek, my assistant and former daughter-in-law, asked for the dozenth time.

"I don't have a choice," I told her as the limo wove through Manhattan traffic.

This was our second meeting with the league's higher-ups, and it had been a long, grueling two days of meetings.

But I was done and about to head home to Los Angeles.

"I need to get home," Sloane said quietly. "Johan and I are going to Slovakia to see his family."

"I know." I smiled over at her. "I'll be fine."

"You need another assistant. Someone local."

"I know that too, but until I can find someone I trust, you'll have to do."

She laughed. "Thanks a lot."

"As long as you're available online, I'll handle the rest."

"You can't do it all, Harper. You're drowning in work as it is, and based on the backlash you're already seeing, it's going to be a long off-season."

"I'm heading to the entry draft in Vegas at the end of the month, then I'll focus on the back-office changes. Henrik and Victor are going with me to Vegas, so I won't be alone." Henrik Vanek was my new head coach. He and his fiancée were in the process of moving to L.A. this month, and I hoped to have a handful of trusted colleagues in my corner in the near future.

I would have preferred to fire my general manager immediately. Howie Fornier was a womanizer, an asshole, and didn't share my vision for the team, but I didn't have a replacement yet, and the truth was I couldn't go into the draft without help. The Phantoms would have the first overall pick, since we'd finished dead last in the standings this past season. There was no doubt who I wanted for that first pick, but the waters got murky after that. So I needed Howie whether I liked him or not.

"Call Dom," Sloane said as we parted ways at the airport.

She'd read my mind.

Although I didn't yet know if I would be able to coax him to come to L.A., I knew who I wanted to be the new general. Dom Gianni had been a problematic player early in his career, with a temper both on and off the ice. Until his coach from college brought him to Las Vegas and helped him turn his life around. He was retired now, with a wife and a couple of kids. He'd been a scout for a couple of seasons, but rumor had it he didn't like being away from his family as often as the job required, so he'd quit.

He wouldn't need to be on the road that much as my GM, but from what I'd heard, he and his wife liked their life in Vegas and had a big support system. It would take some bargaining on my part to get him on board, so I planned to make him my first call tomorrow.

As soon as I was settled on the plane, I opened my laptop and found an email from my OBGYN.

"...if you're serious about trying artificial insemination, we should start the process soon. Did you decide on a donor yet? I know you don't want to hear this, but you're not getting any younger and with your history, we may have to try several times. I think you'll have better success with a younger donor. Edward just didn't have a high enough sperm count..."

I didn't care about the other details, so I closed the email program and stared out at nothing, oblivious to everything going on around me.

I'd made the decision to have a baby on my own but pulling the trigger was harder than I'd thought it would be.

Choosing a random donor from a sperm bank seemed...*icky*. There was no other way to describe it.

A literal stranger knocking me up.

Without the fun of one-night stand sex.

I'd been through this before, so I knew what was ahead, and

this time there wouldn't be my kind, loving husband holding my hand. Cheering me on. Crying with me when it didn't work.

Dealing with all of that alone, while simultaneously taking over the team and handling the shit storm that was undoubtedly coming my way once I started firing people, would be intense. Trading players. Creating a whole new internal vibe. It was going to be a lot. The timing honestly couldn't have been worse.

I'd just taken over the team in March.

I was turning thirty-six in July.

Pre-season would start in September.

I didn't want to wait another year.

But I might have to.

I didn't see any other choice.

AFTER A GOOD NIGHT'S SLEEP, forty-five minutes of yoga, and two cups of my favorite coffee, I felt better. Like I could take on the world.

The first order of business was Dom Gianni.

So I called him.

"Dom, this is Harper Barrowman."

"Hey, Harper." He sounded friendly but cautious. "My agent told me you'd be calling."

"Yes." I paused, taking a figurative deep breath and putting my business cap on. "I have a proposition for you and wondered if you'd have time to discuss it with me."

He hesitated. "I'm willing to listen to anything, but I can't make any promises."

"I had a whole speech planned," I admitted, suddenly switching tactics. "But my gut tells me you'd prefer me to shoot straight."

He chuckled. "Yeah, I don't like game-playing unless I'm on the ice."

"I'd like to bring you on board as my General Manager."

I could all but see his eyes widen and feel his sharp intake of breath.

I'd caught him by surprise.

Good.

"I wanted to bring you and your wife to L.A. to discuss the possibilities and present an offer."

"If you want both my wife and me to come, you'll need to wait a week. This is the last week of school, and my wife is room mom. She's got Field Day and the class party and while I don't organize it, my presence is both demanded and required. According to the kids."

I grimaced.

I needed him now.

Yesterday.

But if I gave him an ultimatum, I already knew his family would win.

"I can wait," I replied smoothly, "but then I need to know if it's at least possible. If you'd consider relocating your entire life to move to Los Angeles. I have several other people in mind, but I won't pretend that you're not at the top of my list."

He hesitated again. "Can I ask you why? Why me? I don't have GM experience."

"No, but you have player experience and scout experience. The prospects you brought to the Sidewinders were top-notch, telling me you have an eye for talent and visions for a team. I also wanted to bring younger men into the organization, instead of the white-hair club that seems to rule the league. It's time for a change of the status quo, and I'm not the only owner who feels this way. Money is money, and if you can afford a team, you can buy one. But management, coaching, and all the rest of it, it's time for changes. More women, more people of color, and a younger demographic."

"So you're planning to clean house." There was no censure in his voice as he said it.

"Yes." Lying would be ridiculous if I wanted him to become my right arm. "If you take the job, you and I will work closely together.

That's part of the reason I want to meet your wife and build a relationship with her as well. No matter how forward-thinking I am, I know what the optics could be, so I want to make sure she's on board as well."

"Molly is a straightshooter as well," he said with a laugh. "I think you two will get along."

"Excellent. So, you're interested."

"When I heard you were going to call, I'd already planned to listen to your offer, which I was assuming would be either another scouting position or an assistant coach, and give you a polite no. But this is something I wasn't expecting, so yes. I'm interested. I need more details, and Molly and I have to sit down and think about the logistics for the kids. Brian just turned eleven and Alyssa will be ten in December. They have a lot going on, including sports. They both play hockey, Bryan swims in the summer, and Alyssa takes ballet as well."

"If you're seriously considering the position, I have a whole package prepared. Salary, bonuses, real estate, schools, and more. I want you to *want* to be here. It benefits no one if you and/or your family is miserable."

"Exactly. Can you send me salary information? There's no point in wasting either of our time if the move to L.A. won't work for us financially."

"Absolutely. Give me your email and I'll send you the basics."

"And I'll see you next week."

"Tell me your availability and I'll arrange the fights. Would you rather fly in and out in a day or spend the night?"

"Let me talk to Molly and I'll get back to you."

"Perfect. Thank you for your time, Dom."

"You're welcome. I'm looking forward to meeting you."

"As am I." Movement on the video screen covering my front door made me frown.

Oh, shit.

I had a visitor.

Gabe.

Christ.

"I'll, uh, I'll talk to you soon," I said quickly. "Take care, Dom."

I disconnected and stuffed my phone in the back pocket of my jeans. I hadn't planned on seeing anyone today, so I was dressed down, with my hair in a ponytail and no makeup, which always made me feel half-naked.

What the hell was Gabe doing here?

He rang the bell again and I breathed in deeply.

On the rare occasion we saw each other, we were like oil and water.

I padded to the front door, wishing I at least had shoes on.

For some reason my bare feet left me feeling more vulnerable than usual.

Of course, the big, good-looking jerk had always made me feel vulnerable.

I opened the door with what I hoped was a friendly smile. "Gabe. What are you doing here?"

His lips quirked up in a cocky smile. "Moving in."

2

———————

G *abe*

I ALMOST LAUGHED at the look on her face.

"Ex-excuse me?" She blinked, squinting in the bright sunlight.

"You said I could live in your guest house this season."

"Yes, but... you've been living in the team apartment."

"Yeah, but I gave it up at the end of the season when I went on vacation. That's why I stored my stuff here. Now I'm back and ready to move in."

I couldn't tell what was going through her mind, but myriad emotions flitted across her face.

"I, uh, I'd forgotten," she said at last.

"That was part of the deal," I reminded her.

"The deal was me getting Brittany off your back," she said. "Which I did."

"And living with you for a season, until I decide if I'm going to retire or not."

"I thought by getting Brittany to back off, your financial issues went away, and you could get your own place."

I shrugged. "What you thought and what you said are two different things."

She let out a frustrated huff. "Jesus Christ, Gabe. Do you know what it's going to look like with you living here?"

"Like two exes who ended on good terms and are now working together?" I suggested sarcastically, arching my brows.

She frowned at me.

"Do you think I could come in for a minute? Or should we continue to stand in the doorway debating it all afternoon?"

She hesitated but then stepped back. "Fine. Come in."

I stepped inside and followed her through a bright living room with floor-to-ceiling windows and expensive flooring. She'd done well for herself. Better than me, and my body took a beating every day. Which was why I hadn't played since I'd been in L.A. A bad hit left me with yet another concussion, so the doctors had been strict about me not getting back on the ice until they deemed me ready.

"Shoes off," she called over her shoulder.

I glanced down at my sneaker-clad feet and then slipped them off.

She led me into the kitchen and motioned to one of the stools by the island. "Have a seat. Are you hungry?"

She was nothing if not a good hostess.

"No, I only have a few minutes." I looked around, taking in her open laptop and the piles of papers everywhere. The Harper I'd been married to a decade ago never would have left such a mess. She'd changed more than I'd thought in the years we'd been apart.

"So." She lifted a coffee mug to her lips and took a sip, studying me carefully. "You want to live in my guest house."

"I mean, I'm happy to live here in the main house, but I figure that might get a little uncomfortable for us, with one or both of us running around half-naked all the time. Well, for you more than me, probably."

Her cheeks turned red, but her eyes flashed with annoyance. "Don't do that, Gabe. You're not going to come into my home, asking to live here, and be an obnoxious ass."

Banter with Harper was always a blast, but I was tired and just wanted to get settled, whether it was here or somewhere else. Technically, I could afford to rent an apartment or condo, but she *had* promised I could live in her guest house. So why wouldn't I take her up on it?

"Look, we had a deal," I said. "Is it really that big of a deal for you to let me live in the guest house?"

She sighed, rubbing her temples. "No. I guess not. I just…"

"What?" I asked. "Just say it. You know I'm not actually going to come into the main house naked."

"The rumor mill," she said finally. "It's going to go nuts. No matter how we handle it, the team is going to give you shit about living with your ex-wife. You went straight to the injured reserve when you got here, so you haven't had a chance to play, but I can only imagine what they're saying about me in the locker room."

"You knew that was going to happen," I said quietly. "Right? There's no universe where you take over a pro hockey team—with your looks and those tits—and expect to be taken seriously."

She bristled. "You don't get to talk to me like that, Gabe."

"Hey." I held up my hands in a conciliatory gesture. "I'm not saying I agree with it, but people who don't know you are going to take one look at you and make assumptions. There's no way around it. Edward was, what? Twenty-five years older than you?"

She looked away. "Thirty-two."

"Jesus. Well, you can get prissy all you want, but from the outside looking in, a woman in her late twenties marrying a guy in his sixties is only about one thing."

She sighed. "Money."

"Money for you, sex and/or a midlife crisis for him."

"Is that what people are saying?"

"Of course." I said it matter-of-factly, but the truth was, I'd heard much worse things. About her, about them, and about someone like her taking over the new team. She didn't have an uphill battle; she had a trek up the side of a mountain at a ninety-degree angle.

"Shit."

The sound of footsteps made her turn just as a voice called out, "Dad? I'm hungry!"

"Brandy." I quickly got up, turning to my nine-year-old daughter. "I told you to wait in the car."

"I'm *hungry*," she reiterated emphatically.

"I know. We'll stop for food on the way to Anaheim. Can you just wait outside?"

"Hi, I'm Brandy." She ignored me and held out her hand to Harper.

My daughter was way too much like her mother, with selective hearing sometimes.

"Hello, Brandy. I'm Harper. It's nice to meet you." Harper seemed startled but smiled as she shook her hand. "If you're hungry, I can make you a sandwich."

"No, it's not—" I began.

"Yes, please!" Brandy said at the same time.

Fuck.

I hadn't wanted them to meet like this.

Honestly, I hadn't wanted them to meet at all.

But I'd needed to know whether or not I had a place to live before we left for our mini vacation.

"I can make grilled cheese, peanut butter and jelly, or ham and..." Harper rummaged in a drawer in the refrigerator. "Either American or Swiss."

Brandy wrinkled her nose. "I'm allergic to peanuts and I don't like Swiss cheese."

"Grilled cheese it is!" Harper didn't seem at all put out as she got a loaf of bread out of a cabinet.

"Harper, you don't have to do that," I said, giving my daughter the stink eye.

She was oblivious though, happily perching on the stool next to mine.

"It's no problem," Harper replied, her back to me.

"Your house is pretty!" Brandy said, looking around. "Is this where you're going to live, Daddy?"

"I don't—" I began.

"He'll be living in the house out there," Harper interjected, motioning to the guest house, which we could see through the kitchen windows.

"Oh!" Brandy's eyes widened. "It's like a playhouse. It's so cute!"

"It's only one bedroom," Harper said, glancing at me.

I nodded. "I know. Brandy won't be here very often, and when she comes, we'll be doing stuff like going to Disney. Which is what we're doing today. We'll be gone the next three days, then two days in San Diego. We'll come back here for one night before I fly her home."

"I'm little," Brandy said, grinning. "I can sleep on the couch."

"I'm going to buy a pull-out couch for next time," I told her. "But I think we'll stay at a hotel when we get back. The guest house is a mess with all my crap everywhere and there's no food."

Brandy giggled. "You never have food when I come visit."

I playfully rolled my eyes at her. "Well, you only eat like, three things, so does it matter?"

"Five things," she said primly. "Steak, chicken nuggets, spaghetti, pizza, and mac and cheese."

"And grilled cheese," Harper pointed out. "So that's six things."

The two of them laughed like old friends.

"Yeah, yeah." I ruffled her hair.

I'd never wanted to be a dad, but once my ex had gotten pregnant, I'd fallen in love with the little blob on the ultrasound screen. The fact that her mother and I had divorced when she was just a year old hadn't deterred me, and I'd done my best to be present in her life. It wasn't easy, with me living in another state and on the road during hockey season, but I tried to be there for her in the off-season. Luckily, her mother, Tricia, looked forward to getting a break so she didn't prevent me from taking her on trips or spending time with her.

"Here you go." Harper put a plate in front of Brandy with a sandwich and some kind of chips that didn't look familiar to me.

"What are those?" Brandy asked, wrinkling her nose.

"How about you try them before you make a face?" Harper responded without missing a beat.

"Okay." Brand held up the funny-looking chip, inspecting it before taking a tentative bite. She chewed thoughtfully. "It's a little sweet, but salty too."

"They're sweet potato chips," Harper said. "They're my favorite."

"They're okay." Brandy nodded, taking a bite of her grilled cheese.

"What do you say?" I prodded her gently.

"Thank you!" She grinned up at Harper, who smiled back.

I hadn't planned on the two of them meeting, and certainly not like this, but it seemed to be going okay. I'd worried how Harper would react since my stance on having kids was one of the things that had come between us. I'd assumed she would be furious, and maybe she was, but even so, she would never take it out on Brandy. She wasn't like that. She annoyed the crap out of me, but she wouldn't be mean to a kid.

"You're welcome." Harper washed her hands and dug something out of a drawer. "These are the keys to the guest house and a remote for the garage, if you want to use it. I only use one of the three spaces."

"Thank you." I nodded. "I appreciate this, Harper. This really helps me out." I glanced at Brandy. "I'll, uh, explain more after I get back."

"Don't worry about it." She looked at something on her phone. "Well, I have a call in a few minutes. You guys are welcome to finish eating or whatever."

"Thanks." I nodded. "I'll see you when I get back."

"Have fun at Disney!" Harper said to Brandy.

"Thank you." Brandy waved as Harper left the room.

I followed her retreating figure with my eyes, taking in the curve of her ass, long slender legs, and the way her hair moved as she walked.

We hadn't been great together when we were married, but she was still the most beautiful woman I knew.

"All right, finish eating and then make sure you wash your dish," I told Brandy.

"I will." Brandy inhaled the last of her sandwich, stuffed the last few chips in her mouth. Then she got up and went over to the sink.

Leaning against the counter, I watched as she turned on the water and started washing the dish. Tricia was doing a good job with her. Sometimes I wished I could be around more, but it was probably better that I wasn't. I loved her, and made sure she had everything she needed, but I often wondered if I was a good dad since I only really saw her in the off-season.

As I waited for Brandy to finish washing the dish, I glanced at the papers strewn across the island. I wasn't trying to be nosy, but one folder in particular got my attention.

#Donor 67891

Donor?

Was Harper sick?

Was this something left over from her husband's illness?

Curiosity won out and I couldn't help but open the file.

The information in front of me was confusing.

Eyes: Blue

Hair: Dark blond

Height: 6'2"

Weight: 195 lbs.

Ethnicity: Polish, Slovak

What the hell was I reading?

I skimmed the rest of the sheet and suddenly it clicked.

Holy fucking shit.

Harper was looking for a sperm donor.

3

———————

H*arper*

MEETING GABE'S daughter had been jarring. I had known she existed, of course, but seeing a petite little female version of him in person had been unexpected. She looked just like him with dark hair and silver-gray eyes. They had the same smile too, despite her missing a few teeth. Well, that was the same too since I knew he was missing his two front teeth as well. He simply wore a bridge, from what I remembered.

God, it seemed like a million years ago that we'd been married.

We'd been so in love once upon a time.

Until everything fell apart.

Losing him had been so hard.

When I'd met Edward, he'd soothed my battered heart, showing me a gentleness I'd never experienced before. He'd been sixty-one to my twenty-nine, but we'd clicked. He'd made me feel safe and cherished, something I'd never gotten from Gabe. But Edward's sons hated me, my friends thought I was crazy, and his friends had tolerated me like an annoying pet, but we'd been happy. Even with the failed artificial insemination attempts and his cancer diagnosis, we'd been a team.

Then the cancer came back, terminal the second time, and I'd lost him within a year.

It still didn't feel real sometimes.

"Hello, Harper. How are you?" Henrik's voice brought me out of my reverie, and I forced myself to focus.

"Hey, Henrik. How's the move going?"

"I think we're finally settled," he replied.

"So, you're good to go to Vegas in two weeks?"

"Absolutely."

"I also wanted your opinion on something."

"Sure."

"What do you think about Dom Gianni for GM?"

"That's an interesting choice. I don't know him personally, just by reputation, but Toli Petrov talks about him as one of his best friends, so I'm sure we'll get along. As far as his skill set for being a GM, I have no way of knowing that, but I trust your judgment."

"I think he's perfect for the job," I said. "I just want to make sure you two don't have any issues from when you were playing and scouting. I should have asked you before I spoke to him, but I was anxious to get the ball rolling."

"No problem at all. Our paths never crossed."

"Great. He and his wife are coming to town next week and I'm going to do a formal interview. Assuming things go well, I'll invite them to dinner. If that happens, I'd like you and Autumn to join us. Is that possible?"

"Sure. I'm looking forward to meeting him."

"Thanks. I'll text you details once I know them."

"Anything I can do to help."

"I appreciate that. And let me know if you need anything." I paused. "Have you filed for full custody yet?" He and his fiancée were planning to get custody of his eight-year-old twin boys.

"Yes. Last week. My ex is pissed. The boys are with her now and she won't even return my texts. I'm sure it's going to be a battle."

"I'm sorry. I hope it's not too much of a shit show. I know first-hand how court cases can be."

"My attorney says it may be difficult to take them from her, especially since Autumn and I aren't married yet, but we're working on that."

"If she doesn't want the whole big wedding, Vegas is the perfect place to do it," I said, chuckling.

"That's what we're debating. She had a huge wedding planned when she was engaged to her ex, and it put a bad taste in her mouth. I don't want her to give up her dream wedding because it would be more convenient for my custody battle, you know? So we're batting around some different ideas."

"Absolutely. But if she loves you, and I'm sure she does, she's going to want something that works for both of you."

"Yeah. For sure. That's what we've been discussing. In the meantime, I'm going to emphasize the fact that Lydia's boyfriend doesn't like the kids, how her new job takes her out of the country regularly, and how much more freedom she'll gain if she lets me have primary custody."

"I hope it works out," I said gently. "I'm sure it's been stressful."

"We'll get through it."

"I'll be in touch soon. We'll need to meet before Vegas."

"Just let me know."

"Take care."

We disconnected and I wandered back to the kitchen, grateful that Gabe and Brandy were gone. She was a sweet kid, but I needed to keep my distance from him. We always wound up arguing, so it was best to just keep things casual. Even if he was going to be living practically on top of me.

I'd have to set some boundaries.

He and his daughter couldn't just wander in and out of the kitchen whenever they felt like it.

He had to stay in the guest house and pretend like I wasn't even here, barring emergencies.

It would simply be easier that way.

As I walked into the kitchen, I noticed that one of them had washed the dish her sandwich had been on.

That was when I spied the napkin sitting on top of one of my files, immediately recognizing Gabe's scribbled handwriting.

Thanks for making Brandy lunch. Appreciate it. Gabe

It shouldn't have been a big deal.

Except it was sitting on top of one of the files I'd received from the sperm bank.

Shit.

There was no doubt in my mind Gabe had seen it.

It wasn't any of his business, and I didn't care what people thought of me, but it was still a little weird. It reeked of desperation, as if I couldn't find a man to have a baby with.

I guess that was somewhat true.

Dating had always been hard for me.

Yes, I was attractive and had no problem getting men to pay attention to me, but I'd only loved two men in my life, and everyone else paled by comparison. Gabe had been rough and immature and a terrible husband, but he was also funny, so good-looking it almost hurt to look at him, a successful professional athlete, and an incredible lover. He had many faults, but I wasn't perfect either, so I didn't put all the blame on him. Loving him had been easy. It was just the reality of our disparate lives that had become a problem. Not to mention how much he'd loved to party.

And now we were going to live together again.

I nearly rolled my eyes at the irony.

Then there had been Edward.

He'd been handsome for someone in his sixties, kind, generous, and the most attentive man I'd ever known. He liked to shower me with gifts, but he also enjoyed spending time with me. Playing chess, talking about sports and business and current events. We'd had a lot of fun together.

Our sex life had been fine until he'd gotten sick, but I hadn't held that against him. I would have been happy, even without sex, if he'd lived because he'd been an amazing human being.

Unfortunately, I'd lost both men I'd loved, and the handful of dates I'd gone on since Edward's death left me convinced I was better off alone. I'd found love twice in my life, which was more than most people, so I harbored no illusions that I'd find it again. My new career and hopefully a baby in the next couple of years would be plenty.

I didn't need anything else.

~

DONOR #68966 sounded boring even on paper, and my eyes blurred as I scanned the information that had been sent to me. So many nameless, faceless men. It was nothing but statistics. Hair color, eye color, height, and weight. There were other variables, like blood type and such, but mostly it boiled down to looks. Did I want a man with blue eyes like mine, maximizing my chances of having a blue-eyed child? Did it matter if he was six-one or six-five?

I wanted a baby so badly, but the more I looked through the papers, the less enthused I was about doing it this way. I had a handful of male friends who probably would have been willing to donate their sperm to my cause, but how did you ask someone to give you a child and not be part of its life?

I didn't like to think about the past, or my useless mother, but I couldn't help it sometimes. Especially lately. I already had a good idea of all the things I never wanted to do in that regard. The bigger question these days, in the wee hours of the morning or when I was in the shower, was what kind of mother I *did* want to be.

My mother hadn't been able to care for me and one day when I was ten, she simply decided I was too much. I'd come home from school to find a social worker waiting for me, and my life had never been the same.

I'd never been the same.

I wanted to be there for my child, no matter what, but there were a lot of things to consider.

How would I handle the time constraints of being a hands-on

hockey team owner with a child who needed and deserved my attention? When they were sick or had trouble with homework or a baseball game? My mother had never bothered to do any of that, so I had no experience with it, but I assumed it was time-consuming. And I wouldn't have a lot of that going forward.

I closed the files and stuffed them into my junk drawer.

As much as I didn't want to put off trying to get pregnant, I needed one season to find my footing as the new owner and, at least right now, acting president of the L.A. Phantoms. There was no time for pregnancy or a newborn. It just wouldn't be smart. There were only so many obstacles I could tackle at once, and the Phantoms were a big one.

In addition, I would have to be more careful with what I left lying around in the future. I planned to tell Gabe he couldn't come in without knocking, but I still wanted to be mindful of things left out in the open. I had contracts and other things related to the team he didn't need to see either. For the dozenth time, I wondered why I'd agreed to let him live here.

If I was honest, it probably had to do with keeping him in my corner.

That was a little more self-serving than I'd planned, but if I had something to hold over his head—like kicking him out— maybe he'd do exactly what I hoped he would in the locker room: Defend me. Keep the guys from talking shit. Or at least keep them from being overly crude. It was a pro sports locker room. Crude was part of their DNA. But there were limits. And I needed Gabe to be that gatekeeper.

His leadership abilities and years in the league were the main reason I'd brought him here. He was a great goalie, elite back in the day, and young players looked up to him. My hope was that in addition to what he'd bring to the team in net, he'd also be good for morale. He was at the end of his career, turning thirty-seven soon, so if I was only interested in skill, there were quite a few goalies that were better. However, there weren't any that had his experience and skill that I had an in with, though.

So, if there was a slight loss of privacy by having him live here for the season, I'd deal with it. The good far outweighed the bad.

At least, that was the plan.

Not that Gabe played by anyone's rules but his own, so I'd have to keep an eye on him. He could be stubborn and self-absorbed, which meant he would be focused on whatever his priorities were instead of mine. And that made sense.

As long as there was some loyalty to me, that was all I needed.

Hopefully, our past wouldn't interfere with the present.

4

____

G _abe_

BRANDY and I had a great time visiting Disneyland and San Diego. I liked spending time with her because it had begun to occur to me that she was growing up faster than I'd anticipated. It felt like just a couple of years ago that she'd been born, but now she was walking, talking, playing softball and tennis, and was developing a huge personality. I loved her because she was my daughter, but I also liked her.

Maybe my opinion was slightly skewed since I only saw her on vacations. There was no day-to-day interaction where I had to deal with homework, report cards, or any of the other things my ex did on a daily basis.

I was lucky in that respect, which was why I never bitched about child support and always sent extra when it came time for school supplies, extracurricular activities, birthdays, and other holidays. I was aware that I didn't have to deal with the hard stuff, and I was the fun dad. Sometimes I rationalized, telling myself it was better that way, but in the back of my mind, I wondered if it would be a good idea to move to Milwaukee when I retired. That way, I'd be around more, could see her more, and could help out Tricia, my ex.

I wasn't quite ready to retire though, so for now, I had to focus on the mess that was my new home.

I'd taken Brandy home yesterday and gotten back to L.A. late last night. After a good night's sleep, I had a ton of work to do. There were boxes everywhere, the place needed a good cleaning, and I wanted to get my TV mounted on the wall ASAP. I wasn't overly fussy about my living space, but a California king bed and a big-screen TV were non-negotiable.

The place was a disaster because Harper had been using it for storage so maybe she'd be able to help with getting it clean. I was sure she had a cleaning service, so I'd be willing to pay extra for them to include me in whatever her cleaning schedule was.

I also needed groceries and to figure out if the stove worked. Harper had said it hadn't turned on the last time she'd tried it, and though I preferred to grill if I had to cook, there were always exceptions to that. I'd gotten used to being a bachelor, which meant having a fully functional kitchen.

Since it was after ten and I figured Harper would be up, I walked across the patio and peered into the kitchen. I was just about to knock on the sliding glass doors when I realized she wasn't alone.

There was a guy with her.

Shit.

My fist was in mid-air, frozen in place as I debated whether or not to knock, when the guy seemed to spot me. He said something to Harper, and she turned. Then she came over to the doors and slid them open.

"Hey, Gabe. What's up?"

"Good morning." I tried to keep my voice neutral. "I had two questions and need a favor."

"Start with the questions." She didn't appear to be in any hurry to invite me in or introduce me to her friend.

"Does the oven in the guest house work? I tried turning it on and nothing happened, but I wasn't sure if I should try to repair or buy a new one or what?"

"It's old," she admitted. "How about we buy a new one? Do you want input, or should I just make it happen?"

"I'm not super picky," I replied. "And I'm happy to pay for it."

"I'll take care of it today, and don't worry about payment. I want a working oven in there regardless."

"Okay. The other question is whether you'd be willing to have whatever cleaning service you use include me? And if they can come sooner rather than later, because the place is a mess."

"Oh. Yes, of course. I'll call today and ask if they have time to squeeze you in and get a price for your share."

"I appreciate that."

"And the favor?"

"Could I make a cup of coffee? My Keurig isn't unpacked, and I don't have any groceries. I don't think I can function without coffee."

She sighed, a look of annoyance on her face, but then she motioned me inside. "Come on in. I just made muffins."

I followed her inside, and the guy sitting at her island stood, extending his hand. "Hey, Gabe."

It took a moment for me to realize who he was.

My new head coach, who'd been an assistant coach when I'd played for the Lauderdale Knights.

"Hey, Coach." I shook his hand. "I didn't recognize you at first."

"No problem." Henrik smiled. "Harper was just telling me that you moved into her guest house."

"Yeah. I just got back from taking my daughter home to Milwaukee and realized the place is a disaster."

"Moving is a pain in the ass. Autumn and I just got settled into our new place. We're staying in corporate housing for a year before we decide if we want to buy something, but moving is never easy."

"You got that right."

"Espresso or regular American coffee?" Harper interjected.

"Regular old American," I replied. "Thank you. And black is fine."

She nodded. "Help yourself to a muffin. They're cranberry apple."

"Sounds great." I plucked one from a basket on the counter and settled on a stool next to Henrik. "So, you looking forward to being a head coach?"

"I'm looking forward to turning this team around," he replied. "We've been bottom ten the last five seasons. That stops now."

"You think you can make that happen in one season?"

He chuckled. "I think we can finish somewhere in the top twenty instead of the bottom ten, you know?"

"Hey." Harper put a cup of coffee down in front of me. "Being so bad last season gives us the opportunity for the first pick overall. If we can get Connor Brooks, he'll be a fantastic addition to help us start rebuilding."

"In with the new, out with the old," I murmured, taking a sip of coffee.

"You're not on your way out yet, are you?" Henrik asked.

I lifted one shoulder in a mini shrug. "I mean, I don't have a foot in the grave or anything, but I'm definitely in the twilight of my career."

"Hey, at least you made it into your thirties. I blew out my knee at twenty-seven." Henrik met my gaze. "I made the best of it, though."

The last thing I wanted to think about was injuries. I'd had another close call this past season, and though I'd recovered, it had been a blatant reminder that I wasn't as young as I used to be.

"You were young," I acknowledged. "But you became a scout, right?"

Henrik nodded. "Then I coached in Sweden for a few years."

"And you jumped up to head coach in three years?" I chuckled. "You lead a charmed life, Coach."

"Gabe." Harper's voice held a warning, and I rolled my eyes at her.

"I'm just busting his balls," I told her, getting up. "Anyway, thanks for the coffee and muffin. I'll bring the mug back later."

"You're welcome." She gave me a tight smile.

"If you need anything, let me know," Henrik called to me.

I paused by the sliding glass door. "You know, I could use a hand hanging my TV. I need an extra pair of hands while I screw it into the wall-mount. If you have ten minutes, that's all it'll take."

"Sure." Henrik nodded. "Let me finish my coffee and I'll come find you."

"Thank you. It's just out back." I glanced at Harper. "Thanks again for breakfast."

"You're welcome."

Our eyes locked for a moment, and I wondered what the hell the look in hers meant.

Did she still hate me for what had happened when we were married?

No, hate was probably too strong of a word.

She definitely disliked me.

But not enough to tell me I couldn't live in her guest house or turn down my request for breakfast.

For some reason, that made me feel better.

She was a ball-buster and I'd moved on a long time ago, but I still cared about her.

I heard the door slide shut behind me as I stepped onto the patio, and I couldn't help but wonder what she and Henrik were talking about.

Me?

The rest of the team?

Who she was going to fire next?

It was going to be a crazy off-season once we got past the entry draft and she could start trading players. I had a feeling there were going to be a lot of unhappy guys in the league.

Or maybe not.

Playing on the worst team in the league was undoubtedly a bummer and they'd be happy to move on. Older guys, especially the married ones with families, tended to want to stay put once their kids were in school. It couldn't always be avoided, but they'd be annoyed if they got traded simply because the new owner had something to prove.

Not that I disagreed with her decision.

She needed to shake things up because the status quo wasn't working out and the previous coach had been useless. The current GM was also useless, so I hoped she planned to get rid of him as well. I'd gotten here toward the end of the season, and he'd sat me down—even though I had a concussion and couldn't play—giving me some song and dance about how my ex-wife owning the team wouldn't save me if I fucked up.

Whatever that meant.

I was no angel, but I showed up for work and did my job.

And I did it pretty damn well.

So he could kiss my whole ass.

The thought of her potentially firing him made me grin and I gulped down the rest of my coffee.

I needed to finish putting the wall mount up so Henrik could help me hang the TV.

Then I'd take my time unpacking and getting settled.

It wasn't like I had anything else to do until hockey season started back up.

5

———————

H*arper*

DOM GIANNI WAS a big guy and imposing in person.

Six-five and well over two hundred pounds, with piercing dark eyes and sharp cheekbones that made him look intense. However, the moment he smiled, it changed his entire demeanor, and I couldn't help but smile back as I shook his hand.

"It's nice to meet you," I said.

"Likewise." He pulled his wife forward. "This is my wife, Molly."

"Nice to meet you." I shook her hand too. "Harper Barrowman. Shall we sit?"

"Yes, thank you." Dom and Molly followed me into my office at the arena and we settled in the small sitting area off to the side. I had a desk and credenza, along with one wall of built-in bookshelves, but there was also an anteroom with more comfortable chairs and tables, where we could talk and potentially eat.

"How was the flight?" I asked politely.

"Quick and easy," Dom said.

"It's one of my favorites," I told him. "You're descending almost immediately after reaching flying altitude. Up, down, out."

"Absolutely." He nodded.

"So. I don't want to waste time." I handed them each a file. "Did you have a chance to review my proposal?"

"We did." Dom glanced at his wife. "You've given us a very enticing offer."

"But?"

"There's no but," he said slowly. "It's more a matter of biting the bullet, so to speak. My wife has a support system in Las Vegas, with friends and help. Now that I'm not working anymore, it's not as necessary, but obviously that wouldn't be the case if we move here."

"I know that's a concern," I replied. "And I can't really help with that. It would be a leap of faith because I don't know many of the wives and girlfriends yet. There are also going to be a lot of changes in the coming season, so it wouldn't make sense to get to know people who will be traded. However, that's one of the bonuses. If there is anyone from the Sidewinders you'd like me to consider bringing on board, you'll have the power to do that."

"Most of my friends' husbands are retired now," Molly said gently. "And I don't think any of them want to move to L.A. But I'll be okay if we decide to make the move. I'm more concerned about the kids."

"We did some research into schools and there are some great private schools."

"Real estate is ridiculously expensive, but we're prepared for that," Molly said, a faint smile on her face. "We have plenty of equity in our current home."

I was watching them carefully, and my gut told me they were on board, so I wasn't sure where we were going with this conversation.

"Have you made a decision?" I asked quietly.

"We've made a tentative decision," Dom said. "I think my bigger concern is longevity. If we uproot our life, and the kids' lives, I need to know that this isn't some sort of trial run. I'd like to say we can turn this team around in a couple of years, but you and I both know that's not realistic. If I take this on, I'd like to know I'm going to be here for a while. That you don't plan to sell in a year because running a professional hockey team isn't what you thought it was going to be. For me, it's not a big deal, but for Molly and the kids, it's a lot."

"I have no intention of selling anytime soon," I replied honestly. "Edward asked me to take over his team and my goal is to turn us into champions within five years."

"That's a hell of a goal, but I can work with that." His eyes gleamed with what I could only call excitement, and that was exactly the passion I was looking for.

"I'm pretty self-sufficient," Molly said. "The kids and I are a well-oiled machine, but they're used to seeing their father and Dom and I feel strongly about him being a part of their lives."

"Absolutely," I nodded. "He told me he left scouting so he wouldn't be gone all the time, and that's the beauty of this position. Yes, there will be some travel, and home game attendance is expected, but in general, you'll have plenty of time to coach your son's hockey team or see your daughter's ballet performances or whatever."

"The kids are definitely busy," Molly said, shaking her head. "We're all about hockey and softball and swimming. Not to mention ballet and they're also learning to ski."

"They sound like chips off the old block," I said. "I look forward to meeting them."

"What's the timeline?" Dom asked. "We'd like to be settled before school starts."

I nodded. "Actually, I'd love it if you started immediately. Could you be prepared to assist me at the entry draft next week if I fire Howie today?"

Dom didn't bat an eyelash. "Absolutely. I've already been thinking about the prospects."

I smiled as I held out my hand. "Welcome aboard, Mr. Gianni."

～

I fired Howie that afternoon. He'd known it was coming but that hadn't made him any less unpleasant and I was exhausted when I got home. It was almost eight o'clock, I was starving, and I still had dozens of emails that required my attention. Sloane went through them every morning and deleted the garbage, made sure I paid attention to the important ones, and highlighted ones she wasn't sure what to do with.

I had a separate email address for personal things, but sometimes they overlapped, and the fertility clinic I'd spoken to about finding a sperm donor had reached out, asking if I'd made any decisions.

I had to tell them I'd changed my mind.

This wasn't the best time for a baby.

Even though I wasn't getting any younger.

Even though the potential for problems and birth defects and such increased after the age of thirty-five.

Would one more year really make that much of a difference?

I needed a year to get this team running smoothly.

Or at least on the road to smoothly.

And there would be a lot of stress coming up.

I didn't want to wait, but I had to.

It was the smart, mature decision.

"Hey." Gabe's voice made me jump and I realized he was standing outside the kitchen on my patio.

"Jesus. You have to stop that," I muttered, holding a hand over my heart.

"Sorry. I saw you pull up and thought you might be hungry. I was about to grill a steak, but I have two and I'm happy to share."

I hesitated.

Gabe and I didn't need to be spending one-on-one time together.

He wasn't supposed to be anything more than a tenant and an employee.

But I was starving.

And I had to talk to him about paying rent.

Not a lot of money, but his share of utilities and such.

I was wealthy but I was paying him a fuck-ton of money.

"That would be great," I said finally. "I have potato salad in the fridge, if you want me to get it out?"

"Perfect. I was also planning to grill corn."

Corn cooked on a grill was one of my favorite things and he'd obviously remembered.

"Give me a few minutes to change and I'll be right out."

"No rush." He turned, and I went into the bedroom, pulling on shorts and a T-shirt. It felt good after wearing a suit all day and I padded back to the kitchen in my bare feet.

I'd made the potato salad for a night like this, so I could throw a burger on the grill or make a sandwich and be done. It wasn't the healthiest meal in the world, but it was food, for days like today when I was gone for twelve or fourteen hours.

I'd hoped to take Dom and Molly to dinner, but they'd wanted to get home to their family—and to start planning the move—so I'd dropped them at the airport before heading home. I would head to Vegas a day early next week so Dom and I could finalize our strategy for the entry draft, and I sent Henrik a text to let him know the updated plan.

"Steaks are almost done," Gabe called out. "You still like yours medium?"

"Yes, thank you!" I yelled back, pulling plates and utensils out. "We can eat in here, if you want."

"Sure. Everything will be ready in about five minutes."

I set up two place settings on the island, put a serving spoon in the potato salad and pulled a couple of bottles of Sam Adams out of the fridge since I knew Gabe drank it too. Well, I wasn't positive he still drank it, but he had when we'd been married.

"You still drink Sam Adams?" I asked, holding up the bottle of Summer Ale as he came into the kitchen.

He nodded. "I do."

"Perfect." I opened both bottles and settled on the stool at the island. "That smells amazing."

"Nothing better than steak on the grill in the summer," he said, taking a pull from his beer.

"You still eat your steak still breathing?" I asked with a wry smile.

"Oh yeah. The rarer the better."

"Gross." We'd had this same conversation a million times when we'd been married, and he must've realized it at the same time I did because our gazes all but crashed together.

Shit.

We needed to stop this weird trip down memory lane.

"I fired Howie today," I said instead, cutting into my steak.

He made a face. "How'd he take that?"

"About as well as you'd expect."

"What will you do next week?"

"Dom Gianni is the new GM."

He looked surprised. "Damn. You moved fast."

"I've known who I wanted for months. It was just a matter of making it happen. I wasn't sure I could convince Dom and his wife to leave Vegas, but they seem happy to do it."

"I played against him a lot early in my career," he said. "He was as tough as they come. Too tough sometimes."

"He's still tough, just in a different way now. I think he's mellowed since he became a dad."

"Yeah, it happens." He looked thoughtful. "Never thought I'd like being a dad, but it's not as annoying as I thought it would be."

I had a million things to say, since he'd been adamant he didn't want kids any time soon when we'd been married, but that would open up a can of worms I wasn't interested in trying to wrangle back into the can.

"Hopefully, I'll find out one day," I said lightly, scooping potato salad onto my plate.

"You involved with anyone?" he asked, his eyes gleaming despite the lightness to his tone.

"Not that it's any of your business, but no. Who has time? Dating is way too much work."

"Agreed."

For some reason, we both chuckled.

"Every time I go out with someone new, I have high hopes.

Like maybe he won't be an asshole interested in my money, my connections in hockey, or nothing but sex. And every damn time I'm disappointed."

"Same. I keep hoping there's a woman out there who isn't interested in my money, the status of being a pro athlete's girlfriend, or some other thing I can do for her. But I'm not interested in having a fourth wife. Maybe someday I'll live with someone again, but I'm done with marriage."

"I don't think I'll get remarried either," I said after a moment. "Twice was enough."

"That why you want to use a sperm donor to get pregnant?"

6

———————

G *abe*

THE QUESTION SLIPPED OUT UNEXPECTEDLY and I nearly cringed at the fury on her face.

"Did you go through my stuff?" she demanded, eyes wide and blazing with heat.

"Noooo." Shit, I was in trouble, so I backpedaled. "Brandy knocked the file off the counter, and I read it when I was picking it up." Yeah, I was a jerk for throwing my kid under the bus, but that seemed safer than telling her I snooped.

"It's none of your business!" she hissed, glaring at me.

"Look, it was an accident." I really was a great liar when I had to be. "And it's not like I'm going to tell anyone. I'm just curious as to why."

"Again, not your business." She stuffed a piece of steak into her mouth and then took a long pull of her beer.

"There are *much* more fun ways to make a baby," I said lightly, hoping to change the direction of the conversation.

She rolled her eyes, shrugging. "Sex is overrated."

I burst out laughing. "You did *not* just say that."

"What? It is. Guys are so predictable. They want you to blow them and then give you a lackluster, perfunctory fuck before kissing you on the forehead, taking off, and you never hear from them again. And that's fine if you're up for a one-night stand. But Jesus, you go out with a guy three or four times, you start getting to know each other, and then bam, he gets what he wants and he's out. I don't need that bullshit at this stage of my life. At least be fucking honest about your intentions."

"Yeah, but wouldn't it be more fun to get knocked up that way instead of picking a name out of a book and doing it in a doctor's office?"

"More fun, sure, but you never know if the guy is going to want to be part of the baby's life. That's what I don't want. With a sperm donor, I know for sure he won't."

"You'd rather raise a kid on your own instead of having any kind of father in their life?"

She hesitated, the anger all but visibly draining from her. "I think so. If we're not going to be a couple anyway, why add the complication? I have the resources to give him or her the best of everything, so I don't need the stress of some absentee father coming and going, potentially letting both of us down."

"Not all of us are like that," I said, suddenly feeling the urge to defend my gender. "Brandy's mom and I were terrible together, but we've worked hard to never let Brandy see it. I do my best to be there for her in the important ways, even if it's not on a daily basis. I send more money than the court mandates, and I spend time with her in the off-season. It's not perfect, but she knows I love her and will do anything I can for her."

"Most men aren't you, Gabe." She said it so softly I almost missed it.

It had been a long time since she'd given me a compliment of any kind, and I was momentarily shocked into silence.

And why the fuck did it feel so good to hear her say something nice about me?

I was an idiot.

I didn't need her approval, or anyone else's for that matter.

Eating together had been a dumb idea even though my only intention had been to smooth the wrinkles of our relationship since we'd be seeing a lot of each other.

"Did it ever occur to you you're being selfish?" I asked, opting to risk annoying her. "A boy needs a male role model. You going to teach him to skate or hit a baseball or shave, for that matter?"

She made a face. "I have plenty of male friends, and an entire hockey team at my disposal to teach him sports. I'm sure we can figure out shaving and how to put a condom on when the time comes."

I snorted out a laugh.

She really was a ball buster.

"Touche. But I don't know, Harper. It seems like you're doing this for you, without taking the kid's needs into consideration. You and I know firsthand how damaging it can be without involved parents."

That might have been a low blow, because we'd both had rough childhoods. She'd grown up in the foster care system and I had an absentee mother who drank too much along with an abusive father.

"I'll never let a child of mine go into foster care," she snapped. "And I sure as fuck won't let anyone abuse them."

"And what if something happens to you?" I shot back. "Then what?"

She gave me a direct look filled with venom. "Remington Knight and his wife will raise him or her. I've already discussed it with them."

Oh, shit.

I'd had no idea she had that close of a relationship with the billionaire owner of the Lauderdale Knights hockey team. No wonder she'd been able to trade for me without any issues.

"I didn't realize you were that close to them," I said after a moment.

"There are a lot of things you don't know about me," she replied, picking up her beer. "But anyway, this entire conversation is moot. I'm going to hold off until next summer and then reassess. I don't have time to be pregnant or have a baby right now." "So, moving on, what we should be discussing is what you're going to pay to live here."

Oh, yeah, I'd pissed her off.

"What are you talking about?" I asked, trying to switch gears.

"You know, your share of the utilities, that sort of thing."

"Right. Just tell me what you think is fair."

"A thousand dollars a month should cover your share of electricity, water, cable, internet, and whatever else I'm not thinking about."

I nodded. "Sure."

"And you can pay the cleaning service directly. Della said she would talk to you once she got an idea of what you needed. She's coming Tuesday morning. I'll be in Vegas, so will you be here to talk to her?"

"I'll make sure I am."

"Great." She got up and carried her plate to the sink, rinsing it before putting it in the dishwasher.

I watched her work suddenly feeling like an ass.

We'd been having a nice dinner and I'd gone out of my way to piss her off.

That hadn't been my intention, but it seemed to happen organically when we were together, almost like I couldn't help myself. It had started the last year of our marriage and apparently it was still going on even after nearly a decade apart.

That was our M.O.

Everything would be fine and then one or both of us would say something to aggravate the other and, before we knew it, we'd start fighting. Of course, back then fights would be followed by makeup sex.

Sex so good it was worth all the arguing.

Until it wasn't.

Until the fighting and silent treatments and tears had gotten to be too much.

Until she'd accused me of doing something I hadn't done and refused to believe me.

I would never deny I hadn't been the ideal husband, but I'd loved her and had been faithful. I'd done a lot of *other* dumb shit, but I'd never cheated.

And I'd never forgiven her for losing faith in me.

"Thanks for dinner," she said abruptly, as if she knew exactly what I was thinking.

"Oh. Well. Uh, I was cooking anyway." I paused. "You didn't eat your corn."

She frowned, as if she'd forgotten about it. "I guess I didn't."

"Come on, you know I like to make you crazy, but grilled corn is your favorite. Don't miss out just because I can't shut my mouth."

She gave me a wry smile. "Yes, you do like to make me crazy, and yes, it's still my favorite." She grabbed a paper towel and then came back to sit beside me, plucking an ear of corn off the platter and biting into it. "Mmm. Yum."

Christ.

She was beautiful, with a body made for fucking and a face that could've graced magazine covers, but the simple act of watching her eat corn on the cob was somehow incredibly erotic. Or maybe it was the little sounds of pleasure she was making, which reminded me of how she sounded when I was inside of her. It could have also been the delighted twinkle in her eyes as she went to town, entirely unconcerned with the little kernels spotting her cheeks or the butter dripping down her chin. Which of course reminded me of things I absolutely did not need to be thinking about.

My cock disagreed, though.

He'd sat up and taken notice, forcing me to cross my legs to prevent embarrassing myself.

"I haven't had this in a long time," she murmured. "It's *so* good."

"I'm glad you're enjoying it." I playfully handed her a napkin. "Maybe a little too much, though."

"Oops." She quickly wiped her face before digging in again.

There had always been something about her that lured me in.

We'd met at one of my hockey games when we'd been in college and there hadn't been a chance in hell I wouldn't take her home that night. So, I'd done it. And she essentially never left. She unofficially moved in that first night and we'd been together until the day she'd told me she was filing for divorce. I'd let her go because I'd been hurt and pissed off. In retrospect, I'd never loved anyone else the way I'd loved her.

I wouldn't even try to pretend she wasn't the reason my two subsequent marriages had gone bad.

What a shame it was that we'd never get back the magic we'd once had.

Not being at each other's throats every minute would be a nice change, though.

I had to work on muzzling myself.

She finished the corn far too quickly, getting up and washing her hands in the sink.

"Well, that was deliciously messy," she said. "Are you done? I need to clean up and do some more work."

"I can help," I said, strangely reluctant to go back to my incredibly quiet guest house. I usually preferred to be alone, but it was different with Harper. She still had a hold over me I couldn't explain.

It was ridiculous.

It was even more ridiculous how nice it felt to be in her kitchen, eating together, helping her put everything away, and just hanging out. We weren't even talking but we didn't seem to need to.

We'd had a lot of moments like this when we were married.

Being with her had been so easy back then.

Oh, what the hell was wrong with me?

I needed to go out and find some sweet young thing willing to let me do dirty things to her until I fucked Harper right out of my system. Things that would make me forget how comfortable it was to spend time with her. Or how relieved I was that she wasn't going to make a baby with some stranger.

If anyone got her pregnant, it should be me.

The thought nearly made me drop the plate in my hand.

Where the hell had that come from?

I didn't want any more kids.

I barely had time for the one I had.

A baby with Harper would be a huge disaster.

And yet, it wasn't the worst idea in the world either.

Why couldn't I be her sperm donor when the time came?

She wanted to raise the kid on her own anyway, and I'd have the option of being in its life without any pressure.

Right?

Fuck, what was I thinking?

This was a bad idea.

A *terrible* idea.

"Harper, let me..." She was reaching up to put something on a high shelf and my hand brushed against the side of her breast as I moved to help her. My arm briefly skimmed hers as I took the bowl from her, and it was like a jolt of electricity whipped through me.

How long had it been since I'd touched her?

And why had I thought it would somehow be less enticing after all this time?

I had to get out of here.

Immediately.

Before I said and did something stupid.

Something I couldn't take back.

"Dinner was great," I said abruptly, wiping my hands on the dish towel. "But I need to do a few things myself. I'll see you later, Harper." Without another word, I grabbed the platter I'd brought the food in on and made a beeline out the door.

7

____

H*arper*

THE AFTERMATH of the entry draft was intense.

Everything in Vegas was a party, but there was a lot of business that went on as well. Business that probably wouldn't have included me had it not been for my friendship with Remy Knight and the fact that I had Dom and Henrik with me. Most of the other owners smiled politely and then talked around me. It was incredibly annoying, but short of being rude, it wouldn't be easy for me to break into their circles.

Many of them had known Edward, and they'd always treated me like a pretty arm adornment. It had been frustrating then, but that was how I'd gotten friendly with Remy and subsequently his wife Noelle. There were a couple of others who were nice, like Gage Caldwell, who owned the Alaska Blizzard, and Lonnie Finch, who owned the Las Vegas Sidewinders. The rest avoided me like the plague.

"You need to go down to the bar and play nice," Remy

murmured in my ear. "I know it's hard, but you'll never earn their respect if you run and hide."

I nodded, steeling myself. "I know. I'm on it."

"Don't worry." Noelle squeezed my arm. "I'll stay nearby in case you need to be rescued before you say something scathing."

I laughed. "So you'll be glued to my side all night?"

"If necessary."

"I appreciate it."

"Look, you know what you're doing," Dom said quietly. "Don't let the good old boys' club get to you. Talk about what you know—which is a lot. Discuss your plans and vision for the team. You don't have to give away the details, just let them know you're actively working to make us better."

"I will." I took a deep breath. "Okay, let's go."

We moved to the hotel bar en masse, and while it was nice to have my core group of friends as protection, for lack of a better word, I needed to do this on my own. I needed to show the hockey world I deserved to take over the team. That I was more than just Edward Barrowman's rich widow.

God, it was hard feeling like I had to constantly prove myself just because I didn't have a penis.

To be fair, there was also the added factor of not being an athlete and never having worked in hockey before. I had an MBA, so I was educated for the business side of things, and I'd spent five years working as a marketing manager for a small software company. I didn't know if that would impress anyone, but at least I gave a shit about the team. Not like some of these guys who used them as tax write-offs.

"How's it going, Harper?" Stan Remick, the GM for one of the teams in New York, approached me with a smile, holding out his hand. We'd met on several previous occasions.

"Hi, Stan." I shook his hand. "I'm doing well. Nice to see you."

"Leanne and I were sorry to hear about Ed." His eyes held genuine sympathy. "I hope you're doing okay."

"Time heals all things," I responded, nodding. "It gets a little easier every day."

"Well, it's nice to see some new blood around here. I get tired of looking at the same faces, year in and year out. Everyone treating you okay?"

I chuckled. "I think you know the answer to that. But at least their mistreatment mostly consists of ignoring me."

He made a face. "Don't worry. Just focus on what you're doing for the team. Everything else is just bullshit and background noise."

I smiled.

Bullshit and background noise.

That might be my new catch phrase.

"Thanks, Stan."

"Talk soon."

He ambled off and I moved to the bar, ordering a tumbler of bourbon with an ice cube in it. True bourbon drinkers would have something to say about watering it down, but I didn't give a damn what anyone thought about how I drank my whisky. I had more important things to worry about.

"Still pretending to like bourbon." The voice behind me made me freeze.

Fuck.

"No, Eddie, I'm not pretending anything," I said quietly, turning to face my former stepson. "I actually enjoy bourbon. What are you doing here?"

"These people are my friends. I was invited." He smirked.

I was reeling on the inside, but I'd be damned if I let him see it.

It was so hard to look at him because he was the spitting image of his father, just thirty years younger. Sometimes I found it impossible to believe a kind, articulate man like Edward had raised not just one, but two complete assholes. Of course, according to Edward, they were like their mother.

"Have a good time." I turned to go, but he snaked out a hand and grabbed my arm.

"Just because you won the court case doesn't mean you've won everything," he hissed. "These people will never accept you, will never make deals with you, and will never respect you. The team is going to fall apart with you at the helm. Is that what you think my father wanted?"

I shook my head. "I know it's hard for you but try to keep up. I'm *already* accepted and making deals. And I don't really give a shit if they respect me. I'm going to love laughing all the way to the championship." I yanked my arm free and turned on my heel.

He said something as I walked away, but I was moving too fast to hear it.

Asshole.

~

VEGAS HAD BEEN exciting but exhausting.

Seeing Ed had been frustrating.

There had been a lot of nice people too, though.

Friends of Remy's and Gage's, people Dom and Henrik knew, and a few people I met for the first time, so I'd expanded my professional circle quite a bit. Some of those people probably didn't know what to think about me, but as long as they didn't make negative assumptions, I didn't mind taking the time to build those relationships.

I'd met a lot of people as Edward's wife, but it wouldn't surprise me if they didn't even recognize me. Older men with attractive, much-younger wives were a dime a dozen in this world, so I had to forge my own road now that I was in charge of the Phantoms.

It had been a brutal couple of days, wining and dining and putting on my professional face day in and day out. I'd never been so glad to get home and sleep in my own bed. I had things to do around the house and needed to get to the office at the arena for a few hours, but I took a day to get a manicure and pedicure, along with a massage and facial. Finding my Zen and trying to push away all the stress had seemed necessary for a multitude of reasons.

I'd let a lot of things go while Edward had been sick, focusing on spending as much time with him as possible and making sure he had everything he needed. I'd put on a little weight and stopped working out, but at least that was under control. It was the mental and emotional parts that were harder to deal with. Coping with loneliness was new to me, and even the grief counselor I'd spoken to hadn't been able to give me any advice that helped.

Time and finding new friends and hobbies were the only cures for that, and there weren't enough hours in the day to make new friends. I did have a few, though, and I needed to foster those relationships. Since Edward's death, I'd been laser-focused on upholding the terms of his will and taking over the Phantoms, letting many other things fall by the wayside.

That ended now.

Impulsively, I picked up the phone and dialed my friend Cheyenne.

She was one of the top supermodels in the world, and we'd met at a charity fundraiser last year. She was only twenty-three, so a lot younger than me, but we'd spent weeks as co-sponsors of the fundraiser, and had gotten to know each other well. It had been not long after Edward's death, and she'd been sweet, understanding, and seemed to know exactly how to distract me from my grief.

I hadn't seen her in months, but that wasn't entirely my fault.

She traveled the world doing photo shoots, fashion shows, and other appearances, so she wasn't in town that often. I'd seen she was in L.A. on social media, which was why I'd thought to text her.

HARPER: Hey! I see you're back in town. Do you want to get together?

CHEYENNE: Hi! Absolutely. What's your schedule like? I've left the next week free, so I can decompress after being gone for two months, but I'd love to get dinner or a movie or something.

HARPER: Isn't there a new movie with The Rock? We could see a matinee and then go to dinner?

CHEYENNE: Sounds amazing and perfect. Tomorrow?

HARPER: Sure. I'll pull up movie times and text you.

CHEYENNE: Great. Can you drive? My car is in the shop. Apparently, leaving it in the garage for three months kills the battery.

HARPER: No problem. See you tomorrow! I'm really excited to see you. I have lots of news.

CHEYENNE: Oh good. I have nothing interesting to tell you, but I can't wait to hear all your news.

HARPER: See you tomorrow.

Making plans to see a girlfriend made me so happy, it was almost embarrassing.

I padded into the kitchen, pondering which movie theater to go to, when I spotted Gabe outside.

Holy crap.

He'd always had an incredible body, and apparently that hadn't changed as he'd aged.

Hell, if you asked me, he looked even better than he had in his twenties.

And I was here for it.

I didn't have to like the man to appreciate the gloriousness of his physique.

He was in low-slung swim trunks that showed off the "V" of his oblique muscles and his six-pack abs. The muscles in his thighs moved as he walked, his lean body strong and sure as he dove into the pool. He glided almost the full length of it underwater before coming up, making a turn, and doing it again.

I was mesmerized as I watched him.

After three times across the pool, he came up and started to swim, picking up speed as he swam from one end to the other. The muscles in his arms and upper back bulged with each stroke and I momentarily remembered what it was like with those strong, muscular arms around me. What it felt like when he was above me, holding himself up as he stared down into my face.

His broad shoulders.

The dark hair on his chest.

Knock it off, Harper.

The angel on my shoulder was stern in her admonishment.

It had been too long since I'd had sex, so I was obviously in need of a fantasy.

But he's no good for you. Not even for the best sex of your life.

I took a deep breath and turned away from the window.

Nope.

There would be no more fantasizing about Gabriel DeLugo.

Not today or tomorrow or any other day.

I had no intention of making the same mistakes of my past.

8

___

G *abe*

ONE OF THE good things about having been in the league for so many years was the number of guys I'd played with. I'd been on teams with Americans, Canadians, Russians, and more, and those guys were now scattered all over the world. Some retired and went back to their home countries, while others were playing for teams all over North America.

A small group of them were still my friends.

I wasn't the friendliest guy, a loner by nature, and there were probably a lot of reasons I didn't let people get too close. My fucked-up childhood was at the top of that list. I tried not to dwell on it, but it wasn't hard to see the correlation between me keeping people at a distance and how abusive my parents had been. I'd become quiet and reclusive as a child, only coming out of my shell when I'd found my passion for hockey. But even then, I couldn't get close to any of the other kids because I didn't want any of them to see how fucked up my home life was.

Then I'd met Harper and she'd gotten past all the walls I'd put up, making me realize I wasn't that scared little boy anymore. I was still somewhat reclusive, but for the first time, I'd started to allow myself to make friends, both in college and once I got to the pros.

One of them had been a Russian player named Ivan Rochenko. He was six or seven years younger than me, and I'd been his off-ice mentor his first year in the league. He was a fun guy who liked to party, and though my job had been to keep him out of trouble, we'd managed to find our share whenever we were together.

He'd been traded to the Phantoms early this past season. We hadn't had a chance to hook up yet because I'd been on the injured reserve suffering from another concussion when the trade went through, and then I'd gone to Wisconsin to spend time with Brandy while I recovered. I'd reached out to him a few times and he'd said to text him when I got back to town, so that was what I'd done.

We'd made plans to get something to eat and then hit a couple of clubs he liked. I figured it was time to think about female companionship since I was going to be here for a while. Nothing serious, but it would be nice to find a few ladies I could take out once in a while, who might not mind casual sex. I was getting a little old for constant one-night stands, but my libido was having a hard time reconciling the two.

"Good to see you, man." I hugged Ivan when we met up at the bar of a popular but low-key restaurant in Hollywood.

"You look good!" he said, heartily clapping me on the back. He had a faint accent, but you had to really listen for it. "Are you settled yet?"

I made a motion with my hand, wobbling it from side to side. "Mostly. Bedroom is set up, kitchen is close, and I hung the TV in the living room. Still have a little to do but the place is less than a thousand square feet, so it won't take long. I just need to do some shopping, and you know that's my favorite thing."

He arched his brows. "A thousand square feet? Why so small?"

"I don't know how long I'll be here," I admitted as we settled at the bar. "Why would I spend the money to buy a house or even rent a big place? This is easier. And cheaper."

He frowned. "Why didn't you ask me? I have a guest room."

"I didn't want to be a third wheel. I assumed Marina wouldn't be thrilled with it."

"She's gone," he said quietly. "She left right before Christmas."

"Seriously?" I stared at him.

"Long story."

"Stop it," I told him before turning to the bartender. "Two bourbons. Four Roses. Straight."

"It's been over for a while. Not a big deal. But the point is, I have plenty of room if you want to move in."

"You bought a house?" I asked curiously.

"Condo. But it's big."

"It's all right. I've got a sweet deal living in Harper's guest house."

He stared at me, his face expressionless other than the slight twitch of his upper lip, which told me he was on the verge of bursting into laughter.

At least he waited a few seconds before giving in. "Seriously? I knew it! I knew there was more to the story of you coming to L.A. than you getting a nice contract."

"That's all there was to it," I protested. "Really. Well, that and her getting Brittany off my back."

"What?" He looked confused.

"Brittany found a loophole in the prenup. She wanted... a lot. Basically, everything I had that wasn't in trust for Brandy. I told Harper if she wanted me in L.A., the only way I could afford to move here was if she got Brittany to back off. And she did. I have no idea how—I didn't ask—but she gave up the lawsuit and I haven't heard from her since."

"Damn." He let out a low whistle. "I didn't realize Brittany was going after you."

"She never forgave me for not loving her the way she loved me," I muttered, taking a sip from the tumbler the bartender had just put in front of me.

"She was a bitch," he said wryly, shaking his head. "But we both know you never got over Harper. I mean, Brittany looks a lot like her. First time I saw her I thought it *was* Harper. You were looking for a replacement, and I'm sure that was a disappointment for everyone."

I looked away. "Brittany could never be Harper."

"That's for sure. And now you're living with her. Tell me everything."

"There's nothing to tell. I don't know if my body will allow me to play more than one season here, so I'm living in her guest house. That's it. It's clean, has everything I need, and all I'm paying is utilities. I've done some really dumb shit with money. This is a chance for me to get caught up."

He eyed me. "You've also *made* a lot of money over the years, my friend. Did you really blow through all of it?"

I looked away, almost embarrassed to admit how stupid I'd been.

"Between two divorces, taking care of Brandy, and how much I spent trying to keep Brittany happy, yeah. I blew through almost everything except Brandy's trust, my 401K, and a couple of small investments. I'll probably be working into my seventies if I'm not careful."

He grimaced. "Well, if you need a place to live, you've always got a room with me."

"Speaking of empty rooms, tell me what happened with Marina." Marina had been his longtime girlfriend. They'd been together nearly a decade.

"Eh. You know how it is. This life isn't for everyone."

"So after, what? Eight years? She suddenly got tired of it?"

"We got together young. She missed Russia and was ready to go home. I was not."

"She was that unhappy?" I questioned.

"She was lonely. It was hard for her to make friends in Detroit. The other wives didn't like her and, to be fair, she didn't make it easy for them. Her father's a high-ranking officer in the Russian military, so she was raised to be cold, aloof, to keep people at arm's length. That doesn't work here in North America. She pushed them away and they weren't going to beg her for friendship."

"And now?"

He met my gaze with a smirk. "Now I am sowing many, many oats, as you like to say in English."

"No chance of reconciliation?"

"I don't want her back," he said quietly. "Since I've started dating women who are *not* Russian, I see how cold she was. How indifferent. And honestly, now that I've had a taste, I'm not interested in more of that. I've discovered I like a woman who can show me how she feels. Even if it's just for the night, or friendship or whatever. Being stoic isn't nearly as hot as I thought it was at nineteen."

"Not all Russian women are like Marina," I pointed out.

"No, but there aren't a lot of single Russian women here in L.A. So, I'm exploring my options."

"Same." I looked around. "And there are some lovely options here tonight."

"This place is good. You have to have a little money to come here, because it's not cheap. But it's not a celebrity hangout either, so you tend to meet ladies who are professional. Who can buy their own drinks. Who'll talk to you without expectations. And who mostly don't recognize you."

"Damn, is this place heaven?"

He laughed.

WE TALKED at the bar for the next hour, ordering food and more drinks.

It had been a couple of years since we'd hung out and it was nice to catch up.

He told me stories about the guys that played for the Phantoms, along with some of their escapades and that of the coaches. It seemed like there was the usual mixture of really good guys and assholes, with a handful that were hard to read or not as friendly as the others. I wished I'd had a chance to meet the team, but I'd come to town, met with the doctors, and then headed to Wisconsin. If I couldn't play, I'd wanted to spend time with my daughter, but that left me floundering as the new guy.

And if I was going to take on the leadership role Harper wanted me to assume, I had to start getting to know everyone. Of course, Harper was going to trade a lot of guys, so maybe we'd all be newbies together.

"Jensen Bang is hilarious," Ivan told me. "But he's solid. You can count on him, both on and off the ice. He's big and as tough as they come. He'll have your back."

"Good to know."

"Laurie's good too—Evan Laurentz," he clarified. "You know there won't be any shenanigans when he's on the ice. Although he's not as talented as Big Bang."

"Big Bang?" I asked curiously.

Ivan grinned. "Yes. Jensen is very large. He's also a fan of that TV show."

"The Big Bang Theory?"

"Yes, that one."

I'd never seen the show.

Apparently, I was getting old.

"So, you and Harper getting along?" he asked.

"Ish."

"You'd think after ten years the two of you would have mellowed."

"She's still a ball buster, man." I paused. "Haven't you talked to her?"

A lot of regret crossed his face as he shook his head. "She hasn't been down to the locker room at all, and I didn't realize your Harper was Mr. Barrowman's widow until the court case hit the news. Then I stayed away because it was a hot topic in the locker room." He narrowed his gaze on me. "And *you* didn't give me a head's up."

"Sorry. I thought you knew." I paused. "So...were the guys talking about her?"

"Did you think they wouldn't? They're talking about you too. Our text chat blew up when you got traded here. And then you didn't even come by to say hello."

"You guys were in the middle of a road trip when it happened, and the doctors told me I was out for the season. Two concussions less than a year apart—and my fourth ever—they didn't want me anywhere near the ice. Technically, I still haven't been cleared to play."

"How much longer?" Ivan asked quietly.

"They think I'll be fine by September, but nothing is guaranteed. I've started swimming and running again. I'm going to hit the weights if I get clearance at my next appointment."

"I had no idea it was so bad."

"Yeah, this one was scary. I was fine at first, thought they were making a big deal out of nothing. Then the headaches started."

"Shit."

"I haven't had one in two weeks," I said, knocking on the wooden bar. "Knock on wood."

"Let's hope it stays that way." He downed his drink as his gaze landed on something—or someone—by the door. I followed his gaze and found him staring at a stunning blond.

Tall.

Supermodel thin.

Perfect features.

Great smile.

There was something familiar about her, but that probably happened a lot in L.A.

"Jesus. It's *Cheyenne*," Ivan murmured.

"Who?"

"The supermodel. You know, Sports Illustrated? Victoria's Secret?"

Well, that made sense.

Cheyenne turned and grinned at someone, and I froze.

No fucking way.

Harper was hanging out with one of the biggest supermodels in the world and they looked chummy.

"She's with Harper," I whispered.

"What?" He hesitated for a moment and then grinned. "Let's go say hello!"

Before I could stop him, Ivan got up and headed in their direction.

9

H*arper*

CHEYENNE and I were just heading for the door when I heard someone calling my name. I turned in confusion and it took me a minute to recognize Ivan Rochenko. I'd known Gabe's old friend played for the Phantoms, but I hadn't wanted to reach out until I was done making trades, and he hadn't made any attempt to contact me either.

"Ivan." I smiled, leaning into his embrace as he hugged me and kissed my cheek.

"Look at you." He grinned. "As beautiful as ever."

"Thank you. You don't look bad yourself."

"Hey, Harper." Gabe looked decidedly uncomfortable.

"Hey, Gabe." I tugged Cheyenne forward. "Guys, this is my friend Cheyenne. Chey, this is Gabe DeLugo and Ivan Rochenko, from the Phantoms."

"Hi!" Cheyenne smiled politely.

"Nice to meet you."

"Girls' night out?" Ivan asked.

"Yes! And we just found out that Nobody's Fool is playing a top-secret gig at Stowaway! We're headed there now. You guys want to tag along?"

I wanted to strangle my friend, but it was too late.

"What's Stowaway?" Gabe asked, frowning.

"New club not too far from here."

"I love Nobody's Fool," Ivan said. "We have to pay our bill, but I'd love to see them."

"Why is it a top-secret gig?" Gabe asked me as Cheyenne and Ivan chatted animatedly about the up-and-coming rock band.

I shrugged. "I guess it's like a practice thing before their tour or something. Chey used to date someone who knows them, and he texted her. I guess it's a word-of-mouth thing since the club wouldn't be able to handle it if they officially announced they were going to play."

"I didn't think you liked hard rock," he said, frowning.

"I don't, but Chey does, and it's cool to go to a concert that's kind of a private, by-invitation-only thing."

"Do you want me to bow out?" he asked after a moment. "I think Ivan was so mesmerized by Cheyenne, he forgot you and I are divorced."

I shrugged. "You're welcome to come along. I don't mind."

"Are you sure?" He stared down at me intently, and for a moment I was lost in his gorgeous silver eyes.

"Positive." I quickly averted my gaze, pretending to be looking at something on my phone.

"Are we ready to go?" Ivan asked as he and Cheyenne rejoined us.

"I'll drive if you guys want," I said. "I only had one glass of wine, so I'm good to go. I don't mind being the designated driver."

"Sure." Ivan nodded and we headed outside to where the valet was just pulling my car up to the front. "This works for me because I like to drink."

"You want me to drive?" Gabe asked me. "I've only had a couple and we ate, so I'm good for now."

I hesitated.

I hated driving at night in Hollywood. Traffic was always a nightmare, and I didn't know if there would be valet parking where we were going.

"You sure you're okay?"

"Absolutely."

"Thanks. That would be great." I ignored Cheyenne's raised eyebrows and got into the passenger seat while she and Ivan got into the back, chatting like old friends.

I smiled to myself because Cheyenne was the sweetest, most gorgeous woman you'd ever meet, but she friend zoned *everyone*. She was hyper-focused on her modeling career and had zero interest in a relationship. So, if Ivan was looking for more, he would be sorely disappointed.

Of course, there was always the option of a one-night stand, but Cheyenne had told me she wasn't a fan of those.

"This is nice," Gabe said, pulling my new Lucid Air into traffic.

"She's my baby," I said, grinning. "Zero to sixty in three seconds, and four hundred miles to a charge." I loved driving an electric car.

Ivan whistled from the back seat. "Damn. That's impressive."

"It's a great car. Sleek, fast, and luxurious."

"I never considered an electric," Gabe admitted. "I thought they would be slow, cumbersome, and need to be charged every twenty miles or something. I knew that wasn't the case intellectually, but somewhere in the back of my mind, I'd automatically decided I wouldn't like one."

"Remy Knight has one and he let me drive it," I said, laughing. "That was it. I was hooked."

"I'm pretty hooked too." He glanced at me. "She handles like a dream."

"She does."

"Can I drive it sometime?" Ivan asked.

"On a day when you're not drinking, sure," I replied.

"Fair enough."

Despite being surprised and slightly annoyed that they'd joined us, I had to admit it was nice to be out with a couple of strong, take-charge guys so that I didn't have to do anything but enjoy. I didn't even have to drive. It wasn't that I couldn't. I drove all day, almost every day, and I loved my car. But sometimes it was a relief to let someone else take charge. Just for a little while.

I'd been in control of so many things, for so long, something as simple as Gabe driving on a night out allowed me to breathe. To truly relax for a couple of hours. Gabe was many things, but stupid wasn't one of them. Maybe I was a romantic fool, because Gabe had been my first love, my first lover, my first almost everything, but I trusted him. He would never do anything to hurt me or our friends, and despite our differences, I knew he would be vigilant about our safety at the club.

I wasn't expecting trouble or anything, but it was always a crap shoot with Cheyenne. She had a well-known and easily recognizable face, and men flocked to her like the proverbial moths to a flame. That was why we'd gone to a movie and dinner, hoping to keep things low-key. But then she'd gotten the text about the concert and really wanted to go, so I'd agreed. Especially after she'd pointed out I needed to get out more.

Now I was out with my ex-husband, and Cheyenne was hanging out with his buddy, and it was a little too much like a double date.

Except it was comfortable and easy.

I'd known Ivan for years, and though we hadn't seen each other in a long time, he was a good guy. Easy-going and well-read, we could talk about literature or sports or even politics. He always had something to contribute to a conversation. And Gabe was a lot like that too. He didn't talk politics much, but he did like to read. When we'd been together, I'd made him read "Pride and Prejudice," and then we'd discussed it at length.

Having him read me passages from my all-time most beloved book, while we were naked in bed, was one of my favorite memories from our marriage.

"I'm on the list," Cheyenne said as we approached the entrance. She whispered her name to the burly security guy at the door and he took one look at her before swinging open the door.

"I like hanging out with her," Ivan stage whispered.

"Me too." I laughed.

I felt Gabe's hand at the small of my back and a rush of pleasure washed over me.

It was so fucking easy to fall under his spell because when Gabe wasn't being an ass, he was magnificent. Tall and sexy, with a charming smile and expressive eyes that appeared to be looking right into your soul. He could be funny when he wanted to and serious when the occasion arose, and despite how things had ended between us, I'd missed his company.

"I'll get us drinks," Ivan said. "You guys find a place to settle."

The club was bustling with activity, a crowd gathering in front of the stage as they awaited the start of the show.

"There are high-top tables!" Cheyenne pointed and we followed behind her. She waved to someone she knew, excused herself and hurried over to talk to them.

I watched her go in amusement.

As much as I adored her, she was a force of nature sometimes.

She knew everyone, talked to almost anyone, and in some ways, was unaware of the impact her beauty had on the people around her. Obviously, she knew she was a supermodel and that people thought she was beautiful, but when she wasn't working, she seemed to think there was a switch that flipped off. As if she was somehow less gorgeous because she wasn't in front of a camera.

It was one of the things I loved about her.

"This is so not my scene," I murmured as someone stepped on my foot.

Gabe chuckled, moving closer to me so I was against the table and he was between me and everyone else in the room.

"Why did you come?" he asked, looking at me intently.

"I don't go out enough. I wanted to spend more time with Cheyenne. It seemed kind of fun in theory. Now that we're here and there are eleventy-billion people, I'm less enthralled."

"Same." He looked around. "We might be getting old, babe."

I couldn't help but laugh.

"Speak for yourself!" I teased.

"I am!" His laughter transported me to another time.

To when we'd been dating.

Falling in love.

When nothing had mattered but how we made each other feel.

Sometimes I really did feel old.

Everything had been so simple then.

These days, everything was complicated.

And for just one night, I wanted my life to be *not* complicated.

At the very least, less complicated.

"Do you want to dance?" I asked him impulsively. That was something we'd both loved when we'd been together, and I was willing to bet he still enjoyed it.

There was a flicker of surprise on his face but then he just took my hand and led me out to the dance floor. Half of it was filled with people starting to crowd the stage, but the rest still had people dancing to the Matchbox Twenty song that was playing.

"Now I feel a little less old," I said, swaying against him as we moved to the rhythm.

"We're not old, babe. Just a little more seasoned."

"Seasoning is exhausting," I admitted, leaning closer to him.

He slid an arm around my waist, pulling me in. "How can we enjoy the good times if we don't have bad times to compare them to?"

There was the Gabe I missed.

This right here was one of the things that made me fall in love with him.

"It's time!" Cheyenne grabbed my hand as she brushed past us, pulling us toward the stage.

I wanted to protest, and tell her I'd watch from the back, but it was too late.

The music stopped, the lights went out, and there was nowhere to go but forward.

"Hang onto me," Gabe yelled, his fingers closing around my other hand, since Cheyenne was still pulling us toward the front.

I nodded, grateful for his strength as we were jostled and

nudged by everyone trying to do the same thing we were. Well, I was just trying to stay upright; Cheyenne was the one who apparently had a death wish.

Except she didn't.

Somehow, she got us all the way to the front, standing behind one row of people. And when the lights came up, we were close enough to touch the stage.

"Wooo!" Cheyenne's hands were in the air when the band came on stage, and despite this not being my thing, I found myself caught up in the excitement.

Or maybe it was the excitement of having Gabe's strong arms wrapped around me from behind, keeping me steady.

Whatever it was, this night hadn't gone the way I'd thought it would at all, but I was having too much fun to worry about it.

Fun with Gabe.

Fun with my ex-husband.

This was going to go wrong twelve ways to Sunday.

And for some reason I didn't care.

I'd been sorely lacking in fun since Edward's death, and for just one night, I was going to enjoy myself.

What could go wrong?

10

————

G*abe*

I'D BEEN a teenager the last time I'd been in the front row of a rock concert.

I tended to listen to more jazz these days, music that kept me calm and centered. I enjoyed a little pop when I worked out, even some country if I was in the mood, but Nobody's Fool hadn't been anywhere on my radar. Yet I enjoyed the hell out of it. Having Harper wiggling against me half the night probably had something to do with it, but I wasn't going to overthink things.

It felt like we were becoming friends again, and I didn't know if that was a good thing or a bad thing.

Dating your ex-wife was never smart.

There was a reason we were divorced.

Probably a lot of them.

Dating your boss was also a bad idea.

My teammates and the hockey world would have a field day if they caught on.

And yet, here we were, dancing and singing, drinking and having a great time.

It felt too good to stop even though my brain was screaming that I was an idiot.

My heart told my brain to fuck off, and when Ivan pushed through the crowd with four bottles of beer, I didn't hesitate to partake.

Alcohol would make me stupid, especially when it came to Harper, but what the hell. I'd already lost her so it wasn't like things between us could get worse. I was probably tempting fate just thinking that, but this felt too good to worry about anything other than tonight.

On top of the fantastic company, Nobody's Fool was incredible.

The guitars and vocals were on point, and the melodies were catchy.

I might have to broaden my musical horizons because these guys were great.

Not as great as spending time with Harper, though.

We were in dangerous territory, but my traitorous body was far too excited to listen to my more cautious brain. My heart was cautious but totally on board, which was a pain in my ass.

And I didn't give a shit.

One night with her might remind me why we weren't together anymore. The sex would undoubtedly be good if we got to that point, but everything else would blow up.

That should have been a deterrent, but it wasn't.

As far as I was concerned, you only lived once.

So, I pressed myself against her, put a hand on her hip to keep her close, and lost myself in both the woman and the music.

I was so caught up in the show, and Harper's proximity to me, a feeling of loss washed over me when it was over. The lights came back on, music started blasting through the speakers, and the crowd around us started to dissipate. And with it went the little bubble of pleasure I'd been in.

Except I didn't want it to end.

"That was bloody amazing!" Cheyenne said, her eyes sparking with excitement. "Did you have fun? What did you think?"

"They were un-fucking-believable," Ivan said, nodding. "I was already a fan, but now I'm an even bigger one."

"I had so much more fun than I thought I would," Harper admitted. "Thank you for inviting me."

"It was great," I agreed. "Thank you, Cheyenne. I plan to pick up one of their albums."

"I'm going backstage," she said. "But I can only bring one of you. Do you want to come, Harper?"

To my surprise, Harper shook her head. "No. I don't need to go backstage. Why don't you take Ivan?"

Ivan's eyes widened. "Are you sure?"

"Of course. Go on. You guys are actual fans."

"You're the best!" His grin spread from ear to ear.

"See you later?" Cheyenne hugged her.

"Have fun. I don't know how long we're staying, but don't worry about me."

"I'll make sure she gets home okay if you guys take off before we're done." Ivan nodded at us before following in Cheyenne's wake.

Harper watched them go with a fond smile. "I feel like a mom sending my kids out on their first date." She snorted. "Is that ridiculous or what?"

"You think she's into him?"

"I doubt it, but what do I know? He's good-looking, so maybe."

We started to walk toward the high-top tables where we'd been earlier in the evening.

"You ready to leave?" I asked after a moment. "Or would you want to hang out for a while and...dance?"

She turned, her gorgeous blue eyes meeting mine. "I'd love to hang out and dance with you, Gabe."

So that was what we did.

We danced and drank and talked and laughed.

It had been years since we'd done anything like this, but it almost felt like yesterday. The decade since our divorce had gone by in the blink of an eye, and we were right back to where we'd started. That was how it felt as I twirled her around the dance floor and then did shots of tequila.

I didn't know what had changed, but I didn't care.

We'd had a lot of issues as a couple but being together like this had never been one of them.

"Let's do a shot," I told her, tugging her toward the bar.

"Anything but tequila," she said amiably.

I chuckled, because she obviously remembered how hungover I got when I drank tequila.

"Let's do something lighter," I suggested. "Lemon Drop?"

"Sure."

I ordered from the bartender and handed her one.

"What are we drinking to?" she asked, meeting my gaze curiously.

"Renewed friendship," I replied. "A clean slate."

She clinked her glass against mine. "To a clean slate."

We downed the citrusy liquid and before she could protest, I ordered two more.

∼

WE DRANK LATE into the night.

When Cheyenne and Ivan came back to join us, we all went onto the dance floor, alternately drinking and dancing until the lights came on, telling us it was time to go. So, we took an Uber to an after-hours club that Cheyenne knew of, where we drank more, danced more, and got cozy together.

Cheyenne and Ivan didn't appear to be hooking up, so I wasn't sure what was going on there, but they looked happy and comfortable together, which was all that mattered.

Not that Harper and I were hooking up.

There had been some touching and handholding, but it was hard to tell if she wanted me or if there was simply a familiarity there that was impossible to ignore. We'd been friends, lovers, married, enemies, and everything in between. We'd known each other for more than sixteen years and there was no way to separate the past and the present. Good or bad, we had a bond that was impossible to ignore.

When the music slowed down, Harper moved into my arms seamlessly, as if we slow danced regularly.

"Still pretty light on your feet for an old man," she teased.

"I do okay," I replied, resting my hands on her hips as I gazed down at her.

Her eyes drifted up to mine and the spark there was unmistakable.

It was probably the alcohol diminishing my self-control, but I couldn't stop the next words out of my mouth.

"What happens if I kiss you, Harper?" I asked, leaning toward her.

A faint smile played on her lips.

"I guess we're going to find out." Her eyes fluttered closed as she tilted up her face to mine.

I took a moment to take in how beautiful she looked, with her lips parted expectantly, and then I dropped my mouth to hers.

She tasted sweeter than I remembered, her lips soft and pliable against mine. I nibbled on them, trying to keep things chaste, but I was drunk and horny and she was sexy and delicious.

There was no way to resist her once I touched her.

I used the tip of my tongue to trace the seam of her lips, taking my time to reacquaint myself with what she liked. It seemed like a lifetime ago that I last kissed her, and yet it was so familiar. Her taste, her scent, the way her breath hitched when I deepened the pressure of my lips. Her mouth opened, her tongue coming out to meet mine as she wound her arms around my neck. I toyed with her a little, retreating as she pressed into me, and then surging ahead when she backed off.

A delightful game of cat-and-mouse kissing that had always gotten her worked up in the past.

And it seemed nothing had changed in that regard.

I let one of my hands drift down to her denim-clad ass, cupping it lightly as I drew her against the erection behind my shorts. She rubbed her body on mine, digging her fingers into the hair at the back of my neck.

Fuck.

This was so damn good, I was going to embarrass myself if we kept this up.

I reluctantly pulled away, taking in the glassy look in her eyes as I pushed her hair back behind her ear.

"It's almost three," I said gruffly. "If we're going to continue this, we should take it somewhere private."

"Yes." That one word held so much more meaning than simply leaving.

"Home?"

"Absolutely."

I took her hand and headed for the exit as I pulled up the app to call for an Uber.

"My car," she whispered when she realized what I was doing.

"Baby, there's no way either of us is getting behind the wheel tonight," I said. "You want Ivan to take it home with him? He stopped drinking a couple hours ago because we figured someone had to be sober."

"Oh." She hesitated but then nodded. "I really don't want to leave it at that lot."

"Okay. Let's take care of that and then get out of here."

"You realize what we're doing is crazy, right?"

"What fun is it if you don't have a little crazy in your life once in a while?"

11

———————

H*arper*

THE UBER ARRIVED fifteen minutes later, and I tumbled into the back seat of a little Honda, with Gabe crawling in after me. His long legs were cramped in the small car, but he didn't seem to mind as he slid his arm around me, turned his head, and pressed his lips to mine. It was hard to think when he was touching me, and though I had enough presence of mind to not want to give the poor driver a show, I didn't want Gabe to stop touching me.

I was drunk and horny, my inhibitions nowhere to be found as I leaned over and licked the spot behind his ear. His neck had always been sensitive, and I felt the goose bumps break out on his skin as I nibbled and lightly sucked.

"I wish you were on my lap," he growled against my ear in a low voice that made my girlie parts clench in anticipation. "Grinding on my dick while I finger you." He squeezed my thigh, his eyes burning into mine as we stared at each other. He brought his other hand up to cup the side of my face.

"You sure about this, Harper? We're both pretty drunk."

"Sober enough to know we're probably going to regret it but drunk enough not to care."

I would have sworn I saw a look of regret flash across his face, but then he was kissing me again and I couldn't think. Or breathe. Or do anything but kiss him back.

By the time the driver pulled up to my house, we were breathing hard.

"Sorry about the PDA," I murmured to the driver. "You'll get a good tip."

"Have a good night!" The driver laughed as he drove away, and Gabe and I stumbled into the house.

Before I could think about our next move, he had me up against the nearest wall, kissing me with purpose. There was nothing chaste or cautious about these kisses, his mouth and tongue pillaging mine. I moaned into him, kissing him back with reckless abandon, as if my next breath depended on it.

Every swipe of his tongue brought my dormant libido to life, the ache between my legs getting stronger by the minute. My heart raced and the blood running through my veins felt like liquid fire, every sensation heightened as he groped and kissed me.

"Please," I moaned.

"Please what?" He trailed his lips down my throat, nipping at the skin. "You have to say the words, Harper."

"I need you," I whimpered. "It's been so long... *please*."

"Say it," he growled. He sucked on my collarbone, grinding his hips into mine. "Tell me what you want me to do to you."

I'd never been one to talk dirty, even though I'd loved it when Gabe did it. For some reason, it was difficult for me to get the words out.

Apparently, not when I was drunk.

The alcohol took away my inhibitions and the words tumbled out before I could stop them. "Fuck me, Gabe. I need to feel you inside of me."

"Right here?" He started to unbutton his pants.

"Yes." I wiggled out of my top.

And then we were touching each other everywhere, re-establishing possession and finding our groove. He bent his head to nuzzle my cleavage as he unhooked the back of my bra, letting it fall away. My breath left me in a rush when he closed his mouth around one of my nipples, sucking lightly. I pressed my nails into his scalp, scraping them softly across the skin and watching as he sucked and kneaded my breasts.

Everything seemed to move in a rush of frantic groping, kissing, and touching. I shimmied out of my jeans with his mouth attached to mine and the next thing I knew he'd lifted one of my legs and pushed into me. I still fit him like a glove, and we moaned simultaneously. My fingers clutched at his shoulders for balance as he started to move.

He felt so damn good.

I wiggled, desperate to have more of him, and he reached down, lifting me off the ground and guiding my legs around his waist.

"Like that?" he whispered against my mouth.

"More," I pleaded.

He slammed into me recklessly, over and over, the sound of our bodies slapping together bouncing off the walls.

It was primal.

Brutal.

Borderline painful.

Exactly the way I liked it.

My heart thumped against my chest, and I squeezed around him, taking him as deep as possible. I loved the way it felt when he bottomed out, our bodies crashing together with beautiful symmetry, making us one. Bringing us to a point of no return.

"Fuck, yes!" Gabe grunted as I began chanting his name.

"Gabe-Gabe-Gabe!"

"Come for me, baby... just like that..."

The roaring in my ears told me I was done, and my orgasm was an explosive detonation of pleasure. So much so that I nearly blacked out. All I could do was hold on and howl, barely aware that he shot off inside of me a moment later.

"Fuck, Harper." He was still breathing hard, holding me

against the wall, our bodies still tightly connected.

I felt him pulsing inside of me with each aftershock, my vagina convulsing a little each time he did it. Still perfectly in sync. Even after all this time.

"Let's go to bed," I whispered when I caught my breath.

He scooped me up in his arms and carried me down the hall to the primary bedroom, unceremoniously dumping me on the bed.

"Ready for round two?"

THE POUNDING behind my eyes woke me, along with the screaming of my bladder, and it wasn't until I tried to roll over that I realized I was tangled with a warm, hard body. A moment of panic washed over me as my eyes popped open, but then I saw who it was, and I felt a mixture of horror and relief.

Gabe.

I was naked in bed with my ex.

I stared at him in disbelief, despite taking in his chiseled features and the scruff of his five o'clock shadow. How was it possible he got better looking with age? Was that what had drawn me in last night? Along with too much alcohol?

Jesus.

I needed to get a grip.

I'd been lucid enough to know there would be regret, but I hadn't anticipated how much.

Okay, that wasn't entirely accurate.

What I was feeling was regret, but not because of what I'd done.

My regret was the *lack* of regret.

My first inclination, once I got my wits about me, had been to smile.

At how handsome he was.

At how good he looked lying here in my bed.

At how I wanted to jump on him again, since I knew he always woke up with morning wood.

Shit.

I tried to slip out of bed, but his arm tightened around me.

"No running away," he murmured in a sleep-laced voice.

"I have to pee," I whispered.

"Hold it. We both know once I let you out of this bed you're not coming back."

I sighed but relaxed against him.

He had a point.

I was absolutely, positively never doing this again, so I might as well enjoy it.

"Now isn't that better?" he whispered, closing his arms around me. "This is so much nicer than arguing all the time."

I couldn't disagree, so I nestled against him.

If there was one thing Gabe was good at—well, there were a few things, but I was talking about non-sexual things—it was cuddles. Hugs. When he put his arms around me, there was nothing better. He was strong and warm, muscular enough to feel safe but not so much that it was intimidating. As a goalie, his focus was on stamina and agility more than speed or strength. And that translated to other aspects of his life as well.

"Don't start thinking," he warned. "We're just having some morning-after snuggles, which I seem to remember is your thing. Well, it was. Is it still?"

I chuckled. "Yup."

"When you watch movies too?"

"Of course."

"I'll keep that in mind."

"Gabe, this isn't the start of something. It's more like...unfinished business."

"Is that so?" He didn't sound impressed.

He was going to get annoyed now, and then we would argue, which I didn't want. I had enough stress in my life.

I turned over so I was half-sprawled across his chest and could look into his handsome face.

"Let's not fight. Last night was awesome. A much better way of saying goodbye than how we did that day at the courthouse."

The day we'd signed our divorce papers and went our separate ways.

That day had sucked.

Today he sighed heavily, as if the memory was emotionally taxing. "This is definitely better than that, but we can't just say goodbye, Harper. I basically live with you. Work for you. We see each other every day."

"Yes, but we're not going to sleep together every day."

"Every other day?"

"Stop it. Let's just chalk it up to a night of fun and put it behind us. Please?"

"If that's what you want."

"It is. It has to be. You know that. Casual sex between us would be a nightmare. Especially if we ever got caught."

"We're consenting adults. Who's going to catch us, and if they do, what are they going to say? Oh, wow, two single people in their mid-thirties are fucking—that should stop immediately."

I sat up shaking my head. "As you pointed out, I'm your boss. I'm about to shake this team to its core. You think the news that we're sleeping together is going to help in the locker room?"

"I don't really give a shit what the guys think about me in the locker room."

"But I need you to care," I said softly. "I need you to be a leader, to—"

"You *want* me to be your spy," he interrupted dryly, his eyes narrowing. "You don't need me to do shit, but that's what you want, and I told you from the get-go, I wasn't going to be your pawn."

"You did not," I said, scowling. "You said you couldn't afford to live here and that you wanted to retire in Florida. You never said you wouldn't do what I asked of you in the locker room. I handled your money problems and have made your life here pretty damn comfortable. All I ask in return is that you play to the best of your ability and make sure things don't spin out in the locker room. I don't want you to be a *spy*—I just want you to make sure the rumor mill doesn't go wild and that there's a modicum of respect early on."

"You have to earn respect. You know that. Especially in a locker room."

"Yes, but that takes time. Which is why I said early on. They don't have to respect me, per se, but they have to be *respectful*."

"Look, no matter what, I was never going to let anyone talk about you inappropriately. That's not who I am, even if you weren't my ex. Beyond that, you're on your own, darlin'. It's not my job to fix this for you."

"I didn't ask you to fix anything. I just told you what I needed from you."

"Whatever you say, Harper." He swung his legs over the side of the bed and padded across the room toward the bathroom.

I wanted to tell him to use the other bathroom, since I really did have to pee, but I was too damn distracted by his gloriously naked body.

The guy was Adonis personified.

And I absolutely had to stop thinking about that.

I got up and stubbornly followed him into the bathroom.

I refused to be locked out of my own bathroom out of some ridiculous sense of modesty. After all the things we'd experienced together? There was very little he could do to shock or surprise me.

Watching him urinate was oddly intimate, though, and I averted my eyes as I brushed my teeth.

How many times had we done this exact routine when we'd been together?

More than I could count.

But that ended now.

"Could you give me a little privacy?" I asked as he washed his hands.

He arched a brow. "What, you can watch me take a piss but I can't watch you?"

I huffed out a breath. "Gabe."

"Harper." He met my gaze in the mirror.

Apparently, we were at a standoff, and I didn't know if it was worth the energy to fight it.

"You know I get stage fright," I finally said.

"Fine." He wiped his hands and walked out, leaving me blissfully alone.

Except when I sat on the toilet, I felt the strangest moment of discomfiture. As if his departure from the bathroom was indicative of something else. Something more permanent.

And I fucking hated it.

Everyone fucking left me.

My parents.

Gabe.

Edward.

Even friends, like Sloane, who'd moved to Fort Lauderdale, and Cheyenne, who was only in L.A. a few months of the year.

Why did everyone leave me?

I closed my eyes and breathed in deeply through my nose, counting to eight.

I was using a technique my therapist had taught me because abandonment had been a recurring theme in our sessions.

Then I breathed out through my mouth.

People weren't leaving *me*.

My parents had been young and incapable of raising a child.

Technically, I had been the one to leave my marriage to Gabe.

Edward hadn't wanted to die.

And Sloane and Cheyenne had lives, careers, and relationships that took them away physically, but we still had close, if not geographically challenged, relationships.

I had to remember that.

Slowly opening my eyes, I'd just gotten up from the toilet when reality hit me.

Holy fucking shit.

There had been... evidence of last night's sexual encounter on the toilet paper.

Which meant Gabe hadn't used a condom.

Holy fucking hell.

I was going to kill him.

12

———————

G *abe*

"GABRIEL DELUGO!"

I was in the kitchen making coffee when I heard her yell and I winced.

Now what?

I probably should have made my escape while I'd had the chance, but now she was pissed about something. Had I missed the toilet when I took a leak?

"What?" I asked, irritated at the turn the morning had taken.

"Did you use a condom?" she demanded, storming into the kitchen with her hands on her hips.

I stared at her, desperately trying to recall if I had or not. It was usually second nature, but things had escalated quickly last night.

The minute we walked in the door.

Up against the wall of the foyer.

There had been no time for a condom.

Shit.

And despite papers that said otherwise, in my heart, Harper was still my wife.

There was no concern about diseases or a paternity suit.

Condoms hadn't even crossed my mind.

"Uh..."

"Gabe!" She glared at me. "Are you serious right now?"

"Hey, it takes two to tango." I glared right back, running a hand through my hair in frustration. "We were both drunk. I didn't use one... I mean, I don't think I did, but you don't have to worry about diseases. I'm not twenty anymore. I'm cautious."

"Apparently, you're not even *a little* bit cautious or we wouldn't be having this conversation."

"It's different with you," I muttered.

"Different?!" She threw up her hands. "You know I've been contemplating getting pregnant, so I'm not protected! Jesus fucking Christ, how irresponsible was this? Have you grown up at all since college?"

"You didn't say anything either!" I shot back, folding my arms across my chest. "I asked you if you were sure and you said you were. In fact, I seem to recall you—"

"This isn't about consent, dammit! This is about pregnancy. Oh, my fucking God, what have you done?" She clapped a hand over her mouth.

For some reason, I smirked.

The asshole in me was strong sometimes.

It was one of many reasons she hadn't believed me when I'd denied cheating on her. One of many reasons she'd divorced my ass without a backward glance. Probably one of the many reasons we fought like cats and dogs. When we weren't fucking anyway.

Once I got pissed off, there was a huge disconnect between my brain and my mouth, and I said things I probably shouldn't.

"You think this is funny?" she demanded.

"Well, getting knocked up by me can't be worse than by some random dude who jizzed into a cup for money. At least you'll know where to find me if the kid needs a kidney or something."

Her mouth fell open.

Then her eyes narrowed, fury racing across her features as she pointed a finger at me. "You did it on purpose." She looked shocked and angry.

"I didn't, but in retrospect, I probably just did you a favor."

"Are you kidding? This was incredibly irresponsible. I'll take on some of the blame, because you're right that I didn't ask you to use protection, but you were always in charge when we were together."

"We haven't been together in a long time," I pointed out.

"So, if I had been a random hook-up, you wouldn't have been worried about knocking up some stranger?" she snapped.

"Of course, I would have. But you aren't a random stranger and there's a level of comfort between us that doesn't exist elsewhere."

"So, you *did* do it on purpose."

I rolled my eyes. "Yeah. Because making another kid I won't have time or money for is at the top of my list of priorities. Not to mention this particular kid's ball-buster mom who'd make my life miserable."

Oops.

There went my mouth again.

"Get out." Her voice had a deadly edge to it as she pointed to the sliding glass door.

"Harper." I tried to backpedal. "I didn't mean to—"

"Out." Her finger was shaking a little and I realized I might have gone too far.

"Harper, come on. Let's just take a minute—"

"I said to get out! Now!" She wasn't kidding and I held up my hands.

"Okay. Fine. I'm leaving." I grabbed the cup of coffee I'd just made and opened the door. "But we're going to have to—"

"Out."

I shook my head as I walked toward the guest house.

Shit.

I'd left my wallet and phone on her nightstand.

The wallet that had a perfectly good condom in it.

I really was an asshole.

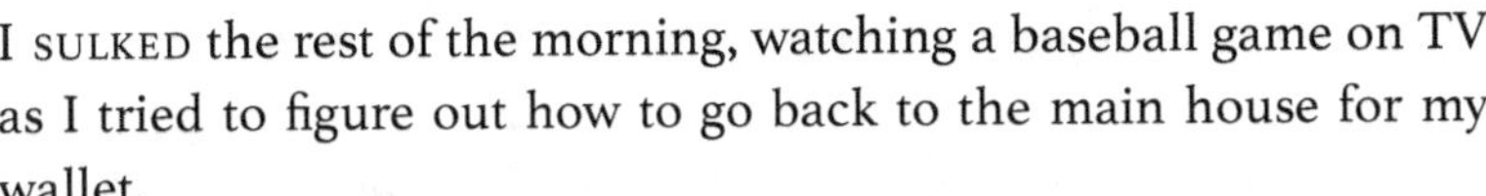

I SULKED the rest of the morning, watching a baseball game on TV as I tried to figure out how to go back to the main house for my wallet.

Harper was really pissed.

And I didn't blame her.

Condoms had truly never crossed my mind, as if I'd subconsciously been doing it on purpose. I'd never admit that to her, but I'd never done that before. No matter how fucked up I got, I always used condoms. And my gut told me Harper did too. I doubted she was a fan of one-night stands, but I figured she'd had a few over the years, and she would have been careful, no matter what.

Historically, Harper had never been able to hold her liquor, but she was different now. Older, more mature. More sure of herself. We'd been having a good time last night, but it was hard not to notice that there was still a tiny trace of the innocence she'd had back in our college days, when we'd first met and fallen in love. Pain, wariness, and a touch of sadness lurked beneath her bright smile and beautiful face. And for some reason, I'd wanted to erase that.

Probably because I'd caused some of it.

The end of our marriage had been ugly.

Tumultuous.

A freakin' nightmare.

A group of us from the team I'd been playing on back then had gone out. It had been a wild night. Yes, there had been strippers. Yes, we'd been drinking heavily. Yes, I'd probably been a little inappropriate with my flirting. But I'd loved my wife. I never would have cheated on her. It was a gray area, but sticking twenty-dollar-bills into a stripper's G-string wasn't cheating. It just wasn't. It was the kind of thing any couple would probably fight about, but at the end of the day, I hadn't touched that woman. Or any of them.

The problem, of course, was the pictures.

My hand on her thigh.

The laughter on my face as I slid the money into the tiny bit of cloth at her hip.

The way she'd been licking her lips as our eyes met.

Fuck.

Even now I got pissed off about the whole thing.

I'd been dumb, but I hadn't cheated.

I'd come close to the line, but I hadn't crossed it.

But Harper hadn't believed me.

I'd begged, pleaded, and offered to go to marriage counseling.

Nothing had moved her, and she'd walked away without a second glance.

She'd said she couldn't stay married to a man she didn't trust.

We'd yelled and argued and said ugly things.

In the end, none of it mattered because she still left.

It had been the end of our marriage, our relationship, and the best part of my life.

I'd tried to find that same love and happiness two more times, hurting both Tricia and Brittany, and bringing a child into the world who only had her dad around for a few months of the year.

I wouldn't intentionally do it again.

Would I?

A knock on my door startled me and I looked up to see Ivan.

"Hey. What are you doing here?" I asked as I opened the door.

"I brought Harper's car back to her, and she asked me to give you these." He held out my phone and wallet.

"Thanks." I took them from him as I motioned for him to come in.

"I can't stay long but look at this place. It's small but nice."

"What do I need more room for?" I asked. "This is perfect. There's a bedroom big enough for my bed. A bathroom with a nice shower. A kitchen and a grill that allow me to cook. And a place for my TV." I shrugged.

"I guess you have a point." He cocked his head. "So, you want to tell me what happened with you and Harper that she couldn't bring you your wallet herself?"

I shrugged. "The usual. We fucked and then we fought."

"Was the sex bad?"

"No, you asshole. We just... you know. This is why we're not married anymore."

"You're not married anymore because you allowed her to think you cheated instead of fighting for her."

"I did fight!" I protested. "I offered to go to therapy. I begged her to give me another chance. I—"

"Those are the actions of a man who's *guilty*," he interrupted quietly. "An innocent man would have let her talk to his teammates, who could corroborate his story."

"Like she was going to believe them? Especially when they were all in trouble with their significant others too? Besides, guys lie for each other all the time."

"Yeah, but a couple of those guys didn't like you enough to lie for you. Not much back then and not at all now."

"You think I should reach out to Rich Sentry or Vinnie Massimo to tell my ex-wife that I didn't cheat?" I laughed. "To what end? We're not getting back together."

He shook his head. "You're going to sit here and tell me you don't still have feelings for her?"

"Sure. There are feelings. She's beautiful. Smart. Successful. The type of woman a man gets stupid over. But I've already done that. Three times. I'm done. I need to finish my career without any more concussions, save up some money, and think about what I'm going to do after hockey, because that day is coming whether I want it to or not."

"That's all you want in life? To work and be a part-time dad to a pre-teen? You don't want companionship? Someone to talk to late at night? Sex that you don't have to go looking for? I mean, what the hell kind of sad, sappy bullshit is that?"

"Did you come by to lecture me?" I muttered.

"No, but it looks like someone needs to."

"I'm fine, man. I don't need a father or a big brother."

"You'd be the big brother in this scenario. Regardless, you should go apologize for whatever you did. You live on her property. You play for her team. You're going to be seeing a lot of each other, whether you like it or not, so it's going to get really complicated come September if you guys are fighting like this."

"I'll figure it out. I always do."

He looked like he wanted to protest but just shrugged instead. "Whatever you say, my friend. I think you're making a huge mistake, but you're a grown man. You've got to figure out your own shit one of these days."

"Have I ever told you you're a pain in my ass?"

"Probably."

"You want to hang out or are you leaving?"

"I have to go," he replied. "I'm getting ready to head to New York for a few days. But I'll see you when I get back."

"What's in New York?"

"A woman." He grinned. "What else?"

13

———————

H*arper*

THERE WERE options after having unprotected sex.

The morning-after pill was the most logical, but I wanted a baby so doing that seemed counterproductive.

I did not particularly want Gabe's baby but if it had happened, it wouldn't be the end of the world.

We'd draw up a custody agreement of some kind and then I'd finally get to be a mom.

Of course, it would add a level of complication to my life that I didn't relish. If people in the hockey world found out Gabe had fathered my kid, and we weren't together, there would be gossip for days. Weeks. Probably the entire season. The focus would be on my personal life instead of the team, which was the opposite of what I was trying to do.

And yet, that didn't bother me as much as I'd thought it would.

I was used to it now.

There had been a lot of horrible comments and gossip when I married Edward. I was a gold digger, a shrew, pregnant, unable to get pregnant, responsible for his cancer. Some of it had been so ludicrous we'd laughed. Other parts of it had made me cry. I'd had Edward then, though, so I hadn't felt alone. He'd always had my back, and even after he got sick, he'd been fierce in his protection of me.

That was one of the things I'd loved most about him.

He was kind and gentle, but also determined and no-nonsense. He didn't take shit from anyone, including his children. He'd never let anyone talk down to me, or about me if he could help it, nipping all the bullshit in the bud early.

I didn't have him anymore, but I did have the lessons he'd left me and the memories of how he'd handled the nastiness. How he expected other people to treat me, and by extension, how he'd wanted to be treated. Both personally and professionally.

It wasn't easy behavior to learn or to implement, but I intended to try. I had to be a million times tougher than people were expecting, and I couldn't rely on Gabe to protect me in the locker room even though I hoped he would. He needed to focus on his play and being an unofficial morale officer. He tended to be broody and sarcastic, but younger players looked up to him and veterans respected him, even if they didn't necessarily like him. That was the main reason I'd brought him here.

Somehow, I had to find a way to be friends with him, without arguing and letting him get on my nerves. Without him potentially getting me pregnant. Without us falling into bed every time— Sloane's name on the screen of my phone interrupted my scattered thoughts and I answered with as much energy as I could muster up.

"Hey."

"Wow, you sound excited to be alive."

"It's early," I muttered.

"Must've been one hell of a movie." She knew I'd been planning to go to the movies with Cheyenne.

"Well, dinner and a movie turned into drinks and a rock concert with Gabe, and Ivan Rochenko."

"Wait, what?" She sounded confused. "How did a simple girls' night at the movies turn into a double date at a concert?"

"It wasn't a date."

Until it was.

"But?"

"I slept with Gabe!" I blurted out.

She burst out laughing.

"You suck," I muttered. "I'd fire you if I didn't need you so badly."

"I wish I'd bet on this because I'd be rich right now," she said. "I *knew* you were going to do the horizontal bop with him. I knew it!"

"*I* didn't even know!" I protested. "How could *you* know?"

"I knew because you always get a dreamy little look in your eyes when you talk about him. Unless you're mad about something he did, but even then, there's a passion in you that I rarely see anywhere else. Gabe is the only person who brings out every emotion in you, so in my head, it was inevitable that you two would sleep together again. If not get back together at some point."

"Well, it gets better." I told her about having unprotected sex. She already knew I wanted to have a baby, so if anyone might have good advice, it would be her.

"Oh, shit, girlfriend. When you want something, you really go for it."

"I didn't do it on purpose!" I said in frustration.

"No? Not even subconsciously?"

I hadn't considered that.

Had I, in the dark, shuttered recesses of my mind, somehow wanted this to happen?

Had I thrown caution to the wind because I trusted him and had been willing to risk it?

Edward and I had started trying as soon as we got married and I'd never gotten pregnant. Then he got sick and the chemotherapy had wreaked havoc on his system, leaving him with a low sperm count and zero sex drive. Artificial insemination hadn't worked either, but by then he'd been too sick for me to think about seeing a specialist. So, I didn't know if I was the problem.

"Harper?"

"I don't know," I admitted slowly. "I mean, no, I didn't go into it with that in mind. When we were together, he was always in charge of birth control, and I just assumed he would be again. Which was stupid."

"So you didn't discuss it at all?"

"No. One minute we were kissing, the next he was inside of me and that was that."

"How many times?" she asked.

"Uh, three? Maybe four. I don't even remember."

"And then this morning you picked a fight with him when you realized what had happened?"

"Yup."

"If I recall, you accused him of something else he may not have done that caused the end of your marriage. Don't you think you might want to give him the benefit of the doubt this time? I mean, why would he do that? You guys aren't together, so intentionally getting you pregnant sounds a little far-fetched. Even for Gabe."

"I know," I said miserably. "I was embarrassed and hungover and frustrated. And he was so smug, the bastard."

"That's who he is, though, isn't it? From what you've told me, he's always been that way, smug and arrogant and all that."

"Yeah."

"Would it be the worst thing in the world if he became your baby daddy? And doing it the old-fashioned way, instead of in a doctor's office paying tens of thousands of dollars, sounds like a lot more fun."

"That's true."

"Not to mention, your kid would have the opportunity to know his dad. He or she would have a mother and a father, even if he was only around in the summer or whatever."

"In theory, it sounds perfect," I said. "But I'd already made the decision to put it off. I don't have time to be pregnant and I'll have even less time to be the mom to a newborn. I have to take a year to get the team running on an even keel. The plan was to circle back to this next summer."

"Well, be that as it may, it's possible you're already pregnant, so you guys need to talk. Please note, I said talk, not yell or fight."

I wrinkled my nose even though she couldn't see it. "I know."

"Tell him the truth, Harper. About all of it. There might already be a baby. You can't pussyfoot around that issue."

"But do we have to talk about it before I know for sure? All we do is fight."

"Apparently, that's not *all* you do. And you're right to have reservations, but at this point, what do you have to lose? You can lie to him and to yourself, but you still have feelings for him. No matter how deep you've buried them. Maybe it's time to put it all out there."

"I do," I said softly. "I wish I didn't, but I do. Every time I see him, my heart beats a little faster. Just like when we first met."

"Talk to him, Harper. You have to communicate."

"I know you're right. It's just hard."

"Most things worth having are hard."

"He's mad at me right now."

"Start with an apology and go from there."

And food.

He liked food, especially when I baked.

"He likes muffins," I mused aloud.

"I'm sure he does," she said, laughing.

"I'm talking about the kind I bake," I said, chuckling.

"Bake some muffins and then go over and talk."

"Tomorrow," I said finally. "I need some time to mull it all over. And I have a conference call at two."

"Yes, you do. You also have to look at Shane Finnegan's proposed offer. It's in your email."

"Got it. Okay, gotta run. Thanks for listening."

"Anytime."

"Talk to you later." I hung up and opened the email on my laptop, but it was hard to concentrate.

What if I was pregnant?

What if there was already a baby growing inside of me?

Gabe's baby.

Something I'd dreamed of many, many times.

We hadn't been ready for kids when we'd been married, and while I'd wanted a big family, he'd waffled on whether or not he wanted any. One of many things we'd fought about.

Now I'd be lucky to have even one.

But that would link Gabe and me for the rest of our lives, and I had to think hard about whether or not I could live with that. It was one thing to have him in my guest house and on my team. Sharing a child with him would make us family.

Forever.

And that would be torture for me.

I'd loved Edward deeply, but I'd never loved anyone the way I'd loved Gabe. It was widely accepted that you never got over your first love, and I never had. In fact, I was positive I never would. Gabe owned me, body and soul, no matter how hard I tried to get over him.

My love for Edward had been different.

Softer, more mature, less all-encompassing.

We'd had a friendship that gradually became something more. I'd loved the fact that he was protective and kind, because no one else had ever protected me. Not even Gabe. So those two things had been what had won me over, and his generosity and intelligence made Edward a wonderful husband. Someone I would have been happy to spend many years with.

Fate had other plans for me, and apparently Gabe was part of them.

14

———————

G *abe*

I'D JUST GOTTEN up and was fighting with my aging Keurig machine when there was a knock on the door. I padded in that direction, surprised to see Harper standing there with a basket of some kind.

"Hey." My gaze drifted down to the basket. "What's up?"

"Breakfast." She thrust it in my direction so quickly, she would have dropped it if I hadn't grabbed it in time.

"Easy, turbo," I said, peeking in to see the contents. "It's not a bomb, is it?"

"No. I, uh, well, I need to talk to you."

"Okay. Come in."

"Thanks." She brushed past me and immediately started to pace.

"You okay?" I asked curiously.

"I owe you an apology, but it's hard for me, so just let me talk, okay?"

"Okay." I put the basket of what appeared to be muffins down on the small counter that separated the kitchen from the main part of the house.

"I overreacted yesterday morning, and I'm sorry. We were both responsible. You just always took care of birth control, and I assumed you would again."

"That's on me. I should have—" I began.

"Just let me talk!" she snapped, before closing her eyes. "Sorry. I just, please... let me get out what I have to say."

"All right." I watched her curiously. Harper was rarely nervous. Even if she was feeling it on the inside, she was good at hiding it, so this was an interesting turn of events.

"I've wanted a baby for a long time," she said. "You and I never could decide what we wanted in that regard, and then with Edward it never happened. Now I'm getting older, already high-risk as far as pregnancy age goes, so my biological clock is going off big-time. I thought using a sperm donor would be safer, less personal. This would be my decision, my baby, my everything." She took a breath, finally looking at me. "But making that decision was so much harder than I thought it would be. Picking a number from a file, using nothing but eye and hair color to create a life...it felt so fucking impersonal and weird."

"Well, looks like you don't have to go through that anymore," I added, trying to make a joke although it seemed to fall flat.

"Please don't do that," she whispered. "I'm trying to be serious, trying to apologize and communicate. For once."

"Sorry. Keep going." She went hot and cold so often, sometimes all in one conversation, it was hard to know how to behave.

"There might be a baby now. One that you and I made together. Maybe not intentionally, but this potentially changes everything."

I waited, unsure where she was going with this.

"We can't have a baby and constantly be at each other's throats, Gabe. And can I be a hundred percent honest?" Her voice was soft as she finally looked at me. Really looked at me. It wasn't just with her eyes, but somehow all of her was in this look.

Jesus.

How was she still so beautiful?

"Sure."

"I don't want to fight anymore. Baby or no baby, we work and essentially live together. And it occurred to me that we fight the way we do to mask our feelings. You're many things but careless isn't one of them. You might not have been trying to get me pregnant, but deep down somewhere, you felt comfortable enough with me to go bare. And you've been around the block too many times for that to be an accident."

"What are you trying to tell me?" I asked after a moment, because I was confused.

"That we're both still battling feelings. Feelings that go beyond sex and our history. I've been trying to move on for so long, and the truth is, I never could. Not really. And based on your divorce record, neither have you."

This was a crazy twist in the plot of our relationship.

I hadn't been expecting this at all.

I'd thought she might eventually apologize, tell me we absolutely couldn't do it again, and maybe have a what-if conversation if I'd managed to knock her up the other night. But not a heart-to-heart like this.

"Can I talk now?" I asked after a long moment.

"Yes."

I needed a few seconds to gather my thoughts, so I momentarily deflected. "First of all, apology accepted. It was probably jarring to realize we'd done what we did, multiple times, without protection. And yes, I'm usually very cognizant of birth control, so I feel bad I dropped the ball. We were drunk, and it felt so good... I know that's no excuse, but we've made love a million times. It felt natural to just go with the flow."

"It did." She wasn't looking at me anymore, staring at some invisible spot over my shoulder.

"But, uh, the other thing..." I cleared my throat. "Yeah, of course, there are feelings. How could there not be? But a lot of those feelings are negative."

"I know." She looked up, her eyes meeting mine again cautiously. "That's my concern."

"I do want to make one thing clear, though: If there is a baby, or if we somehow make a baby in the future, I will be part of his or her life."

"You want that?" She looked surprised.

"It would be *our* kid," I said impatiently. "If you need to ask, then we need to be having a different conversation."

"I'm sorry." She walked over to me slowly, chewing the inside of her cheek. "I didn't mean it to be insulting. You never said anything about wanting to be a dad so—"

"I'm *already* a dad," I said.

"I meant, when we were together."

"Look, can we take this back over to your place? My Keurig machine decided to be an asshole and isn't working. And I don't think I can have the conversation we're about to have without coffee."

"You might need to descale the machine."

"I don't even know what that means," I admitted, chuckling. "I'm probably just going to buy a new one."

"I can help you if you want to descale it, but for now, yes, let's go back to my kitchen."

We walked across the patio in silence, with me holding the basket of freshly baked muffins that normally would have made my mouth water.

Instead, all I was thinking about was her.

Being together again.

Making a baby with her.

Becoming a family.

Did I want that?

Did she?

I'd have to rethink everything if Harper was pregnant.

Hell, I had to rethink everything anyway, because it almost sounded like she wanted to be more than friends.

Or was that just wishful thinking on my part?

Harper turned on the coffeemaker and pulled two mugs from the cabinet.

She seemed to be buzzing with nervous energy, pulling butter out of the refrigerator and a jar of something else from the pantry. She gathered plates, napkins and butter knives, laying everything out on the island.

"Hey." I walked over to her, putting a gentle hand on hers, stilling her movements. "Stop a minute. Look at me."

She lifted those gorgeous blue eyes to mine questioningly.

"If the idea of us as parents makes you so nervous you can't stop moving, maybe we need to rethink this. I know we've had our problems, and we'll undoubtedly have more, but I never want you to look like you're ready to jump out of your skin because of me."

"It's not you." She shook her head. "But if I'm pregnant, the timing is all off. If we were going to have reckless sex, it should have been six or eight months from now."

"Sorry," I said wryly. "I didn't realize that was the timeline. You should've given me a head's up."

She looked startled for a moment and then laughed. "Yeah, sorry. I didn't have get-drunk-at-a-concert-and-screw-my-ex-husband on this summer's bingo card either."

Okay, this was better.

I didn't like seeing her stressed out and unsure of herself.

Confident, snarky Harper was more what I was used to.

"Same." I wrapped my hand around hers. "Talk to me, babe. Tell me what you want."

"I don't know. I just know that we seem to fight as a way to mask our feelings, and that's stupid. We're too old and have been through too much for that."

"Agreed."

"I guess I just want to know if you...well, if you want to spend the next month or so, while we wait to see if I'm pregnant, getting to know each other again."

Holy shit.

She did want to try again.

"But you have to think long and hard about it, because if you do, there are going to be rules."

I sighed, pulling my hand away. "Coffee first. Then rules."

I put a mug under the spout and pushed the button.

As much as I wanted to say yes, starting something with her would be complicated.

But I still wanted to.

I didn't know what the hell was wrong with me.

It seemed like when it came to Harper, I lost all sense of who I was.

I became someone I didn't know.

Someone who might want to be in a relationship again.

Jesus.

Fucking.

Christ.

Ivan was going to have a field day when I told him.

And the locker room was going to be wild when word got out.

It wasn't like we could hide it if she was pregnant.

Even if we kept our relationship on the down low, there was zero chance I'd let anyone talk shit about her or the fact that she was knocked up. If that happened, we'd absolutely have to make an announcement.

When we both had mugs of coffee in our hands, I arched a brow at her. "So. Rules for dating your ex. Let's hear them."

"It's about more than dating. If I'm pregnant, you'll sign something giving me primary and physical custody. And unless I die, you will never sue me for custody."

"That's fine," I replied. "But I'm not signing away my parental rights and I expect to have unlimited, within reason, visitation."

She arched her brows for a moment but then nodded. "That's fair." She drummed her fingers on the counter.

"Talk to me, Harper. I already figured we'd have to talk about custody and all that at some point, but this isn't about that. What's on your mind? If you need help asking me out, I can take that out of your hands."

She smiled, dipping her chin. "No, that's not it. Well, okay, that's part of it. Like, where do we go from here? The timing is all wrong, but we've potentially already set things in motion by our carelessness the other night, and it feels like we're closing that barn door after the animals already escaped."

"What if we just go with the flow," I suggested lightly, reaching for her and drawing her close to me. "Let's get to know each other again, spend time together, and not worry about a baby unless and until we have to. No pressure, you know?"

"We had a lot of problems, and I don't think it'll be any different now. Are we prepared to do that again?"

"Do we have to? I mean, can we try to do it better this time? For us to be better this time?"

"I'd like that. Really. But..."

"Spit it out, Harper."

"I want to spend time together, see what there is to see, but... we can't tell people. We can't let it get out. There's just too much at stake."

"So... you want me to fuck you on a regular basis but I'm going to be your dirty little secret?"

15

———

H*arper*

WHY DID my lady parts clench with excitement when he talked to me that way?

And when he looked at me like he wanted to have me for breakfast.

I enjoyed it far too much.

This was going to be a problem going forward.

Maybe not short-term, but in the long run, I couldn't let him continue to arouse me with just his voice.

Especially when we argued.

"We have to keep things casual because I can't just start sleeping with one of my players," I said as nonchalantly as I could manage with him so close to me. "Even if that player is my ex-husband."

"Casual and ex-husband." He dropped his head slightly, rubbing his nose against mine. "Not two words you hear in the same sentence very often."

"Gabe, please," I pleaded softly. "I need time and if you're honest with yourself, you do too. Casual is the smart way for us to handle it this time around."

"Maybe, but there's no such thing as casual once I touch you. I was the first and I have every intention of being the best."

He brought his mouth to mine and lightly teased my lips with his.

"What...are you doing?" I whispered breathlessly.

"If the goal is to get to know each other again, we should make the most of the off-season." He tugged my lower lip between his teeth, biting down just enough to make me suck in my breath. "Before hockey season starts."

"We... there are still... more...rules..."

"Do any of them involve how many times I'm allowed make you come?" One of his hands drifted beneath the fabric of my T-shirt, caressing the bare skin of my stomach.

"N-no."

"Then you can tell me the rest of your rules later." His mouth captured mine fully and he slid his tongue between my lips. One hand moved to cup the back of my neck while the other continued to touch and caress my torso. His fingers were warm and firm, but his touch was light, giving me goose bumps. Our mouths worked in tandem, tongues and lips dancing in perfect harmony.

He was such a good kisser.

His mouth told a story, simultaneously giving and taking. There was nothing better than having Gabriel DeLugo making love to your mouth. Except when he was deep inside my pussy, making me scream out his name.

Without breaking the kiss, he unsnapped my shorts and tugged them down, taking my panties with them. He pulled my T-shirt over my head next, though my bra didn't quite make it over my head. Giggling, I wiggled out of it while he yanked his own T-shirt off.

"Up." He patted the countertop.

"What?"

He lifted me onto the counter. "Open for me, baby."

"Gabe, not on the—"

He silenced me with another mind-bending kiss that made my world tilt sideways.

My legs opened on their own and he moved between them, hands on my sides as he kissed and kissed me. He moved from my mouth to my neck, pausing to lick and suckle the skin there, and then slipping down to my collarbone. His thumbs were doing wicked things to my nipples, circling and teasing until they were stiff peaks that were so hard they almost hurt.

By the time he got to my bellybutton I was squirming with need, biting my lip to keep from crying out.

And he continued to take his sweet time, exploring my torso one inch at a time.

Every kiss, nibble, and lick quickened my pulse and had me whimpering in anticipation.

He used his hands to spread my thighs apart and dropped down so he was eye level with my most intimate parts.

"Time to get reacquainted," he said in a low, gravelly voice.

"Gabe, please."

"This what you want?" The first touch of his lips on my delicate skin made my hips jerk up to meet him and his groan of satisfaction warmed me. He flicked the tip of his tongue around my clit, circling it with slow, lazy swirls that made me groan.

"Fuck, Gabe." I ran my fingers through his hair as he continued to lick his way up and down my slit. It was soft and gentle at first, exploring every inch of me, before slowly increasing pressure in time to the movement of my hips.

He pressed a finger inside of me and curled it, finding that magical place that always made me see stars.

"Oh, fuck," I moaned, pressing against his face.

A second finger joined the first and he picked up speed with his tongue, flicking it repeatedly around my clit until everything crashed around me. A primal sound left my throat as my orgasm raced down and out, the continued pressure of his fingers sending me into a never-ending spiral of pleasure. I felt the gush of liquid and heard his satisfied rumble of laughter as I collapsed against the counter.

"Damn. When did you become a squirter?"

"Fuck." I dropped my arm over my eyes, unsure if I was mortified or aroused all over again.

I'd never done that before but was too wrung out to formulate any other words.

"Ready?" He was asking as I lay there trying to recover.

"For what?" I asked, not moving my arm.

I jumped when he slid his cock up and down my slit.

"For the non-baby-making portion of this relationship." He held up an empty condom wrapper.

Then he pressed into me slowly, giving me time to adjust, but all I could do was moan.

Again.

"Gabe..."

"That's a good girl," he whispered. "Take every inch of my cock."

Despite having just gotten off, he'd brought me right back to a state of arousal, my pussy clenching around him. He brought my legs up, holding my knees together and pushing them toward my chest. Then he pounded into me, each thrust deeper and harder than the last. And there was nothing for me to do but lie back and enjoy it.

There was a part of me that craved something more, a little more intimacy to go with the ferocity, but there was no time to think because our bodies were already gearing up to detonate. I could feel him speeding up, his body tensing.

"Come for me, baby..." He grunted with exertion. He pressed my knees further back, angled his hips, and when he hit my G-spot, my world went white.

My scream was loud and guttural, this orgasm stronger than the last.

I clutched at the cold granite beneath me, desperate for something to hold on to, and then he let go of my legs. He leaned forward, dropping his mouth to mine as we shuddered through the aftershocks. My arms wound around his neck, pulling him closer, and we lay like that for a long time.

"You okay?" he asked quietly, kissing me softly.

"I don't think I can move," I whispered. "I might be dead."

"But you're smiling," he responded.

"What a way to go, right?"

"Come on." He straightened up, and I couldn't help but cry out when he withdrew, leaving me feeling strangely empty.

"Gabe!"

"I'm right here." He gently lifted me in his arms. "We're going to go soak in the tub, okay?"

I nestled against his chest. "Mm-kay."

He carried me into the bathroom and put me down as he leaned over to run a bath. I watched without saying anything, still a little rattled at how intense what we'd just done had been.

Had it always been like that?

And when had I started squirting?

I didn't know whether to laugh or die of embarrassment.

"Come here." Gabe took my hand, helping me step into the large, soaker tub. He sat down first, and I sank down in front of him, resting against his chest.

"I don't think we've ever taken a bath together," I said after a moment.

"We didn't have a tub in college," he responded.

"And we didn't have one big enough for both of us in our first apartment." Gabe had been drafted at eighteen, but he'd deferred to finish college. After he graduated, he'd played two seasons in the minor leagues, so money had been tight. I'd still been in college and then grad school, so we'd been broke in those days.

Gabe had one arm around my waist while the other rested lightly on one of my thighs. I had a million things to do, we still had to talk about the rules I'd come up with regarding us dating, and I hadn't even had a cup of coffee yet, but all I wanted to do was sit here.

I closed my eyes and relaxed, wishing there were more moments like this in my life, where nothing else mattered. Where I could just enjoy myself without worrying about what was on my calendar, where I had to go, or how many emails needed responses.

Gabe used one hand to cup some warm water and gently drizzle it over my torso.

"That feels good," I murmured.

"I'm glad." He brought his hand up, cupping one of my breasts. "You think they'll get bigger if I knocked you up?"

I chuckled. "That's what they say."

"I'm looking forward to that."

"I thought you liked them the way they are?" I teased.

"I love your tits," he said. "But no guy is ever going to say no to them getting bigger."

"Of course not."

"Tell me the rest of your rules." He was toying with my nipple, so it was hard to concentrate.

"Er, what?"

He pinched my nipple between his thumb and forefinger, making me squirm.

"Gabe, stop that!"

"You don't like it?"

"No, I do. But we just got done..."

"You have a limit on how many orgasms you can have in a day?"

"Well, no, but—" I gasped as he brought up his other hand and pinched both nipples at once.

"Tell me the rules."

"I..." My voice trailed because I couldn't remember them.

Something about boundaries.

My working hours and—holy shit, he was hard again.

I hadn't noticed his erection at first but now it was pressed firmly against my backside.

"Gabe, you can't possibly be ready to go again," I moaned as he shifted, sliding down a little and lifting me onto his lap. He spread my legs, so my thighs rested on the outsides of his, and then he was rubbing his penis along my slit without slipping inside of me.

"Sure I can," he whispered, bringing one hand around to seek out my clit. "But I didn't bring a condom into the tub, so we have to get creative. Because I plan to be inside of you as often as possible."

I tensed, suddenly remembering my number one rule.

"Gabe." I stilled the movement of his fingers by closing my hand around his. "There's one thing that's important. Probably the most important thing of all." It was hard to concentrate, but I had to get this out.

"What is it, baby?" he asked quietly, his voice as sincere as I'd ever heard it.

"If we do this—"

"We're *already* doing it," he murmured, moving back and forth with annoyingly gentle strokes.

"If we *continue* to do this, you can't be with, I mean..." I blew out a breath as I gathered my resolve. "You can't sleep with other women. We have to be exclusive."

16

———

G *abe*

Exclusive.

Of course we were going to be exclusive. Did she really think I'd date other women while we were actively trying to rekindle our relationship?

We didn't have a good track record when it came to trust, though, so it made sense she would want to make some boundaries.

Especially since we were undoubtedly going to be spending a lot of time together.

In her bed.

In her life.

In *her*.

Jesus, I wasn't even inside her, and this felt so good I couldn't think straight.

Had it always been this good?

My memory banks were apparently on the fritz because I

couldn't think of a single time that had felt as good as what we were doing right now.

"Baby, there aren't enough hours in the day for us to do this and for me to go out with other women. You don't have to worry about that."

She relaxed against me.

She'd been concerned.

She didn't *want* me to sleep with other women.

And my gut told me it had nothing to do with the potential for diseases.

She was still the jealous type.

And I was still possessive enough to dig it.

"We don't have a lot of time," I said, going to work on her clit again. "How fast do you think you can come?"

"This will be the third time in... like, twenty minutes!" she protested. "I'm not a machine like you are."

"You'll learn," I teased, pinching the little nub between my fingers as I continued to slide up and down her slit. I made sure my movements kept her on the edge of arousal. She liked rough and deep, and since I couldn't give that to her without a condom, I'd have to compensate some other way.

"Tell me what will get you there quickly," I whispered.

She paused.

"No judgment?"

"God, no. You should know me better than that, Harper."

Instead of telling me, she took the hand that wasn't on her clit and guided it up to her neck. Then she gently positioned it over her throat.

"Not enough to actually choke me," she said. "Just pressure. Like a threat, but not doing anything extreme."

Oh, hell yeah.

I loved shit like that, but we'd both been more naïve back when we'd started sleeping together. She'd been a virgin and I'd only been with a handful of girls, so we'd done a lot of exploring together. Choking, or even faux choking, hadn't been anywhere on our radar.

"Like this?" I squeezed just enough for her to feel it, but I wanted to be sure it was the right amount.

"A little more." She leaned back, completely at ease, and I increased the pressure until she clutched my wrist. "There. No more than that."

"Got it." I loved this trusting but adventurous side of her.

I always had. It was one of many things that had made me fall in love with her. She was so smart and sexy and curious about everything. I'd never met anyone else like her. And for whatever time we had, I was going to enjoy every second of having her back in my life.

She moaned, wiggling her bottom to find the best position.

Once I was relatively sure we had it, I kept the pressure on her throat and continued the sensuous assault on her clit, losing myself in a plethora of emotion and sensation and ecstasy. There was no other word for what it felt like to be together like this.

Her orgasm was more gradual this time, but I felt her start to clench around me and then a long, drawn-out wail left her as she bucked and writhed, with me right on her heels. I shot off in an upward direction, my semen landing on her stomach, both of us watching as I marked her.

Then we just sat there, breathing hard, my hand still on her throat but no longer squeezing.

Just us at our most vulnerable.

Which was equal parts interesting and uncomfortable.

I didn't dare get vulnerable or comfortable around her.

Not yet.

Everything between us was volatile, and while we'd agreed to try to do better this time, saying it and doing it were two entirely different things.

She'd shredded my heart when she left, and though it appeared we'd gotten past a lot of what had happened between us, it still hurt. Trust had been difficult for me since then, which was why both of my subsequent marriages had failed. So I had to be careful.

I wasn't stupid.

No matter the history between us, we were still in unfamiliar and dangerous territory.

She had a lot on the line right now, and us dating on the sly would add a level of complication to a relationship that was already hella complicated.

"I have to get going soon," I said after a few minutes. "I'm meeting up with Ivan."

He'd invited me to join him and a few teammates I hadn't yet met in less than an hour for lunch and a round of golf, and I was almost definitely going to be late. I hadn't planned on an early morning visit from Harper, and I certainly hadn't planned on multiple rounds of sex.

"I have a meeting at eleven," she responded, starting to sit up. "We need to be more cognizant of our time. Which is one of the rules I was going to mention."

I chuckled. "How about we take a quick shower, have our coffee, and maybe meet up for dinner later so we can finish said conversation about rules?"

"You think we can get through an entire conversation without getting naked?" she asked wryly, getting to her feet.

I laughed. "Maybe, maybe not. But we can try."

She padded over to the shower and turned on the water. "Sounds like a plan."

Ivan was waiting outside my house when I exited through the sliding glass doors of Harper's kitchen, and I grimaced. He was going to notice the wet hair. Not to mention the shit-eating grin. Oh, yeah. Ivan would know we'd hooked up.

"Good morning." He looked me up and down slowly, a grin spreading over his face. "Don't you look...refreshed."

I lifted my middle finger as I opened my front door. "Shut up and let me change real quick."

"By all means. I'm happy to wait for your morning-sex shenanigans."

"The shenanigans are over," I muttered. "It'll take me two minutes to change. So shut up."

He chuckled, leaning against the couch as I went into my room.

I pulled on shorts and a polo shirt, grabbed a pair of socks and put my wallet and keys into my pockets.

"I need to get my clubs out of the garage," I told him. "Who's driving?"

"I will," he said, following me as I grabbed my sunglasses and a baseball cap, and headed for the garage.

I got what I needed, threw it in the back of his SUV, and he pulled into traffic.

"Do I even want to ask?" he said after a moment.

"Can you not?" I asked after a slight hesitation. "I'm trying to wrap my head around it all."

"You're a grown man. You can get your heart broken all by yourself without any input from me."

I chuckled. "Yeah, yeah."

Luckily, the country club we went to was only a few minutes away and our teammates were already waiting.

"Gabe, this is Jensen Bang, Phil Lilleberg, and Shane Finnegan, who was just traded here."

"Nice to meet you." I shook all their hands before we headed inside to sign in.

Once we were out on the golf course, Jensen handed us each a beer and we chatted between holes.

"You gonna tell us about the new lady in your life?" Phil asked Jensen. "Or do we have to pry for details?"

Jensen shrugged his incredibly broad shoulders. The guy was like six-five and built like the broad side of a Mack truck. I was glad he played on my team because the idea of him crashing into me in net was a little scary. "We're trying to keep things private while she gets back to her acting career, so whaddaya wanna know?"

"Is it serious?" Ivan prompted.

"Well, yeah." Jensen looked offended at the thought of it being anything else.

"Is it new?" I asked when no one else said anything. This wasn't my kind of conversation, but I figured I should show some interest in my new teammates' lives.

"We've been gaming buddies for over a year," Jensen replied. "I met her in person a few months back and things... progressed."

"Things *progressed*?" Phil asked in a slightly lilted accent I couldn't quite place. Swedish, maybe?

"Look, what do you want to know? She's amazing. I'm in love with her. She's not like anyone I've ever dated before. We're already living together."

There didn't seem to be anything else to say so I figured we were on safer ground until Phil turned to me. "So, what's your deal? Married, divorced, kids?"

If that wasn't a loaded question, I didn't know what was.

"Been married three times," I replied. "Divorced three times. I have a nine-year-old daughter named Brandy who lives with her mom in Milwaukee. Currently single."

Ivan coughed.

"Shut the fuck up," I muttered.

"Well, who is she?" Jensen asked. "If you guys are gonna bust my balls, it's only fair I do it back."

I sighed.

Ivan chuckled.

Phil took a long pull from his beer.

"I don't think they know," Ivan said after a moment.

"Know what? Shane asked.

"Okay, here's the deal." I figured I needed to get this over with. "I'm renting the guest house from Harper Barrowman."

"The owner's widow?" Shane asked, squinting a little.

"The owner," I corrected him. "She owns the team now."

"Holy shit," Phil breathed. "She's... your landlord?"

Ivan coughed again.

I sighed again.

This time Jensen and Shane took long pulls from their beer bottles.

"She's ex-wife number one," I said, bracing myself for whatever the fallout was going to be.

Phil choked on the sip of beer in his mouth, coughing.

Shane stared at me in confusion.

Jensen burst out laughing.

"Oh, this season is going to be fun," Ivan said, grinning.

"You guys suck," I muttered, grabbing my five-iron and heading to take the next shot.

They weren't done with me, though. Ivan was the next to go and while he was doing his thing, my teammates assaulted me with questions.

"Did it end bad?"

"Are you still friends?"

"Why would you rent from your ex?"

"Is she the one you have a kid with?"

"You bangin' her?"

"Jesus, knock it off!" I snapped, shaking my head. "No, she's not my daughter's mother. That was ex-wife number two, Tricia. Yes, Harper and I ended badly but we've grown up a lot in the last ten years so we're friends again. I didn't want to move to L.A. this close to retirement, so she offered to let me rent her guest house for cheap as an incentive. Investing in real estate in L.A. seems risky at this stage of my career, so I opted not to just yet." I was careful not to answer to the question about whether or not we were sleeping together. That was no one's business. Not yet anyway.

"So, you're okay with her taking over the team?" Phil asked.

"Well, yeah. I know it's unconventional, but Harper is smart, well-educated, and knows hockey. She never played but she used to do stats for my college team and the late Mr. Barrowman taught her a lot. He was very careful about whom he chose to leave the team to. And based on the changes she's made so far, I think she's going to do fine."

Phil snorted. "She's brought in a guy with zero head coaching experience to lead us, a guy with zero general manager experience to be the GM, and a goalie with one foot out the door—no offense. It's not giving me the warm fuzzies."

"She brought in a coach who did a hell of a job coaching in Sweden and worked side-by-side with Toli Petrov the last few years," I said, trying to hide my annoyance. "Her GM choice is interesting, but he was both a player and a scout. He knows hockey, knows a lot of the guys in the league, and is tough, which is what we need. As for her choice in goalie…" I smiled. "They don't get better than me."

"Ten years ago," Phil said lightly. "You think you're better than someone like Camden Locke?"

Cam had been the starting goalie in Lauderdale. Twenty-five years old and at the height of his career. It wasn't a fair comparison, but stuff like this was nothing new to me.

"Cam's amazing," I said. "But he didn't have playoff experience and it showed last year. That's why they put me in when he struggled. I've got experience to compensate for my never-ending concussions." I hated admitting that, but everyone knew about my injuries, so there was no point in pussyfooting around it.

"If the goal is to bring in fresh, new blood," Shane said. "Why you? Is there something between you? Did she bring you here so you could be together?"

Christ.

I hadn't been expecting such direct and on-point questions.

And I had to answer them.

Both for myself and for Harper's sake.

But I also had to be careful with how much I gave away.

It was going to be a long afternoon.

17

H*arper*

When Edward was alive, I loved hosting dinner parties.

I'd managed every detail from the food and drinks to the custom place cards and which set of china to use.

Doing it now, as a single woman, was different.

I'd invited four couples over, and I would be the weirdo sitting at the head of the table by myself.

It was my house, and I owned a professional fucking hockey team, so it wasn't like I couldn't handle it. It had just been so much nicer sharing the hosting and entertaining with someone else. I liked being part of a couple, and if that meant turning in my feminist card, so be it.

Gabe was outside swimming, and I longed to call out to him, invite him in, seek out his opinion on the menu I'd chosen, and then ask him to join us for the evening.

But I couldn't.

This was business.

And we weren't a couple.

Not publicly anyway.

I'd invited Dom and Molly, Henrik and Autumn, our assistant general manager Ron Lapointe and his wife Lily, and our Vice President of Hockey Operations, Gerard Macintosh and his wife Gina. These men were the ones I would be working with closely, and I wanted to get to know their wives in an effort to minimize any awkwardness. It was the twenty-first century, so I shouldn't have had to worry about optics, but this was a male-dominated industry, and I was the only female owner in the league. I had to care about things men took for granted.

"Harper, do you want me to start the souffles while you're still eating dinner or wait until after? They take about forty-five to fifty minutes, so it's up to you how long after dinner you want me to serve them."

I paused thoughtfully.

Brianna James was in culinary school here in L.A. and when I'd discovered my usual chef had been unavailable for tonight's party, Molly had recommended her. Ironically, Brianna was married to the drummer for Nobody's Fool, Declan James, and we'd chatted about the show when she'd first arrived.

"Make them while we're eating," I said. "I think an hour is a long time to wait for dessert. And they'll need a little time to cool down, right?"

"Depending on how hot you want to eat them." She grinned at me from where she was cutting up cheese for one of the appetizers.

"Right." I glanced outside at Gabe again, still itching to invite him, but battling with myself over the decision.

"He's very nice to look at," Brianna commented, following my gaze.

"My ex-husband slash current tenant slash starting goalie for the team."

"Oh." Her eyes rounded. "That's not at all complicated."

"Not even a little." I smiled wryly. "I really want to invite him tonight, but it's too complicated. I can't invite him without inviting any other players on the team, and if I do, then people would wonder..." I let my voice trail because I didn't want to get into our current baby-making situation.

"Are you involved?" she asked.

I made a face. "Did I mention it's complicated?"

She laughed. "That's what people who are involved say when they don't want to admit they're catching feelings. No judgment on my part."

"We're...talking again," I said at last.

"But are there still feelings?"

"There were always feelings," I admitted, leaning against the island. "We just had trouble with communication, trust, and our vision for the future."

"Is that all?" She shook her head. "Some relationships aren't meant to be, no matter how much you care about that person."

"Tell me about it." Until I had a better idea what was happening between us, I had to be careful what I said about Gabe and me.

We'd agreed to exclusivity, but that wasn't the same as being a couple.

Falling in love.

Of course, there was no way for me to fall in love with him because I'd never stopped. Not really.

"I have to get in the shower," I told Brianna. "If you need anything, just text me. I'll keep an eye on my phone."

"I'll be here." She smiled and went back to what she was doing.

AFTER MY SHOWER, I dried my hair, put on makeup, and dressed in casual cream-colored linen pants, a sleeveless, button-down linen top in a rich jade color, and matching jade kitten heels. I was aiming for casual but elegant and I'd just turned to go back to the kitchen when a deep voice startled me.

"You look beautiful."

"Gabe." I whirled, my heart racing. "Thank you."

"You look like you're having a party," he said lightly.

Shit.

This was the problem with him living on the property.

"Uh, well, a business dinner. Some of the executive staff from the Phantoms. Henrik, Dom, Gerard, and Ron, along with their wives. Kind of a get-to-know-you thing."

He nodded slowly. "I see."

"I'm sorry," I said quietly. "I would have invited you to join us but that would just open up the door for a lot of questions I'm not prepared to answer."

"Yeah, of course. I understand." He shrugged, though his face was tight.

Shit.

He was mad, but what else could I do? There was too much at risk for us to simply announce we were dating. Unless and until we got serious, things had to stay under wraps. The hockey world had enough to say about me; I didn't need them to jump on my personal life too.

"Are you mad?" I asked, though I wanted to smack myself the moment the words were out of my mouth.

"No." He looked me up and down slowly. "Anyway, you really do look beautiful. Have a good night."

Without another word, he disappeared down the hall, leaving me completely discombobulated. I didn't know why he'd come in, and I wanted to remind him about rules and boundaries but couldn't remember if I'd actually told him not to come in unannounced.

This was such a clusterfuck.

I grabbed my phone off the bed and hurried after him. I didn't know what I was going to say but it felt weird leaving it this way. He was already halfway across the patio when I got to the sliding glass doors by the kitchen and I hesitated as I watched him go into the guest house, closing the door without looking back.

Things were always like this with us.

He was complicated and exciting, sexy and broody, and probably as high maintenance as I was, just in different ways.

We were still like oil and water.

And I still wanted him so much it hurt.

I didn't need him, but I fucking wanted him.

That had always been the issue.

Ten years, another marriage, and practically a lifetime of experience hadn't changed that aspect to our relationship. And it pissed me off that he still had that much of a hold on me.

It didn't help that I'd started sleeping with him, but that was separate.

And maybe if I told myself that a million more times, I'd believe it.

"You okay?" Brianna asked me, her eyes meeting mine. "Your tenant blew out of here at top speed."

"Yeah. I think he's mad at me."

She grimaced. "Well, either way, I think your first guests are here."

"Right." I smoothed my hands down my pants and then walked to the front door to greet Dom and Molly.

Henrik and Autumn were right behind them, and I could see Gerard's Corvette pulling up to the gate.

I firmly pushed Gabe to the back of my mind as I greeted my guests and was soon caught up in the fun of my dinner party.

Autumn was young, probably only in her mid-twenties to Henrik's early forties, but they seemed like a wonderful couple. In a way, they reminded me of Edward and me when we'd first met. She appeared completely smitten and he doted on her, even as he kept up with the conversation and ate his dinner.

Dom and Molly made me miss being in a couple all over again. Dom obviously adored his wife, and it was mutual. She was a decade or so older than him, which I hadn't known until tonight, but they had the type of relationship I wanted to have again. Happy. Loving. Comfortable.

Gerard and Gina were older, at sixty and fifty-nine, with adult children and a new grandchild, so listening to them made me want a baby even more. I could picture myself thirty years in the future with a couple of grandkids playing in the pool while my family gathered for Sunday dinner. My kids probably wouldn't have grandparents, especially not if Gabe and I procreated, but they'd have more than enough love to make up for it.

Not to mention aunties and uncles like Sloane and Ivan.

Was I a sap or what?

Ron and Lily were harder to read. She was quiet, obviously used to taking a back seat to her husband and letting him run any conversation or questions directed at them. Even when I asked her something specifically. That was definitely not the type of relationship I wanted, but maybe it worked for them. They'd been married a long time, from what they said.

"Do you need anything else from me?" Brianna asked me at a little after nine, when dessert had been served and the kitchen cleaned up.

"No, you should go," I told her. "Thank you. Everything was perfect. I'll be calling you again."

"Thank you." She smiled. "I appreciate that. Declan keeps pushing me to start my own restaurant, but I don't want to be tied down to one place like that. I think doing jobs like this is more conducive to our lifestyle. Especially once he goes back out on tour."

"Well, keep me in the loop. Whatever you do, I'll be there for it."

"Thank you. Good night." She gathered her things and left through the garage, and I wandered back into the living room where everyone was enjoying after-dinner drinks.

"Do you have a tenant?" Gina asked. "I thought I saw lights on at the little house out back."

"Oh." My cheeks may have turned red but hopefully no one noticed in this lighting. "Yes. I do. He's only been here a few weeks."

"Are you comfortable with that?" Lily asked, speaking up for the first time. "I don't know if I'd like to have a man living on the premises of my home. As a single woman."

"Well, he's my ex-husband," I said lightly. "And he plays on the team. So I think I'm safe with him."

"Your ex?" Gerard gazed at me. "Are you talking about DeLugo?"

"Yes." I figured it was better to get it out in the open. "He's living in my guest house for this season."

"Well, now we know why you brought a guy his age to the team." Ron lifted his glass but didn't say anything else.

Asshole.

I hadn't been sure if I wanted to keep him or replace him but now, I was leaning toward the latter.

"I brought him here because he's an elite goalie," I said, giving him a pointed look. "He has the experience to lift morale in the locker room, which we desperately need, and he's been around enough to keep the team in line should things get rocky as we make the personnel changes that are coming. My personal relationship with him had *nothing* to do with my decision."

"And as far as roommates go," Henrik put in when Ron didn't respond, "he'll be on the road a lot, so you'll barely see him."

"Exactly," I said, glancing back at Ron, who definitely looked annoyed.

"You don't think it's going to cause gossip once word gets out?" Gerard asked.

"Because there isn't already gossip?" I countered. "I've probably been locker room gossip since the day Edward died."

"They're going to sue you again," Ron said, leaning back in his chair. "You know that, right?"

I sighed. "The judge literally told them to stop wasting the court's time."

"If you do even the slightest thing wrong, they'll either appeal the ruling or they'll report you to the league," Ron continued. "I played golf with Tim last week and he was in no way ready to back down."

Frustration manifested itself as a shot of white-hot anger racing through my veins and I had to mentally count to ten before responding.

"Why were you golfing with Tim?" I finally asked.

He turned to me with a guileless, wide-eyed stare. "Because we're friends."

"You don't think that's a conflict of interest?" I asked in a steely voice.

"I've known him since he was a kid; I've only known you a couple of years. I respect your position and our working relationship but that doesn't negate years of friendship with him."

Well, first thing tomorrow, I was going to have to start searching for a new assistant general manager.

And I didn't relish the thought.

18

G *abe*

I DIDN'T SEE Harper for a couple of days. She seemed busy, leaving early in the morning and not coming back until late, and I was still a little annoyed about the other night. It was entirely irrational to be mad about not being invited, I knew that, but it bothered me because I could have offered helpful insight to any discussions about the Phantoms.

I'd been in the league a long time and potentially had a lot to offer any conversations about the upcoming season.

But that hadn't been the purpose of the gathering.

She was building relationships with these people, and their wives, hoping to potentially have allies once the season started. On top of that, no other players had been invited, so it would have been odd for me to be there.

I knew that and understood why she was doing it.

So why did it piss me off so much to have been left out?

If I was honest, it was because I didn't like feeling as if I were some kind of dirty little secret in her life. We were still figuring things out, but I was already part of the hockey world, and it wouldn't take long for people to notice there was more to us than roommates and exes.

How much more remained to be seen.

We'd discussed trying again, but then promptly had that argument about the dinner party, so I hadn't even talked to her since then.

And I had so many questions.

Was it going to be nothing but good sex until it burned itself out or the start of something new?

A continuation of where we'd left off?

When she'd divorced me, a big part of it was because she thought I'd cheated, but it had also been because she'd lost faith in me, and that had hurt me more than I'd realized until recently.

This time around I wanted things to be different.

This time around.

Was there a *this time*?

It felt like we were already falling into our old patterns and that wasn't going to cut it.

As difficult as it was to admit, I still loved her.

I'd always loved her and had two subsequent divorces under my belt to prove it.

I needed to talk to her before I drove myself crazy, so I wandered over to the sliding glass doors just before noon on Sunday.

To my surprise, she was standing there, her hand on the handle, as if she'd been about to come out.

"Hey," I said.

"I was just coming over to talk to you," she said at the same time.

"Good timing, I guess." I stood there, waiting for an invitation inside.

"You hungry?" she asked after a moment, stepping aside.

"No, I'm good." I paused. "So, uh, what's up?"

"I wanted to talk about the other night. And apologize."

"You don't owe me anything," I said gruffly.

Now that she'd apologized, I felt kind of stupid.

Needy.

She could have dinner parties without me.

It was ridiculous for me to be mad about this.

We might be working on things, but we weren't officially a couple yet.

"I don't know what we're doing," she said finally. "But I don't want to do what we've always done, which is fight and make up."

"I was thinking that earlier," I admitted.

"It feels like a lot of the same, and I just don't have it in me for you to break my heart again." She looked at me and then, to my surprise, reached out her hand.

And waited.

For me to take it.

So I did.

"Gabe, everything is so complicated," she whispered when our hands were linked.

"That's kind of our thing, isn't it?"

"I don't want our regular thing to be our thing going forward," she said firmly. "If we're going to try again, and more so if we wind up raising a baby together, I don't want to fight and argue all the time. I want our baby to see love and respect, even if it's not romantic love. It can be friend love. Chosen family love. Whatever we want it to be. But not angry or resentful love. That would suck for all of us."

"It would," I agreed.

"I have so much negativity and adversity in my life right now, I can't add anything else. We've decided to start dating again, but we don't have to if you think it'll be too stressful."

"I don't think that at all, but I do feel like we need to be more specific in defining our parameters going forward."

"Can we start over? Get to know each other again? Try to build something from scratch?"

"That's the definition of dating. I mean, getting to know each other, becoming friends, and making love. We can't discount the sexual part because it's so intense between us. We feel shit when we're together like that. Even an asshole like me has emotions. Just, you know, buried real deep."

She gave me a slight shake of her head. "You're not an asshole. Not all the time anyway."

I chuckled. "Thanks."

"So... are you going to officially ask me out?"

"If that's what you want, yes."

"That's what I need. I need to fall in love with you all over again, Gabe. We can't fall back on the love we had before. If it's going to happen, it has to be new love for a fresh start."

That made me happier than it should have, so I couldn't stop the smile spreading across my face as I leaned in to lightly press my lips to hers. "I like that. But there's one more issue we have to consider," I said after a moment.

"What?"

"What are we going to tell people who figure it out? We can try to be discreet, but people are going to notice how I look at you. There's magic in the room when we're together. And there was an entire conversation about me living here while I was golfing with the guys the other day. I was with Ivan, Phil, Jensen, and Shane. Other than Ivan, they somehow had no idea we used to be married, and once it came up, they had questions."

She grimaced. "Did they talk shit about me?"

I wobbled my hand from side to side. "Not shit really, just expressed concern about your lack of hockey experience, and then some curiosity about me living in your guest house."

"We can't be open about our relationship," she said. "Not at this early stage. We need to know what we want and what's going to happen before we open that can of worms. I have to earn respect and trust within the organization. I have so much to prove and sleeping with one of the guys on my team will make it ten times harder."

"What happens if you're already pregnant?" I asked. "You'll most likely be starting to show early in the season and having everyone find out a year from now, versus in real time, could be even worse."

"Can we cross that bridge when we come to it?" she asked. "Please? I need a little time to find my footing professionally while simultaneously going back to the beginning with you."

"Then how about I take you to lunch?"

"Oh, I have plenty of food in the fridge. We can just—"

"Babe." I put a finger over her lips. "I'm asking you out. On a date."

"Oh." Her eyes widened and she smiled. "Well, I've got a lot to do, but I guess I could take a couple of hours to go to lunch."

"Let's go somewhere on the water," I suggested. "Do you still love the ocean?"

Her eyes glittered with what I could only describe as pleasure. "I do."

"Leave in an hour?"

"Yes."

I kissed her once more and then headed out onto the patio whistling.

THE NEXT COUPLE of days were nice. Harper and I spent a lot of time together, both at home and out and about. We spent our nights together too, mostly naked and in her bed. Except last night. We'd been naked in the pool, and I'd fucked her on a lounge chair right out in the open. And it had been so hot I got hard just thinking about it.

She was a totally different woman these days, but also the same.

She was still sweet, intelligent, and caring, but now she was tougher. Not to mention more jaded. I was too, of course, and though we hadn't talked in any detail about the relationships we'd had since our divorce, I wondered what had made her so wary and suspicious.

Today she was at the team's main offices at the arena attending a bunch of meetings, and I found myself wandering around aimlessly. I'd gone for a run and then swam fifty laps, I had a video chat with Brandy, and had just put a baseball game on TV, but I was restless.

Back in Lauderdale, this would have been the perfect day for the beach, but it was different here. The weather was better in general, with no rain and barely any humidity, but the Pacific Ocean was cold, even in the summer. I didn't enjoy the beach here, so I'd only gone a couple of times. The pool was nice, but I'd gotten bored lying out in the sun by myself. And Ivan was out of town.

I'd gotten a lot better about making friends over the years, but I still didn't have a ton of them. I had a lot of acquaintances, guys I'd played with and hung out with and traveled with. But we weren't buddies, not like Ivan and me. He was the one guy I'd gotten close to. Before that, I'd focused on loving Harper and then trying to replace her after she left me.

We'd met at eighteen and nineteen, when I was a sophomore and she was a freshman in college. We got married right after I graduated and had been married for four years. I'd married Tricia less than two years later because I'd gotten her pregnant. That marriage had only lasted two years, and I'd met Brittany within six months of our divorce being final.

Like a dumbass, I'd jumped right back in and stuck it out for a little over three years. I'd convinced myself I loved her and could be happy. That I didn't compare her—and every other woman I met—to Harper. That the good times we had blowing through my paychecks would make up for what was missing deep down in my soul.

Once I realized I'd been kidding myself, I'd divorced her and promised myself I wouldn't get married again. It just wasn't worth it emotionally or financially. Harper had saved my ass when it came to Brittany, and I'd been meaning to ask her how she'd gotten her to back off. I was sure money had been involved and, in retrospect, that bothered me. What the hell had I been thinking, manipulating Harper into handling that for me?

I'd still been pissed at her then, annoyed that she was forcing me to move to L.A. when I didn't want to. Annoyed that she was still as beautiful and alluring as ever. Annoyed that I still wanted to fuck her, even though she'd broken my heart.

Maybe that was why I was so determined to try again.

It wasn't completely rational, but there was a part of me that wanted to prove to her I was the man she deserved. The man I should have been when we'd been together.

If I wanted to win Harper back, and I really fucking did, I needed to be the man both of us were expecting.

Too bad I didn't yet have a clue who that was.

19

H *arper*

Firing Ron had been brutal.

He'd been furious and then started threatening to sue.

He'd tried cajoling at first, then apologizing, and finally brought out the big guns, talking about lawyers and court cases and how his alliance with my former stepsons would destroy me. In the middle of it all, I started getting cramps, and when I got to the bathroom, I discovered I'd gotten my period.

And the disappointment was palpable.

I'd been convinced I was already pregnant, that Gabe had done what Edward had never been able to do, even though it had only been a couple of weeks since the first time we'd had sex.

I was far more emotional about it than I'd anticipated I would be, and when I finally got Ron out of my office, I locked the door and burst into tears.

It took about fifteen minutes to get myself back under control and I had to go back to the bathroom to wash my face and do something with my makeup. I had one more meeting today, and I didn't want to let Gerard, Dom, or Henrik see how emotional I was. They would think it was because of firing Ron, and while that hadn't helped, I was far more upset about not being pregnant. And there was no chance in hell I would tell them that.

"You okay?" Henrik asked when he got to my office, studying my face.

"I had something in my contact lens," I lied, shaking my head. "It felt like someone was stabbing me in the eye."

He frowned slightly but then nodded. "So, how did it go?"

"About how you'd expect." I tried to shrug, as if it was no big deal. "He threatened to join Eddie and Tim in suing me. Blah blah blah. Same tired old bullshit."

"You had legal look at his contract, right?"

"Oh, yeah. Legally, I'm covered. Whether or not he reports me to the league and bad mouths me to everyone who'll listen, well, that's something else."

"Fuck those people," Henrik said.

"Who are we fucking?" Dom asked as he came into the office. "And why?"

I chuckled. "Just a rough afternoon. Firing Ron was...highly unpleasant."

"I told you to let me do it," Gerard said as he joined us.

"I needed to do it," I said, sinking into my chair. "I have to avoid the perception that I need the men in my organization to do my dirty work."

"I respect that," Gerard said, "but I think you're making an already difficult job even harder."

"Probably." I leaned back. "All right. Let's get down to business. Do we have suggestions for a new assistant GM?"

"I have a thought," Dom said. "I don't know how you'll feel about this, but I know he and his wife are anxious to get out of Alaska."

I frowned. "Who are we talking about?"

"Drake Riser. He's an assistant coach out there, and while he's enjoying it, it's far from everyone and everything. I don't think his wife Erin is happy there."

"Oh, that's an interesting suggestion," Gerard said. "I was considering Eli Montford, the assistant GM in Jersey, but I don't think he'll make a lateral move. He's ready to move up."

"Exactly." Dom nodded. "And Drake has been coaching for a few years now. He might be ready to make a change to be in the back office. I don't know for sure, but we're pretty tight, so I can ask."

"Let me do some research about him," I replied. "In the meantime, reach out and see if there's interest on his part. No use jumping through hoops if he's not interested anyway. A lot of people don't want to move to L.A. I'll also need to talk to Gage Caldwell, because he and I are friendly, so I don't want to steal his people without a conversation."

Dom nodded. "I'll call Drake this afternoon and feel things out."

"Great." I looked at the list I'd made on the note pad in front of me. "The other thing I want to talk about is Chandler Cormier. Tell me what you want me to do. Keep him in the minors, bring him up for training camp, or trade him and find someone else to back up Gabe." Chandler was a shining star for our minor league affiliate in Portland, but he'd had a rough time during the playoffs.

"I'd like to see him during training camp," Henrik said. "Let him work with our training and coaching staff and see if we can help him get where he needs to be to stay in L.A."

"I agree," Dom said. "He's a good kid with a lot of talent."

"He's only twenty-one," Gerard added. "He has time. Goalies often don't come into their own until their mid-to-late twenties."

"That was my thought too," I replied, making a note on my pad. "If he works out, I won't have to start trying to entice Donovan Legori away from Buffalo."

Dom chuckled. "Does Gabe know about this?"

I laughed. "I don't discuss my business decisions with Gabe, but he knows two concussions in a year is a lot. We need to make sure he has solid back-up."

"Donovan isn't going to give up the starting job in Buffalo to be a back-up here," Gerard said.

"I know. That's why I asked about Chandler. If, God forbid, Gabe gets hurt, we need to have options."

"For the right price, they'll come," Dom said dryly.

We talked about a few more players and salary caps before we adjourned, and I logged out of my computer. I just wanted to curl up on the couch with a pint of Ben & Jerry's and watch something sappy and romantic on TV. I had cramps and was still battling the disappointment of getting my period.

I tried to rationalize it as I drove home.

We'd only had unprotected sex the one night. I'd never paid a lot of attention to my ovulation cycle so I didn't know when I was most fertile. It was probably something I should have been more attuned to, but it had been years since Edward and I had been forced to stop trying because of his illness. Before that, the doctor had been in charge of all those details.

And I didn't want to go through that again.

If we couldn't get pregnant the old-fashioned way, I might have to consider adoption.

Gabe probably wouldn't like that, but this wasn't about him.

This was about me and what I wanted.

But one of the things I wanted was Gabe.

I wanted to become a mom, to help the Phantoms win a hockey championship, and to give it one more shot with Gabe. It would be hard to trust him again, after everything that had happened between us, but maybe it was time to open up about that. How could we move forward if we didn't clear the air? The time for us to have that conversation was long overdue, but I hadn't been interested in rehashing a past that would bring up bad memories.

Now that we were going to try dating again, it seemed ridiculous to continue avoiding what might prove to be a difficult conversation.

I pulled into the garage and got out of the car, tossing the strap of my laptop backpack over my shoulder.

The smell of something delicious hit me the moment I opened the door that led into the kitchen, and I looked around. The sliding glass door was open and music was coming from the patio. I put down my backpack and kicked off my heels, padding in that direction.

Gabe was standing at the grill in khaki shorts and nothing else.

I could get used to coming home to a view like that.

The dinner he was cooking was nice too.

"Hey!" I called out to him.

"Hi." He turned with a smile. "Go change into something comfortable. Dinner will be ready in five."

"What are we eating?" I asked.

"Grilled pork chops, grilled corn, and baked sweet potatoes."

"You're hired!" I said, laughing. "I'll be right out."

I changed into shorts and a tank top, pulling my hair into a loose ponytail. I hadn't been expecting dinner, but it was a thoughtful surprise, which I really appreciated.

"You okay?" he asked as I came out to the patio.

"It was a long day. I fired Ron."

He grimaced. "He didn't take it well?"

"He was pissed."

"Gerard could have done it. That's part of his job."

"I know. But right now, I'm trying to keep a tight rein on everything. This is about me keeping my finger on the pulse of every part of the organization. From now until when the season starts, I can't afford for anything to slip through the cracks."

"Yes, but you also need to show your inner circle, and the men who will be running the team going forward, that you have faith in them."

I sighed, rubbing my temples. "I'm running the team for the foreseeable future. And to be honest, I'm not sure I can trust anyone right now other than Henrik and Dom."

He cocked his head, his eyes searching mine. "Not even me?"

Well, wasn't that the loaded question of the day?

"You're one of the players," I said quietly. "It's different from the back office, the people doing the wheeling and dealing. After what Ron said at dinner the other night. I was blindsided."

"You mean that comment about his friendship with Tim?"

"Exactly. Edward told me I could trust Ron, but apparently not."

"People change. Circumstances change." He put the pork chops on a platter with the corn and turned to me. "The potatoes are in the oven. You want to eat inside or out here?"

"Let's go inside," I said after a moment. "I'm tired and it's hot out here."

"Okay."

We walked inside and I got out plates while he pulled the sweet potatoes out of the oven. Everything smelled so good, my stomach growled.

"I think I'm hungry," I said, chuckling.

"I know I am. I picked up a bottle of cabernet, if you want to open it?"

"Sure." I reached for my automatic wine bottle opener.

"I was going to make a salad," he said, "but I got lazy after I got back from the grocery store."

"This was incredibly thoughtful. Thank you. You have no idea how much I appreciate it. I was planning to curl up on the couch with Ben & Jerry's tonight."

"That's your go-to on the first day of your period," he said, pausing and slowly turning to look at me. "Did you get your period?"

20

———————

G *abe*

THERE WAS no mistaking the disappointment on her face as she nodded miserably, and I quickly put down the dish in my hands to walk over to her. I reached out, wrapping one arm around her waist and pulling her against my chest.

"Hey, it's okay. We weren't really trying. From what I remember, you've never been on a twenty-eight-day schedule, so the chances you were going to get pregnant from one night were low."

She nodded. "It's the same. I still get it about every thirty-two days or so."

"You'd already decided not to go ahead with getting pregnant, right? You said the timing is jacked up."

"Yeah, but I found out right after I fired Ron," she whispered, leaning against me. "And I just sat there and cried. Like an idiot."

"There's nothing idiotic about emotions," I said, stroking one hand up and down her back. "Not to mention hormones."

"I felt so inept. Like I wasn't capable of firing someone without having a meltdown."

"Did you cry in front of him?"

"Hell no."

"Then it doesn't count. You're allowed to be as weak and scared and hormonal as you want behind closed doors. As long as you don't let them see it, you can do whatever the fuck you want. You're only human, Harper."

"I know." She didn't seem anxious to leave my arms and I liked having her there.

"Would an orgasm help?" I asked after a few minutes. "The shower is just a few feet away..."

"Honestly, I'm too hungry for an orgasm," she said. "Maybe after dinner?"

"I can work with that." I used my thumb and forefinger to gently lift her chin. "You're stronger than you think you are, babe. You're one of the strongest women I know."

"You think?" She looked dubious.

"Well, you don't see any other female owners in the league. That's not because there aren't any that are smart enough or rich enough, but because it's *hard*. It's a hard job even for a man. Professional sports is full of adversity, competition, and back-stabbing. Not to mention politics. Add being the only woman into the mix, and why would anyone willingly take that on? I think you've got bigger balls than most men I know."

"Bigger than yours?" she deadpanned.

"Well, let's not get crazy." I put a soft kiss on the tip of her nose. "Come on, let's eat, and then I'll clean up the kitchen while you go relax."

"You're spoiling me, Gabe."

I hesitated, trying to carefully consider what I wanted to say. "I don't think I did enough of that when we were married. If we're going to do this dating thing, I'd like to be a better partner this time than I was last time. No matter what happens between us."

"We both made mistakes," she said. "I wasn't perfect either."

"So we're both figuring shit out in a new way."

"But we're still the same people."

"Are we?" I put a pork chop on each of our plates as she carried the corn and sweet potatoes to the island.

"I don't think leopards change their spots, you know? We grow and mature, but at our core, we're still the same. The sex is still good, the chemistry is even more intense than it used to be, and we still have issues communicating." She held up a hand when I started to protest. "I'm equally responsible. I'm just pointing out that people don't change as much as you think."

"Does that mean you want to give up?" I asked, disappointment jabbing me in the gut.

"I didn't say that. I guess I'm afraid we're going to fall into the same bad habits we had before. Hockey season is starting soon, and I'll be busy with work while you're doing your hockey thing. Just like when we were married. I kept myself busy so I wouldn't miss you and eventually we were both so busy we never saw each other."

"And I missed you so much I did dumb shit."

She pursed her lips as a look of frustration crossed her pretty features.

It was time to bury the hatchet when it came to the issue of cheating.

She hadn't believed me back then, but somehow, I had to make her believe me now.

"I never cheated, Harper. I know you think I did, but I swear to you, I did not. Yes, I went to the strip club with the guys. Yes, I was dancing with the girls and putting money in their garters. But that. Was. All. That. Happened. Was it the way a married man should behave? Probably not. But I did not touch, kiss, or have any type of sexual contact with anyone but you until after you filed for divorce."

She didn't look at me, staring at her plate for an inordinate amount of time. Finally, she lifted her gaze to mine. "There were pictures."

"Yes. Of me laughing and dancing and being an immature ass. *Not* cheating. And maybe some people would say just going to the strip club was cheating, but I disagree. When your friend Sloane gets married, and she has a bachelorette party at some male strip club in Vegas, are you going to say you can't go because we're dating or married or whatever? Will that count as *cheating* because you have a fun night with your girlfriends celebrating?"

She opened her mouth but then closed it again. "No. I guess not."

"So, what's the difference? Yes, I went. Yes, I behaved borderline inappropriately. But I didn't cheat. I swear it. What can I do to make you believe that?"

"The other wives said they heard their husbands talking about how you went into a back room with two of them."

"That's a lie. Tell me who said that. I'll fucking get him on the phone right now." I was pissed. I hadn't known my buddies lied to save their own asses. No wonder she hadn't believed me. Between the pictures and corroboration from my so-called friends, there hadn't been a snowflake's chance in hell she would believe me.

"Honestly, I wouldn't even be considering believing you if I hadn't talked to Brittany. She hates me and I couldn't figure out why. Then she told me how you used to compare her to me, how you talked about me all the time. How you got shit-faced one night and told her the whole story about that night at the strip club. How hurt you were that I didn't believe you."

Jesus.

Brittany had apparently gone off about me. Normally, I would have been annoyed that two of my ex-wives had talked about me, but now I was grateful for how jealous she'd been of Harper. They'd never met but Brittany had blamed Harper for all of our problems, saying I was making her live up to an impossible standard. At the time, I'd thought she was nuts, but apparently there was more to it than I'd thought.

"There was no way for me to know that you would one day have a conversation with her," I pointed out. "She said I compared her to you our entire marriage, and I'd always laughed and told her that was ridiculous. But subconsciously, I probably did."

"Why would you do that?" she asked, knitting her brow in confusion.

"Because I'm an asshole," I said. "I've never denied that. Being a jerk doesn't mean I didn't love you, and it absolutely doesn't mean I cheated. I never cheated on you or Tricia or even Brittany. I'm many things, but a cheater isn't one of them. And I will die on this hill."

"You're serious." She studied my face.

"Very." I paused. "I'm also serious about finding out what you did to make Britt leave me alone. Did you pay her off?"

She shrugged. "Yes."

"I want to pay you back."

"No." She shook her head. "I couldn't pay you any more on paper because of the salary cap and also because I would look like I didn't know what I was doing. Consider the money I gave her an unofficial addition to your salary. She also signed an NDA, so there's a lot of money for her to give back if she runs her mouth."

"I want to do whatever I have to for you to believe in me again," I admitted.

"We're getting there, but it's going to take time," she said softly. "Trust and respect aren't automatic. It might not be fair, but you're going to have to prove yourself to me. I was shattered when I saw those pictures. It hurt like you can't imagine."

"Probably the same way it hurt me when you didn't believe me."

I had a lot to make up for, but so did she.

She looked surprised for a moment but then nodded.

"No, you're right. And I apologize for the way I behaved back then. Even if you'd cheated, I should have been open to discussing it. Going to therapy. Something that wasn't me yelling and throwing all your things into the street."

I tried not to smile but a small one broke through anyway. "Good times, eh?"

She buried her face in her hands. "I'm so embarrassed."

"Nah. We were young and emotions were running high. Plus, we'd been apart so much of that last year, it was inevitable that a huge misunderstanding would happen. We weren't talking, weren't spending time together, weren't doing any of the things that couples are supposed to do to nurture a relationship. We have to do better this time around."

She slowly lifted her head, a smile playing on her lips. "You sound like a grown-up, Gabriel DeLugo."

"I'm trying. If for no other reason than to be a good example for my daughter. It's not her fault her mom and I were careless, and she got knocked up even though we weren't planning to be together."

"Is that why you married her?" she asked.

I nodded. "Yeah. Tricia and I were friends with benefits. She was a nurse, and I was in Milwaukee playing for the minor league team there for a few weeks while I was rehabbing an injury. We were just hooking up. She called me a month later to tell me she was pregnant. And she was a nice girl. I had no reason to doubt her. We decided to get married and at least try. But neither of us was in love. We called it quits after two years. No hard feelings. I take care of Brandy and to some degree Tricia."

"It's nice that you tried," she said softly.

"I never tried to love her," I admitted. "I tried to be a good husband and dad, but love was never going to happen. Not with her and not with Brittany."

"So why did you marry Brittany?"

"Because she was gorgeous, and I liked showing her off to my friends and teammates. Because the sex was fun. Because I was a fucking dumbass. Really, I can't even make up good excuses. I was running away from my past, my anger, and the memories of you."

Her cheeks turned pink, and she dipped her head. "I'm sorry," she whispered.

I reached over to cover one of her hands with mine. "Nothing to be sorry about. You didn't mess up our marriage by yourself. There's plenty of blame to go around."

"I feel like we could have avoided so much heartache if we'd just talked."

"For sure. But if we hadn't done the things we'd done, we wouldn't be here today. It seems like we had to go through those things to get to this point."

"There were a lot of hard years."

"Is that why you married Edward? Did he make your life easier? And I'm not talking about money."

"He did," she said after a moment. "He was older, very stable, and very gentle. With me anyway. And I desperately needed someone who was gentle. And I don't mean physically. Gentle with my heart. Gentle with my soul. Someone who soothed all my battered parts because I had those long before I met you. You know how hard it was for me growing up."

"I know." I squeezed her hand. "So he was good to you? He took care of you in the ways you needed?"

"Oh, yes. He was a good man and an even better husband."

"Did you love him, Harper?" I nearly held my breath as I waited for her to respond.

"I loved him," she said, nodding. "I don't know if I was head-over-heels *in love* with him, but I loved him with my whole heart. He loved me, protected me, and made sure I was happy. He cared about the little things, like whether or not I was sleeping enough. My mom reached out when Edward and I had been married about a year—I think she found out I'd married a billionaire—and I was a wreck."

"Oh, geez." I'd had limited dealings with her mother, none of them good, so I could only imagine how annoying she would be when there was potentially a lot of money at stake.

"And he handled it all. I don't know what he did to make her go away, but she never bothered me again. She still hasn't. Thank goodness."

"I'm glad he was what you needed," I said sincerely. "And that there was someone in your life who had your back. I hope that can be me going forward."

21

———————

H*arper*

Tears stung my eyelids.

How long had I dreamed of hearing something like that from Gabe?

I wasn't ready to trust him with my heart, but I was ready to try.

"Don't cry," he said softly. "I don't ever want to be the reason you cry again."

"We have to go slow," I said, dabbing my eyes with a napkin. "I know that sounds ridiculous considering we used to be married, but I feel like we have to be cognizant of everything we do."

"I know, baby." He was still squeezing my hand. "We can go as fast or as slow as we want."

"Please don't be mad that I don't want a lot of people to know. It's inevitable that some will find out, like Henrik and Dom, Ivan, Sloane, and a few others, but let's not make it general knowledge yet. Can you be patient with me?"

"I'm going to do my best to try," he said. "I'll admit it bugs me to hide that we're together, but I also understand how precarious your position is right now. I talked to Ivan yesterday and he said the troops are restless. The guys are all worried about who's getting traded next, who else is getting fired in the back office, shit like that."

"I know. That's why I don't want to add fuel to the gossip fire. Us being a couple is going to complicate your life in the locker room too."

He laughed. "You think? Babe, I've been on the receiving end of all kinds of bullshit from teammates, coaches, and whatnot. I truly don't give a fuck. They can talk shit about me all they want. But I know it's different for you."

I pushed my plate away, suddenly exhausted.

"I'm so tired, Gabe. I want to go lie down."

"Go ahead. I'll clean up the kitchen and then join you." He paused. "Unless you'd rather I didn't."

I smiled. "No, I'd rather you left the kitchen alone and came and cuddled with me."

"You got it." He got up, took my hand, and we made our way down the hall to my bedroom.

We crawled onto the bed, and I nestled against his chest.

Despite the ever-present attraction between us, I was content to just lie there with him and he seemed happy to let me. Up until things had started to go wrong, he'd always been a calming force in my life. Back in college, when I'd been staying up late studying for finals and running around like a chicken with my head cut off, Gabe was the one who'd forced me to take breaks. Those breaks were often coupled with sex, but that had been what I'd needed. It relaxed and soothed me, and he'd known it.

My needs were different today and yet he seemed to sense that too.

Even after a decade apart, we knew each other well, and I still liked the man he was deep inside. He was a bit of a mess on the outside, but when you dug into who he was beneath the arrogant pro hockey player façade, there was a lot of good. Much more good than bad, which was why losing him had hurt so much.

And now we were getting another chance.

My phone buzzed in my pocket, and I absently reached for it.

DOM: I talked to Drake, and he's interested! Where do you want to go from here?

HARPER: I'm going to do some research on him tonight and, depending on what I find, I'd like to reach out to him tomorrow. Send me his contact info?

DOM: Sending it right now.

HARPER: Thanks. We'll talk tomorrow.

"What was all that?" Gabe asked. "You seem excited."

I hesitated. Could I share everything with him? I probably shouldn't, but how could we be in a relationship if I couldn't talk to him about work?

"I'm considering hiring Drake Riser for VP of Hockey Operations," I told him. "Do you know him?"

"Yeah. We were on an All-Star team together a while back. He's a good guy. Isn't he coaching now?"

"Yes, for the Blizzard. I heard a rumor that he wanted to leave Anchorage and come back to the mainland, and Dom knows him, so he reached out. Turns out he's interested."

"That's great. I've never heard anyone say anything bad about him."

I gazed up at him. "You're going to wind up knowing a lot of things you shouldn't, so it goes without saying you can't repeat this stuff, right?"

"Of course. You've also asked me to pay attention to locker room talk, so confidentiality is going to go both ways."

"I didn't bring you here to be a spy," I said carefully. "I hope you know that. I wanted you for your experience and expertise, but it wasn't to be a spy. Although I hoped you wouldn't let the guys talk about me inappropriately."

"I would never," he said firmly. "Even if we weren't back together, I still wouldn't let them talk about you that way. There are limits to our levels of assholism."

"Is that a word?" I asked, chuckling.

"I'm pretty sure it is!"

"Thank you," I whispered.

"I haven't done anything," he replied.

He'd done more than he knew, but I wasn't ready to tell him that.

I MET with Drake Riser the following Monday and was floored by what a great guy he was. He was another big guy, much like Dom, well over six feet tall and broad-shouldered, though he seemed a lot more easy-going than Dom. He talked about his wife and children a lot, and how difficult it had been to move them from Las Vegas to Anchorage. It was also clear he was ready for a change.

So, I'd filled yet another position and now had to focus on the team. The players. The guys on the ice who would be the ones to score the goals and win or lose the games. At the end of the day, it all boiled down to winning. I could have the best working environment, build a family-like atmosphere, and make everyone happy to be here. But if they couldn't win, it wouldn't matter.

I had to make some hard decisions when it came to the roster, and I'd spent hours looking at advanced stats, analytics, and even personalities. Did we need a guy with a bad attitude if he could score goals? How much was I willing to sacrifice to get the team to where they could win the championship? There were a lot of tough choices, and I couldn't help but wonder why Edward had thought I was the one to take over for him.

We'd talked about it, of course, and the truth was that his sons were idiots when it came to business. He'd unofficially turned the team over to Tim when he'd first gotten sick, and when Eddie joined him, they'd practically run it into the ground. It had been devastating for Edward to watch them make multiple bad decisions, but he'd been positive I could turn it around.

He'd had so many ideas, and so much faith in me, I'd started to believe in myself as much as he did. We'd known it would be difficult for me, both as his much-younger widow and the only female owner in the league, so he'd tried to prepare me. I had dozens of documents and notebooks filled with notes, ideas, stats, and everything in between. Edward had loved hockey and it had been his dream to own a team.

The plan had always been for it to go to his sons.

Then he'd seen how inept they were, and he'd switched gears.

In retrospect, I didn't know that I was the best choice.

I was smart enough, but I wasn't sure I was tough enough.

I *could* be.

Mostly, I didn't know if I wanted to be.

I was already having to do things I hated doing, like firing people and wheeling and dealing behind the scenes. As we got closer to the start of the season, all eyes would be on the team, and by extension, me. The entire hockey world would be watching and waiting for me to screw up. And when word got out I was sleeping with my starting goalie, it would turn into a nightmare.

One of the main lessons Edward had taught me was to mitigate problems before they started, and one of the ways to do that was to get in front of them. So that was what I was going to do.

I'd called a meeting of my executive staff today. I'd even flown Sloane out to be here with me because I needed all the support I could get. We'd ordered lunch and everyone made small talk as they ate and caught up, and finally, I cleared my throat.

"There's a lot going on," I said, looking around the room. "And I'm going to add something to your plate that may give you pause, which is why I'm telling you now. If you have questions, or if this is going to be an issue for you, let me know today. Otherwise, this is confidential information that isn't anyone's business but mine."

I paused, giving everyone a moment to let my words sink in.

"As most of you know, Gabe DeLugo is my ex-husband," I said, keeping my voice neutral. "What you probably don't know is that we're involved again. We didn't plan this, but it happened organically as we've spent time together this summer, so I wanted to put it out there."

"I take it this isn't public knowledge?" Henrik asked.

"No. And I don't want it to be. Not yet. It's still new, and with our history, we're hoping to take things slow. But you know what they say about the best laid plans. Anyway, I wanted to be up front with you guys so you're not blindsided should it get out before I'm ready." I looked around. "Does anyone have anything to say? Questions? Concerns?"

"Who you date is none of my business," Dom said, "but you have to know this is going to be a mess when word gets out. And probably more for Gabe than for you."

I hadn't considered that. "You think?"

He chuckled. "You know how brutal a hockey locker room can be? They give guys shit just for dating some random woman. Dating the team owner? That's going to be epic, from the perspective of gossip and giving each other shit."

"Not to mention a big distraction," Henrik remarked. "You might want to consider letting word get out sooner rather than later. If we start the season and everything is going well, then a bombshell like that gets out, it could derail everything."

Shit.

I wasn't ready to go public, but Henrik had a point.

Now I had an impossible decision to make because while I wanted to protect myself, I needed to protect the team, which included Gabe.

"I think he's right," Dom said after a moment.

"I have to side with the boys," Gerard added. "Sorry, boss."

"All right. Let me think about it and talk to Gabe." Gabe already hated the idea of sneaking around, so he would most likely be happy. I was the one who was going to have to deal with most of the fallout.

"Look, when it comes to this kind of thing, people have short memories," Gerard said. "One minute it's all anyone can talk about, and the next they've moved on to the Kardashians' latest makeup line. Whatever happens, it'll blow over as long as we focus on the game."

"I'm sorry," I said quietly. "We didn't plan this. I know the timing sucks so I'm going to do everything in my power to make this a non-issue."

"Sometimes you just have to go with the flow," Dom said with a wry smile. "Trust me, I have firsthand experience with this."

"But it'll pass," Henrik said. "It always does."

Sloane and I exchanged a look, and hers told me she didn't believe it any more than I did.

22

———————

G*abe*

Sometimes you had to grab life by the balls.

Other times, it grabbed you.

Today, my balls were definitely the ones in peril.

Harper and I had talked ad nauseum about whether or not to go public with our relationship and we'd finally made the decision to let the word get out now. It was early August, with about six weeks until training camp started, so that seemed like a reasonable amount of time to let the gossip and any repercussions die down. There were no guarantees, but the hockey world had to have more important things to talk about than the love life of an aging goalie and his team owner.

Especially when she was his ex-wife.

I wasn't worried about the locker room or my teammates.

There was a reason I didn't have many friends, so this wouldn't be much different than any other room I'd played in. I'd do my job, they'd respect me for it, and we'd get along fine without having to be besties.

Back in the day, having friends had ultimately cost me the woman I'd loved, and though I hadn't framed it that way before now because I hadn't realized just how responsible they'd been, it made sense I'd started shying away from those kinds of friendships after the divorce.

Looking back, I'd been one of only two married guys on the minor league team I'd been playing on when Harper and I had gotten married. I'd been pulled up to the majors after a season-and-a-half, and Harper had thrown herself into her new job as a marketing manager, so I'd started to party. It got to the point where she was too busy with work to get to my games most of the time, and I was too busy hanging out with my friends on my days off to make time for her. None of it had been intentional, but if I'd paid more attention to my wife than my new friends, I would have seen how far apart we'd grown.

I had a better grasp on the work-home life balance these days, but I wouldn't let anything like that happen again.

I slid my feet into a pair of expensive leather dress shoes, put my wallet and phone into my slacks, and grabbed my car keys. I walked across the patio and opened the sliding glass doors.

"Harper? You ready?" I called out.

"How do I look?" She came down the hall in a sexy red number that made my mouth water. It was short and flirty, with a little flared hem that hit her mid-thigh and rhinestone covered spaghetti straps that showed off her gorgeous neck and shoulders. And arms. Not to mention cleavage.

She took my fucking breath away.

"Jesus." I swallowed. "You're fuck-tastically beautiful."

She smiled, shaking her head. "There you go, making up words again."

"You're so gorgeous that the words currently available in the dictionary don't do you justice."

"Well, thank you." She sashayed over to me, and I couldn't help but reach for her. "You clean up pretty nice yourself."

"I try to keep up, but you're way out of my league," I murmured, leaning down to kiss her.

"Don't mess up my makeup. I have to compete with super-models tonight, and it's daunting."

"Baby, there is no competition," I replied, pulling her against my chest.

"Please don't make me redo my lipstick," she whispered, though her eyes were half-closed as if she expected me to kiss her despite her warning.

"I think the limo just pulled up and saved your lipstick," I said against her mouth. "But I'm kissing you in my head."

She laughed, sliding her hand into mine as we walked out the front door to where the limousine was waiting.

We weren't half-assing anything in our quest to go public. She'd planned an elaborate evening out with Cheyenne at the helm, inviting a group of us to join her and some of her super-model friends at some movie producer's private screening and after-party. The ladies had invited Henrik and Autumn, and I'd invited Ivan, Philippe, and a new guy on the team named Lincoln Smythe-Rollins. Cheyenne had said she was inviting a couple of her model friends, and they needed dates, so Ivan had suggested Philippe and Linc since they were both single.

"Hi!" Cheyenne had a bottle of champagne in her hands, pouring glasses for us as we settled in. Henrik and Autumn were already in the car, along with Ivan and two ladies Cheyenne introduced as Stevie and Addison. They were both obviously models, with long hair and perfect makeup. They were also wearing scanty cocktail dresses and high heels, talking and laughing with everyone.

I kept Harper's hand in mine, exchanging a quick glance with her before handing her a glass of champagne. I wasn't a fan of events like this, but if we got photographed at some big Hollywood shindig, it would almost guarantee everyone on the team and in the hockey world would see Harper and I together. That would eliminate the need to tell people individually, and maybe the gossip mill would burn itself out before training camp.

It wasn't likely to be that easy, but all we could do was try.

"Hey, everybody!" Linc and Phil were the last two to be picked up and they were together at Phil's place.

There was no doubt the moment Phil noticed my arm around Harper, but after a quick flicker of curiosity crossed his face, he was focused on Stevie and Addison.

Good.

"So Mikhael Nazarenko is an asshole," Cheyenne said to us as we approached the house where the party and screening was being held. "He's brilliant but he made this movie specifically to be his daughter Natasha's debut. She's supposedly spoiled and difficult, a complete diva raised in Beverly Hills and somewhat unapproachable. From what I hear, Mikhael is spectacularly overprotective."

"And his next move was to put his daughter in a movie and show her off to the world?" Stevie rolled her eyes. "I mean, Natasha's okay. Definitely spoiled but also a little shy. I guess that's to be expected. She was home schooled until college. Now she's at Yale. I think she's majoring in business."

"A business degree to help her acting career?" I asked, chuckling. "I mean, it's good to have an education. I have a degree, which I get *lots* of use out of playing hockey."

We all laughed.

"Hey, any college degree is useful," Ivan said. "I wish I had one. I might start taking an online class just for the hell of it."

I arched a brow at him. "Really? In all your free time?"

"We have tons of down time on road trips."

"More power to you, man." I held out my fist and he bumped it.

"College." Phil shuddered. "Sounds like torture at this stage of my life. I didn't like school as a teen. I can't imagine going back now."

"What happens if hockey doesn't work out?" Stevie asked. "Like, what if it ended today? Do you have enough money to live comfortably into your seventies?"

Phill frowned. "I guess not, but I figure I can coach somewhere. I never gave it a lot of thought."

"We should all have a plan." Stevie wagged a finger. "Life happens."

"You're young to be so cynical," Phil told her.

"I'm young but smart." She grinned.

~

MIKHAEL'S HOUSE WAS STUNNING, a sprawling estate with a tall, golden gate that was open and lined with limousines and sports cars as we pulled up.

"Jesus, this is nuts," I murmured to Harper.

"Welcome to Hollywood," she replied with a wry smile.

"The movie will probably be a yawn," Addison said, "but the food and drinks will be good."

"Great place to see and be seen," Cheyenne added, looking over at Harper.

"Screening is at eight, dinner's at eleven," Stevie said as we started to get out of the limo. "See you then!" A moment later she was gone, with Phil on her heels, and Addison and Linc right behind her. Henrik and Autumn were next, and Cheyenne gave Harper another look.

"You should go after me. They're probably waiting to see who I'm with and what I'm wearing, so you'll get a little less attention if you let me go first."

"Got it." Harper nodded and I sat back, waiting for Cheyenne and Ivan to get out of the car.

I didn't really understand Hollywood or these types of events.

We had a fraction of this kind of attention at hockey-related events, but beyond that, I lived in anonymity. Now that I was in my mid-thirties, I didn't think about fame or celebrity, so it was a little odd to be part of it now simply because Harper and I were together. In my head, she was still the smart, soft-spoken virgin with the great rack I'd met in college. Obviously, we'd both matured and changed, but it was still hard to wrap my head around her being the owner of a pro hockey team and the center of attention.

Flashbulbs and cameras going off made it look like daylight as Cheyenne got out of the limo with Ivan behind her. The paparazzi were calling to her, firing questions at her, and I was glad to see Ivan walking behind her with a protective hand at her back. He swore there was nothing going on between them but friendship, but he was putting out some mixed signals from where I was sitting.

"We're up," Harper said, lifting her chin.

"Remember, we're not doing anything wrong," I reminded her. "We're consenting adults. We're allowed to fuck." I was purposely crude at the end, hoping to make her smile, and it worked.

I got out of the limo first and then turned to offer her my hand.

A few cameras went off, and someone called to Harper by name, but it was very tame compared to how they'd reacted to Cheyenne, which was what we'd been hoping for. I didn't know exactly what she and Harper had discussed ahead of time, but Harper seemed relaxed and confident as we strode down the gold carpet that had been set up instead of a traditional red one. I didn't know what that meant, but I didn't care.

As long as Harper was okay with this, and we'd made our unofficial announcement that we were a couple, I'd put up with the evening's shenanigans.

"We're going to powder our noses," Cheyenne told Harper, taking her arm.

"I'll be at the bar," I said, heading in that direction since I spotted Ivan and the others already there.

The ladies disappeared and I accepted the glass of champagne Ivan handed me.

"Figured you don't need to be mixing drinks tonight," he said under his breath. "You probably need to be on your toes."

"Thanks." I took a sip.

"So, you and the boss, eh?" Phil shook his head. "I should've seen that coming."

"We've known each other a long time," I said. "Been through a lot both together and since we divorced. There's something to be said for finding your first love again after you're all grown up."

He looked thoughtful and then nodded. "I guess you're right. I don't know that I need to see my high school sweetheart ever again, but we were like fourteen when we met. I think college is different."

"For sure." I nodded. "I was an asshole back then. Trying to find my footing in the league, trying to figure out who I was and what kind of man I was going to be. It took a while."

Linc chuckled. "I'm twenty-seven and I'm still not a hundred percent sure who I'm going to be. It's harder than you think it's going to be when you're eighteen."

"I'm twenty-five," Phil said, sipping his drink. "And I honestly never gave a thought to my post-hockey future until Stevie said something in the limo. I mean, I have a retirement account and the stuff they tell us to do, but I never thought about it."

"Most of us don't," Ivan said.

"Well, you don't have to worry about your future," Phil quipped to me. "Now that you're back with Harper. She's rolling in it."

I frowned, an uncomfortable feeling rolling through my gut. Were people going to think I was a gold digger? Fuck. I needed to nip this shit in the bud immediately.

"Rolling in what, exactly? Mr. Barrowman left her the team and some gifts, like the house she lives in. He left the bulk of his estate to his sons, so Harper isn't rolling in anything except the team. And we all know the Phantoms aren't the most profitable team in the league."

Linc frowned. "Rumor has it the old man turned over all of his investments. That's why his boys were so pissed off."

"I don't know the details of her financial portfolio," I snapped, "but I'm telling you that's not true. She's comfortable but it's not what you're thinking." I said the words but realized I didn't know for sure whether or not they were true. Harper lived fairly frugally, from the perspective that she'd been married to a billionaire. I knew the house was paid for, along with her car, because she'd told me Edward had wanted to make sure she was comfortable when he died. As far as I knew, Harper hadn't inherited any cash from him. Just things he'd bought her ahead of time. House. Car. Jewelry.

The only item he'd left her in his will had been the team.

Right?

I was spectacularly uncomfortable not knowing the answers to these questions and I made a mental note to ask her.

"Oh, shit." Ivan nudged me.

"What?" I followed his gaze and froze.

Harper was standing with Cheyenne, a look of fury on her face.

And Tim Barrowman was in front of them waving his arms around like he was yelling.

Oh, hell no.

Not on my watch.

23

H *arper*

I'D BEEN SO DISTRACTED by the gorgeous surroundings, famous faces, and beautiful dresses I didn't see Tim until he was practically on top of me.

"Look what the cat dragged in," he snarled, leering in the direction of my cleavage.

"Well, they let you in," Cheyenne responded, "so the rest of us were a given."

"Why don't you go play with the other pretty arm pieces so Harper and I can have a grown-up conversation?" he said dismissively.

Cheyenne laughed. "I'm not going anywhere, asshole."

"Look, this is neither the time nor the place to rehash the same old thing," I said quietly. "If you want to argue about your dad's will, we can do it at our attorneys' offices."

"You think because the judge ruled in your favor that this is over," he snarled, "but I will *never* stop fighting you. The team was never meant to be yours."

"It was after you practically burned it to the ground," I responded. "Your dad knew you were wholly incapable of running it, so he made a very difficult decision."

"He wasn't in his right mind."

I shook my head.

How many times had we had this conversation in the last year? I was over it.

"Look, we're not doing this here. Have your attorney call mine." I tried to step around him, but he blocked me.

"Listen to me, you manipulative, scheming little bitch. Everyone in hockey knows who and what you are. They will *never* accept you into the fold, never listen to you or respect you. And eventually, the team will turn on you too."

"With the exception of a couple of your buddies, they've already accepted me," I said. "And I already have more respect than you'll ever have. Both personally and professionally. Your father would be so ashamed of you right now."

"You have no idea how my father would feel!" he snapped, moving so close to me I could practically feel his breath on my face. "And he's rolling over in his grave."

"I'm going to need you to step the fuck away from her." I nearly jumped at the steely tone to Gabe's voice, but I'd never been so grateful to see him. Or Ivan, Phil, and Linc.

Tim's eyes widened for a moment and then he threw his head back and laughed. "Seriously? You brought guys from the team to a movie screening? Wait—are you fucking your ex?"

Gabe folded his arms across his chest. "Talk to her like that again and you'll be leaving without your teeth," he said in a low voice.

Seeing him all riled up and protective kind of turned me on.

Was that wrong?

"Are you boys really that bewitched by a pretty face and big tits that you don't see what she did?" he demanded. "She took advantage of a sick old man and—"

"The court didn't believe that," Gabe interrupted him. "So why should we? Give it a rest, man."

"My father never even thought about changing his will until after he was sick. Doesn't that strike you as odd? Can't you see what she did? How am I the only one seeing clearly here?"

"Because you failed and everyone knows it," I said, irritated all over again. "You were a shitty owner and your father saw the bad decisions you were making."

"Those decisions were made by our executive team!" Tim shot back. "It was just growing pains. All teams go through it. We were in an upward trajectory and now she's dismantling it all."

"I'm dismantling the bullshit you put into play when your father got sick," I said. "And like I've said repeatedly tonight, we're not doing this here or now. Come on, let's go." I put a hand on Gabe's forearm.

"Eddie and I are going to make sure you lose everything if you don't give up the team," Tim said, his jaw working with irritation.

"You don't have that kind of power," I replied. "And in the future, please refrain from talking to me directly. Anything you have to say needs to be said through our lawyers."

He narrowed his gaze. "Fancy doubletalk won't change reality, Harper. I'm warning you—if you don't do the right thing and turn the team over to my brother and me, you're going to regret it."

"You're an asshole, you know that?" Cheyenne wrinkled her nose. "Let's go, Harper. Come on, guys." She tugged at my hand and motioned to Ivan. "This douche-canoe is pissing me off."

I followed her because I couldn't stand listening to Tim for even another second. It was so frustrating to be having the same conversations even after a judge had ruled in my favor, but Eddie and Tim didn't seem keen on giving up or giving in.

"I don't like him threatening you," Gabe growled in my ear.

"His bark is worse than his bite," I said. "Edward tried talking to the boys after he changed the will and they were furious, yelling and stomping around the house like toddlers having a tantrum. It was so embarrassing, but it made Edward feel better about his decision. He struggled with it, hoping things would turn around for the team, but they never did."

"You need to be careful, babe," he said. "I wouldn't put it above them to start harassing you at home."

"I have an excellent security system," I said. "I also have you."

He smiled. "Yeah, but once hockey season starts, I'll be on the road a lot and you'll be alone."

"I'll be fine. Don't worry so much." I leaned over and kissed him. "I like it when you go all alpha protector on me, though."

"Yeah?" He arched his brows and wiggled them playfully. "I bet there's somewhere private where you could show me how *much* you like it."

I laughed. "I don't know if I like it *that* much."

I woke to something warm and delicious between my legs.

Gabe.

I sighed and stretched, arching my hips into his mouth.

We'd gotten home late and passed out, but he was making up for it now.

His tongue was circling my clit as he slipped a finger inside me and I reached down, digging my fingers into his short hair, tugging on it as he licked and sucked on my sensitive flesh. He was masterful with his mouth, especially down there, and I came awake quickly.

"Fuck, Gabe..." I moaned when he lifted his head.

"You like that?"

"So much."

"You don't get my cock until you come for me." He dove back in, and it only took a few minutes before I was grinding against his face, my hips undulating in time to the thrusts of the two fingers that were now inside of me. He curved them up while simultaneously biting down on my clit and I went off like a cannon. My orgasm was short and intense, exploding out of me as I screamed his name.

"Not sure what I like better," he murmured, sitting up. "How you taste or how it looks when you come all over my face." He crawled over me and positioned himself between my legs.

"Morning," I whispered.

"Morning." He slid into me slowly but purposefully, filling me in one smooth, steady thrust.

I closed my legs around his back, locking my ankles together, and he started to move. He dropped his mouth to mine, and we were immediately swept up in the moment. The heat. The intensity between us.

I'd been turned on watching him defend me last night, but I was much more turned on now. I loved how it felt when he was inside of me. I'd only ever slept with four men in my life, and none of the others came close to Gabe's skill as a lover. Or maybe it was just our connection. Or the fact that he'd been my first. Whatever it was, it didn't take long for him to take me over the edge a second time, with him right behind me.

"Fuuuuck." He collapsed on top of me. "That didn't suck."

I chuckled. "It did not. Wanna do it again?"

"I do." He hesitated. "But we should probably talk first."

"Talk?" I was momentarily confused, so caught up in the magic of what we'd just done that it took a few seconds for me to understand that something was going on. "Wait, did something happen?"

"Well, you got your wish. About us going public."

"Oh." I tried to wiggle out from under him, but he kept me pinned in place with his larger body. "So that's what the morning orgasm was about."

"The morning orgasm was about sex," he said. "And the fact that I love going down on you. The bonus was that it would relax you ahead of me giving you unpleasant news."

"I don't know how that's working out, but let's hear it."

"You have to promise you won't freak."

"I won't freak out," I protested. Then I reconsidered. "Wait— just how bad was it? Is the press saying bad shit about me just because we're dating?"

"Well, it's not very flattering."

"Shit." I stopped trying to move and let my body mold into the mattress. "Tell me."

"If it's any consolation, the parts about me aren't flattering either."

"Just tell me what was said and by whom."

He slowly rolled off me. "How about we clean up and get some coffee in us first?"

"Gabriel."

He chuckled. "Fine. Eddie spoke to some journalists at the event last night and gave them all the talking points. You manipulated his father when he was sick, he wasn't in his right mind, you stole their inheritance, all the same shit."

"Is that all?" I asked, rolling my eyes as I sat up.

"But wait. There's more. I'm a gold digger at the end of my career, latching on to my ex because I've lost all my money to my failed marriages."

"Oh shit."

"Eddie had a lot to say."

"I thought we were past this," I admitted, sliding off the bed and heading toward the bathroom with Gabe right behind me.

"Look, we were expecting some version of this. Does it really matter if it's members of the press speculating or if it's Eddie spewing bullshit? News about us is out and anyone who pays attention to anything in hockey knows. The whole point of going last night was to put it out there and let it burn itself out. And that's what we did. We have five and a half weeks until training camp—with any luck this will all be over by then and we can start the season fresh."

I made a face. "You really believe that? Eddie said he's not giving up, which means it's going to be one thing after another."

"What's the alternative? He'd be going after you whether I was in the picture or not."

"Have you heard anything from the team?"

"Not yet, no. I'm going to text Ivan in a little bit."

"I need to text Chey and the other girls."

"I think Phil went home with Stevie."

"I don't know if that's good or bad."

"Same."

Our eyes met in the mirror and all I saw in his was concern.

For me.

"I really need coffee," I said after a moment.

"You do your bathroom thing and I'll take care of the coffee." He leaned over and kissed me. "Then we'll do some more of the sex thing."

"Now that's the best news I've heard all morning."

24
______

G *abe*

HARPER WAS SWEPT up in a frenzy of activity, on the phone, checking email, talking to her assistant, so I left her to do her thing while I went back to my place. I wanted to call Brandy, so I figured I'd talk to her while Harper was busy and then we'd meet up around dinnertime.

"Dad!" Brandy's voice was loud and filled with excitement.

"Hey, kiddo. What are you all riled up about?"

"My softball team is going to a tournament in Denver, and I want you to go too!"

"Oh, yeah? When is it?"

"The beginning of September. I don't remember the exact date."

"Are you pitching?"

"Duh! No one pitches better than me in my age group."

I couldn't help but feel proud. I'd taught her to play baseball and how to pitch—I'd loved baseball almost as much as hockey when I was a kid—and it was one of the few things we shared.

"That's really exciting. I didn't know you were playing over the summer."

"Mom said I needed something to keep me busy. And it's fun."

"Well, I need to know the dates so I can try to be there. Find out for me, okay?"

"Wait, here's Mom! She can tell you."

Before I could protest, Tricia was on the phone. "Hey, Gabe. Sorry about that."

"That's all right. She sounds excited."

"She hasn't talked about much of anything else the last two days."

"What's the deal with the softball tournament?"

"It's in Denver, the weekend after Labor Day. Thursday to Sunday, I think. There were dozens of kids who tried out for this team, and not only did she make it, she's the starting pitcher. It's kind of a huge deal."

"Hell, yeah! That's my girl. A chip off the old block."

"She's so much like you." Tricia chuckled. "Sometimes it's terrifying."

"You mean, entirely inappropriate, drinks too much, and a complete asshole ninety percent of the time?"

"Well, actually, now that you mention it... yes!"

We laughed.

"I'm not sure what's going on with the team since that's the weekend before training camp starts, but let me make sure there's nothing I need to be in L.A. for, and I'll get back to you, okay?"

"Gabe."

"Yeah?"

"I saw the news. About you and Harper."

Oh, hell.

I wasn't sure if that was good or bad.

If Tricia had heard about it, that meant it hit mainstream news and not just the sports channels.

"Uh, yeah. It's kind of new so—"

"You've never loved anyone else," she said softly. "I'm happy for you."

"But?" That had almost been too easy.

"Brandy's a little disappointed. I think, deep down, she still hopes we'll get back together. I know it's ridiculous, but she's a kid. She doesn't understand why we're not together."

"Oh, hell, Trish, why didn't you tell me?"

"I don't know anything for sure, I'm just guessing, but that's my intuition. Anyway, that isn't the point. What I was getting at was that I've met someone too. And it occurred to me that maybe Denver would be a good time for the four of us to...spend a little time together. We can let Brandy see that it's okay for us to move on, and that we're okay with being friends and co-parenting. I mean, if you wanted to. If you were okay with it."

"That's a great idea," I said sincerely. "Harper has a lot on her plate with the team and the upcoming season, but I'm going to talk to her about making this happen. If we can be there, we will."

"That would be wonderful. And I think it'll be good for Brandy."

"I think so too. Okay, tell Brandy I love her, and I'll call you in a few days after I talk with Harper."

"Perfect." She paused. "And Gabe?"

"Yeah?"

"Don't fuck it up this time."

WITH NOTHING else to do for the day, I went for a run and then swam fifty laps. By the time I showered and got dressed, it was after five, so I walked over to the main house, calling out to Harper. She was on the phone and held up a finger, indicating I should wait.

"...no, please don't cry. Sloane, I'm excited for you! Would you stop crying? It's going to be fine... yes, of course, I'll miss you, but you're going to have a baby. That's such good news... oh, stop it... what kind of friend would I be if I wasn't happy for you?"

I got a beer out of the fridge and sank onto a bar stool, waiting for her to finish.

Obviously, Sloane was pregnant and quitting.

That was going to be stressful for Harper with everything going on.

It was probably hard for her to hear that her friend was pregnant too, especially since I was pretty sure she and her boyfriend hadn't been trying. Sloane lived with Johan Hajek, who'd been one of my teammates in Florida, and though I'd gotten traded around the time they'd gotten together, Johan was a good guy. I had no doubt he was over the moon about becoming a dad.

I could only hope I'd be equally excited when the time came.

I'd been somewhat reluctant when Tricia had told me she was pregnant, and it hadn't been until I'd seen the baby on the ultrasound that I'd warmed up to the idea, so I wanted a do-over when it happened again.

When.

Not if, but when.

As if eventually getting Harper pregnant was a foregone conclusion.

"You okay?" I asked when she hung up.

"Sloane just gave me her notice," she said glumly, resting her chin in her hand as she leaned against the counter.

"She's pregnant, huh?"

"Yup. Four months already, and she didn't even know!" She made a face. "And here's me, trying for years with no luck."

I grimaced. "First of all, we're using condoms right now, so getting pregnant is off the table. Second, I don't know much about much, but I know stress isn't good for anything."

"My whole life is stress," she said. "What choice do I have?"

"Well." I moved around behind her and put my hands on her shoulders. "Your first choice is deciding how long you can survive without Sloane." I gently began massaging her. "Your second choice is what type of person you want to replace her." I dug my fingers into the tight muscles beneath the skin at the base of her skull, pressing until her head fell forward and her chin hit her chest. "And your third choice is whether or not to let me take you to bed."

Her body shuddered slightly but she relaxed against me.

"I can't, Gabe. I want to, but I still have emails to answer, and I have to book a trip to New York and—"

"Sloane can take care of your travel—she hasn't left yet. Emails can wait. You can bring your laptop to bed later tonight and work on those while I rub your feet. Right now, we're going to get you relaxed."

"Sex doesn't fix everything," she protested as I tugged at her hand.

"Not everything, no, but it's really excellent for stress."

"Okay, Dr. DeLugo."

"The doctor is in—or at least I will be."

Thirty minutes later we were in the bathtub, with her between my legs. I'd gotten her off twice and now she was as relaxed as she ever got, resting the back of her head against my chest.

"That was lovely," she said. "You are the master of distraction."

"Well, maybe you can return the favor during the season, when I'm hyper focused on hockey and my body is reminding me how old I am."

"Are you going to be okay?" she asked quietly. "I know you were cleared to play this week, but that was business. Now things are personal. How are you really?"

"If we take concussions out of the equation, I'm great," I said. "I'm strong, and to be honest, probably in the best shape of my life. When I was younger, I didn't have to work at being athletic—I was born with it. Now I have to target specific muscle groups, pay attention to my stamina and diet, things that I took for granted in my twenties. And honestly, I feel fantastic."

"I don't want you to do this if you really want to retire," she said after a moment. "I mean it. I wanted you here for a plethora of reasons, but if we're planning a future, I need you healthy. Our future children will need a healthy daddy. Someone to play catch with, who'll teach them to skate and swim and all the other things I'm not good at."

I chuckled, running a hand over her breast and then cupping it lightly. "I'm good, Harper. Really. The biggest concern is getting hit in the head again. The risk of CTE gets higher every time it happens, but otherwise, I'm in great shape. Aside from some occasional aches and pains."

"The number one job of the defense is protecting you," she said firmly. "And I'm going tell Henrik he has to make that abundantly clear."

"Let Henrik run the team the way he needs to," I said gently. "I'll deal with the team's D. The defense will protect me because it's part of the job, and because they want to, not because a coach tells them to. It's hard to explain the dynamic on the ice. You form a bond, even if you don't like each other off the ice, because it's an important part of the process. But you can't force it. As guys start coming back to town, or moving here as you trade for them, we'll spend time together and get to know each other. That's when loyalty will happen. Or it won't. And when it doesn't, I'll hang up my skates."

"That's the part of this that's hard for me," she said. "I've never been an athlete, never been on a team unless you count the debate team, and I'm going to go out on a limb and say it's not the same."

I chuckled. "Well, I've never been on a debate team, but I'm going to agree."

"So it's foreign to me in general. Add on the stressors and pressure of being on a *professional* team making millions of dollars a year, and I can't replicate those types of relationships in my head."

"There's nothing else like it," I told her. "I wish I could explain how it feels to you, but I can't. You have to live it and experience the bond, the trust that happens on the ice. Teams that don't play well are missing that piece. The only advice I'll give you for the business side of it is that if you don't build a locker room with trust, loyalty and dedication, to go along with the athleticism and talent, you have nothing. That includes your back office, coaching, trainers, all of it. Even the owners."

She was quiet for what was probably a beat too long. "So you're saying if they don't like and trust me, they won't play well?"

"I don't think they have to like you, but they have to trust in your ability to make the right decisions for the organization."

"I'm trying," she whispered.

"I know you are, baby. And I have full confidence in you."

"Now to win over everyone else."

"One day, one step, and one orgasm at a time."

"Why are you so distracted by orgasms?" she said playfully.

"Is that a trick question? Shouldn't everyone be distracted by orgasms?" I let my hand drift south.

She sighed happily, arching into my touch. "Yes, they should."

25

———————

H*arper*

August flew by in what felt like a flash. Between meetings, interviews, trade agreements, and searching for a new assistant, I was working fourteen-hour days, seven days a week. And Gabe was the perfect househusband. He cooked and shopped and made sure I had regular orgasm breaks. He gave me opinions on players, advice on trade deals, and listened when I was angry or frustrated or overwhelmed.

He was everything I never knew I needed.

Not even Edward had been this in tune to my wants and needs, and I wondered where this version of Gabe had been a decade ago. Had he always been there but I'd been too caught up in school and work, along with my insecurities and fear of abandonment, to notice? Had I sabotaged our marriage out of some deep-seated belief that he was going to leave me anyway?

I also had to consider that hockey was going to change the dynamic of our relationship once the season started because he was going to be busy too. He wasn't going to be catering to my every need like he'd been doing all summer. He'd be traveling and going to games, practices, and meetings. There would be very few lazy mornings in bed or dinner waiting when I got home. Everything was going to adjust once the training camp got underway and part of me worried that we would fall back into the same routine we'd had when we were married.

We'd had disparate schedules, with separate routines, lifestyles, and friends. Eventually, it had caused chinks in our foundation that had been precarious, and when I'd seen those pictures of him at the strip club, along with the stories from the other wives and girlfriends, everything had crumbled. There had been other issues too, with him staying out all night, forgetting to call me when he was on the road, and his out-of-control spending. It had all culminated in me having doubts. In the end, it had destroyed us.

With those negative memories always on my mind, I couldn't help but begin to feel some panic as the start of hockey season loomed.

I was teetering on the edge of emotional overload.

Falling in love with him again was risky, and I couldn't afford to take any other risks at the moment. Everything I was doing with the Phantoms was a risk, so the plan had been to keep my personal life relatively simple.

Things in my life were rarely simple, though. Between taking over a professional hockey team, starting an unexpected relationship with Gabe, and the potential of becoming a stepmother to a nine-year-old, my plan for simplicity was rapidly blowing up in my face.

For the most part, I stayed too busy to overthink my situation, but Gabe and I were supposed to be getting on a plane this weekend to see Brandy play in her softball tournament, and I had fifty other things I needed to do instead. It wasn't that I didn't want to go, but the timing sucked. Training camp started Monday, I'd brought in four more new players in the last two weeks, and though I had people to help them with the transition and the details of moving, I wanted to be more involved than that.

I needed to show both players and back-office employees that I deserved to be here. I deserved to stay at the helm of this team. That Edward had been right in leaving it to me.

So, I couldn't just jet off for a kid's softball tournament every time something came up. Except what if we were talking about my own child? Would I feel as resentful about taking the time off when it was my kid instead of Gabe's? Would Brandy feel bad when we spent more time with our child versus his child? If Gabe and I stayed together, I'd have to take her feelings into consideration no matter what because until now she'd been an only child. I had to keep her needs in mind as well, which was going to complicate my life even more.

And I didn't have time for any other complications.

"Are you listening to me?" Sloane asked. We'd been on the phone for an hour and my mind had wandered.

"Sorry. I was thinking about how I don't have time to go to Denver for four days."

"The timing isn't great," she acknowledged. "I'm so sorry I can't come out to L.A. either. I'm just swamped with the new house, Johan starting the season, and now a hundred doctor's appointments to make up for all the months of not going to any."

"How did you not know you were pregnant?" I asked, laughing. "I mean, you're twenty weeks. Were there no signs at all?"

"There was a little weight gain, about six pounds I couldn't seem to drop, but I thought it was all the travel and eating out we've been doing. I was a little more tired than usual, but I'm busy so I thought it was to be expected. There were other signs, but I was oblivious."

"Like?"

"My boobs are bigger. Apparently, my face is glowing and my nails are growing like crazy. I honestly didn't notice any of that, but Johan did."

"I think it's sweet that he noticed."

"He's the sweetest. One of many reasons I love him."

"You sound happy. I'm going to miss you, but I'm so happy for you. You deserve this after being married to Tim."

"You deserve happiness too, you know."

"I don't know if it's in the cards for me."

"Things aren't going well with you and Gabe?"

"They are, but we've been together in the off-season. Once hockey starts...I don't know. My gut tells me everything is going to change."

"You have to talk about it, and come up with a plan, to make sure it doesn't."

"Our lives are going to be incredibly busy. Just like when we were married the first time. I'm terrified history will repeat itself."

"What does that even mean? You and Gabe are back together. Haven't you discussed what the plan is going to be once hockey season starts?"

I grimaced.

We hadn't talked about much to do with the future.

We'd talked about Gabe potentially moving into the main house, how we were going to address the topic of children next summer if things were going well, and how we would handle locker room gossip if it was still going on once the season got under way.

We hadn't talked about whether we'd get remarried or just continue with the status quo.

We hadn't discussed in any detail how we would handle all the upcoming changes to the routine we'd fallen into over the summer.

What we would tell Brandy.

Or anything really.

We seemed to be living in the present without much regard for the future.

"Harper?"

"I'm here. Just thinking about how incredibly dumb I am sometimes."

"You're not dumb. You can be hyper focused on work, which isn't the same thing."

"I have to talk to Gabe. This is the worst possible time for me to head out of town for a long weekend."

"Brandy's going to be disappointed."

"Well, he can still go."

"I thought you were going to meet Tricia's new boyfriend so Brandy can start getting used to the new parenting lineup?"

"Yeah, I know. I just...I can't. Ugh. Listen, I have to go find Gabe."

"All right. Call me later, let me know your plans."

"I will. Thanks." I disconnected and turned to find Gabe leaning against the doorway.

"What did you need to talk to me about?" he asked quietly, a wary look in his eyes.

"Denver." I approached him slowly. "I know we made plans, but I... this is a terrible time for me to get away."

"I understand that, but it's incredibly important to me," he replied. "And to Brandy. This tournament is a big deal and we wanted to present a united front with our respective significant others in supporting her."

"I know. And I'm so sorry. But there's so much happening with training camp starting next week. A bunch of players are arriving Friday and there are—"

"They're grown men, and the team is taking care of the details. They don't need you to meet them at the airport. Athletes understand this part of the life very well." Now he looked frustrated. Maybe even annoyed.

"I know, and I understand you're disappointed," I said, putting my hand on his arm. "Brandy is important, but the team is important too. I won't ever have a first season as the owner again and I have to do it right."

"And Brandy won't ever have a first travel tournament again."

"Tell me what she likes," I said. "I'll send her a present to let her know I was thinking about her and how proud I am of her. With a note. Or I'll call and—"

"She doesn't need gifts," he said impatiently, moving his arm out from under my hand. "She needs the four of us to be there for her, to show her that her life won't necessarily change just because her mother and I are moving on romantically."

"Gabe, I..." I didn't know what else to say.

I was caught between the proverbial rock and a hard place.

I wanted to go to Denver, but I needed to be here in L.A.

We had meetings and conference calls to finalize everything for both training camp and the season. There were so many details to settle, I couldn't be gone for four days. I hated disappointing everyone, but this wasn't a small thing. This was the beginning of my first season with the team. There was still a huge learning curve, and Gabe knew how important this was to me.

"Is this what you're going to do with our kids?" he asked after a moment. "Is work going to come before their sports events and school plays and all that stuff? Are you going to just let a nanny raise them? Because I didn't realize that was the plan."

"It's not the *plan*," I said, my voice rising in frustration. "It's just this one time. This is all new to me! Going forward it won't be like this. It'll be easy."

"You don't get it, do you?" he asked, shaking his head. "It's not going to be easy. A little easier than it is right now because you're doing it for the first time, but it's never going to be *easy*. Pro sports is a never-ending spiral of stress and frustration and complications. It will never, ever be easy. And at some point, you're going to have to decide how much you're going to sacrifice for it."

I didn't respond because I didn't have an answer.

I didn't know what to expect going forward.

Neither of us did.

We wouldn't know until we were living it.

Of course, we were supposed to talk about the future and how we were going to handle it all. We just hadn't gotten around to it.

And now it was about to bite us on the butt.

"Gabe, I don't want to fight," I said. "Can we just talk about this?"

"I don't know what there is to talk about. If you don't go to Denver, I feel like this is a reflection of what our life is going to be like. We both prioritized our jobs when we were married, but we were young and the only people we hurt were each other. Now we're talking about a living, breathing nine-year-old girl with feelings. How am I supposed to explain this to her?"

"You've put work ahead of Brandy her entire life!" I snapped.

"I have," he acknowledged. "And if you recall, I've been trying to make her more of a priority now. I don't even know if I would still be playing if not for you. You asked me to do this, to come to L.A. and help you launch your inaugural season as owner. And I did it. For *you*. In fact, I've done fucking everything for you this summer. It didn't start out that way, but once we started sleeping together, I realized I wanted more than that. This time around, I want to be the kind of partner I wasn't mature enough to be when we were married."

"I know. And I appreciate everything. I do. If we can just get through the next couple of months—"

"Do you recall another time we said that?" he asked. "If we can make it until I finish grad school... if we can make it until I get through the probationary period at work... if we can get through until the end of the season... do you remember uttering those words once upon a time?"

I flushed.

We had said and done those things.

Repeatedly.

But this was different.

How could he not understand what was at stake here?

Maybe he just didn't want to.

Or maybe this whole thing had been a huge mistake.

26

—————

G *abe*

THERE WAS no mistaking the conflict in Harper's eyes, but I couldn't do this again. Especially not when it came to Brandy. I'd been selfish and oblivious in my twenties. I didn't have that luxury anymore. When we'd decided to start dating again, it hadn't taken long for me to realize how much I still loved her. She'd been my everything once, and no one else had ever been able to measure up.

Somehow, I'd romanticized all the bad parts of our relationship, convincing myself we'd do it right this time. Better. That if I was better, then she would change too. And that had been my mistake. I should have known nothing was ever that simple. Three divorces should have taught me that life didn't work that way.

Fantastic sex wasn't enough.

History and chemistry weren't enough.

Love wasn't even enough.

Harper had broken my heart a decade ago and she was going to do it again.

"I'm sorry," she said softly. "What if I flew out Friday night so I could be there for Saturday and then left Sunday morning?"

"If they make it to the championship, that will happen on Sunday," I said. "So you'd miss out on the most important part. And anyway, this isn't about Brandy. Not really. This is about us repeating history. Because I guess you were right—a leopard doesn't change its spots. No matter how much we've tried."

"What does that mean?" she asked.

"You know what it means." I leaned against the counter. "I think we gave it a shot but it's not going to work."

"It's not..." She stared at me. "We just went public with our relationship and it's not going to work?!" Her voice rose higher with each word.

"We'll mitigate the fallout with the whole 'we've decided to be friends' story," I replied. "I can be friendly if you can."

"Are you serious?" she snapped, her eyes blazing in the way that I normally loved. Except now it just frustrated me. She was so stubborn.

"I don't know what you want me to say."

"So that's it? We hit our first bump in the road and we're done?"

"It's not a bump," I said carefully. "It's a fucking roadblock. And I don't see any way around it. You're going to put your job first, as usual, and I'm done with that. I'm ready to slow down. Yes, I'll give you my all this season. I'll protect your reputation in the locker room. I'd give my left nut to make it to the finals before I retire, and while we both know that's a longshot this season, I'll do anything and everything in my power to get us there. I might even have one more season after this in me, as a back-up. But I'm looking toward retirement no matter how much I don't want to. And from a professional standpoint, this is your rookie season. I get it. I don't begrudge you. It's just not where I want to be in life."

"But Gabe, I—"

"I don't want you to change," I said, cutting her off abruptly. "I love the woman you are. I really do. I've always loved you. Since the first time I saw you. You're beautiful and sexy, but also intelligent and dynamic. A force to be reckoned with. You're going to take the Phantoms to the next level. I believe that with everything inside of me. But that's your life, not mine. It's not where I want to be. And I didn't realize it until just now. That's on me, and I'm sorry. Sorrier than you know."

"Where is it that you don't want to be?" she asked, tears puddling in her eyes. "Here in L.A. with me? Playing for me? Starting a family with me? I'm confused because it sounds like you *do* want those things. Just not *with me*."

"I don't want to be caught up in the rat race," I said. "I don't want to be in another relationship with a woman who's never home. I don't want to be a single dad while you're off dominating the hockey world."

"Oh, but it was okay for Tricia to be the single parent while *you* were off dominating the hockey world?!"

"No, it wasn't." I threw up my hands. "That's the whole point, Harper. I already fucked up once, so I'm trying not to do it again! I want to do better this time and not repeat the same mistakes."

She clenched her jaw and swiped at the tears in her eyes.

"I'm sorry."

"You really suck, you know that?" She snatched a napkin off the counter and dabbed at her eyes. "I fucking trusted you!"

"I know."

"And now you're going to make me look bad. Right at the beginning of the season."

Shit.

I was trying to protect myself, Brandy, and even Harper to a degree. But my intention wasn't to hurt anyone. Least of all her. That was actually the opposite of what I wanted. Ending things now protected both of us, although the optics would admittedly be terrible.

"We can wait to make any kind of announcement," I said. "We don't have to tell anyone for a few months. Then we can say that our schedules made it difficult for us to continue our relationship and—"

"Jesus, you've given this some thought. How long have you

been planning to dump me?" she snapped, tears streaming down her face.

"Don't do that. Come on." I took a step toward her, but she backed away.

"You know what? I don't care. Tell people, don't. Do what you want. You always do anyway, right?"

"That's not fair, Harper."

"Life isn't fair." She shook her head. "You should go."

"Let's come up with a plan," I suggested. "We don't have to tell anyone we're not together or we can—"

"I asked you to leave." She folded her arms across her chest in a defensive manner, even though her eyes were red, and her lower lip trembled slightly.

"All right."

We both needed time to calm down.

Think.

Reassess.

A few days apart might be beneficial all around.

I turned and slipped out through the sliding glass doors and quietly closed them.

Leaving my whole world behind.

I DIDN'T SEE or hear from Harper again before Thursday, and the house was dark and quiet when I left for the airport. She hadn't been home much while I hadn't gone anywhere at all, choosing to lick my wounds in private.

I honestly didn't know if I'd done the right thing.

I loved , and ending things hurt me even more than I'd anticipated.

Deep down, I'd hoped she would capitulate. Change her mind about Denver and surprise me at the airport or something, but that had been wishful thinking. I flew alone, the empty seat beside me a painful reminder of what I'd given up.

In retrospect, it had been a somewhat kneejerk reaction.

I'd been hurt that she was cancelling our plans, not only letting me down but making me look bad in front of Tricia and her new boyfriend. We'd prioritized our careers when we were married, and it impacted everything. Now it was happening again.

And I fucking hated it.

Hated myself for caring so much, for still loving her.

Hated myself for expecting her to want the same future I did.

A decade ago, I'd been frustrated by her busy career, and how much it took her away from me. And like a dumbass, I'd fallen in love with her again, knowing how important the Phantoms were to her. She hadn't lied or tried to pretend to be anything except who she was, and I'd somehow painted her into the perfect little box I wanted. With me as the househusband.

And the summer had been good.

I'd enjoyed having dinner ready when she got home.

I'd loved rubbing her feet and dragging her into the tub to relax after a long day.

We'd had fun talking shop in bed late at night.

Everything had been pretty perfect.

So, what the hell had happened?

Was it me back pedaling because things had gotten so serious so fast?

Had I just been embarrassed that she wouldn't be with me in Denver, because I'd have to explain why to everyone?

I was in a bad place emotionally and didn't handle this kind of thing well.

I'd spent the whole summer trying to be a better father, a better partner, and a better man. And in one fell swoop I'd pretty much derailed all of that.

What the fuck was wrong with me?

I wasn't letting Harper off the hook—she held some responsibility in what was going on—but it was hard to read her sometimes. She could be closed off and temperamental. We tended to butt heads when we fought, and things always escalated quickly.

Ironically, that wasn't what had happened. Not really. Things escalated slightly, and she got a bit emotional, but I'd been calm.

Rational.

Instead of fighting for her, for us, I'd been almost stoic in ending things.

In what universe was that who I was?

Yes, I wanted to be better, but I wasn't inherently a bad guy. Flawed, and more than occasionally immature, but not a bad human being. So why had I been trying so hard to be someone else? And more than that, why had I expected Harper to be someone else?

Fuck.

I'd blown things up for no good reason.

Harper *did* have a million things going on.

The start of this particular hockey season was probably the most important event of her entire career. She had something to prove to literally everyone in the hockey world, starting with the league and going all the way down to the janitors at the arena. Almost everyone, save for a handful of friends like Remy Knight and a couple of people who knew her like Ivan and me, expected her to fail.

And I'd wanted her to take time off to see a group of nine-year-olds play softball.

Was I the asshole here or what?

Except she hadn't tried either.

Not really.

She'd presented her point of view and then dug in her heels.

There was never any compromise with us.

It had always been that way.

That was something I'd assumed would be different this time, yet I was just as guilty as she was of not offering a compromise. In fact, she had offered a compromise, and I'd shot it down. She'd wanted to come just on Saturday, to make an appearance in the name of solidarity, for Brandy if no one else, and that hadn't been good enough for me in the moment.

Now I was rethinking it.

I should have called or texted, and told her I wanted to talk, but my pride and bruised ego wouldn't allow it.

Not yet.

I had to ruminate and mull it over a few hundred times first.

So, I got off the plane and headed for the rental car counter.

It was going to be a long four days until I could get back to L.A.

27

———————

Broken hearts sucked.

Being older, more mature, and having lived through divorce and the death of a spouse didn't make a breakup any easier. In fact, this time I was equal parts angry and heartbroken. Losing Gabe a second time was hard, because I'd never stopped loving him, but the anger this time was much more prevalent. That would probably change as time went on, but short-term I was furious.

Furious for allowing myself to love him again.

Furious that I'd trusted him even though I'd tried not to.

Furious about every-fucking-thing.

And I had no one to blame but myself.

I'd fucking *known* I would fall in love with him again.

And I should have known that it would end badly.

There was nothing to do but put one foot in front of the other and do what needed to be done. I hadn't gone to Denver because I was busy, so my only option was to throw myself into work and hope that I'd be too distracted to wallow in self-pity.

Strong, independent women didn't wallow.

I'd tell myself that as many times as was necessary until I believed it.

I took extra care with my makeup, adding an extra layer of concealer under my eyes to hide how puffy they were.

I used a brighter shade of lipstick than usual, hoping to make me look more confident.

It probably wouldn't work, but I had to try.

I was meeting Autumn for lunch in twenty minutes, so I didn't have time to feel sorry for myself. She'd asked if she could pick my brain because as the head coach's wife, she was falling into a role she didn't feel prepared for, so we'd decided to talk through some of the potential obstacles together.

"Hey." She hugged me when I walked into the restaurant, and then paused, cocking her head. "You okay?"

Shit.

So much for my stellar makeup job.

"It's been a rough morning," I hedged. "But I'm good. How are you?"

"Overwhelmed," she said as we settled into a booth. "Henrik is so busy, and his ex-wife is driving us nuts."

"Exes are difficult," I murmured.

"Lydia is...awful. There's no other way to put it. She lives in San Diego with the boys, and she acts like it's right around the corner. Can you pick them up from hockey practice on Sunday? Do you want to take them Friday night? Oh, but they have to be home by noon on Saturday for a birthday party." She was doing a hysterical job of mimicking Henrik's ex-wife. "I mean, it's a three-hour drive. We can't just drop everything at the last minute and drive six hours roundtrip to get them."

"He's fighting for custody, right?" I asked.

"Yes, but we won't get in front of a judge for months." She shrugged. "I think it's going to be an uphill battle to win custody, but he really wants to."

"And you're okay with it?" I asked. "It's a lot to take on another man's children, especially when you're still so new as a couple."

"Oh, the boys are awesome," she said. "I adore them. I'd love to have them around. God knows, I don't have anything else to do. Being a stay-at-home mom is one thing, but being a stay-at-home wife is another. I can't tell you how bored I am."

I stared at her for a moment as an idea began to take root.

"Is that so."

She frowned. "Well, yeah. I mean, it's kind of fun now, in the off-season, but once hockey season starts, I'm going to be on my own, with no friends, and very little to do. Sure, I'll go to home games and host some events with the wives and girlfriends, but how much time can that take? I'm actually thinking of signing up to become a substitute teacher. I did it in Chicago."

I had to wait as the waitress came and took our orders, but the minute she was gone, I blurted out what I'd been thinking. "What if you came to work for me? As my assistant?"

This time she was the one staring. "Wh-what?"

"The pay is good, and I'd be willing to work around your schedule so you're off when Henrik has time off. Especially in the off-season."

When she didn't respond right away, I continued by telling her how much I was willing to pay her, and her eyes widened.

"You're serious?"

"As a heart attack. My assistant lives in Fort Lauderdale and we've been doing everything virtually, but now she's pregnant and getting married. She just isn't going to have the time."

"Eventually I'm going to get pregnant too," Autumn said. "Probably within the next two years. Henrik is already forty-two, and he wants to enjoy any other kids we have while he's still relatively young. So probably two pregnancies in the next five years, assuming Mother Nature cooperates."

I took a sip of iced tea, averting my gaze. "Mother Nature certainly has a mind of her own. Trust me on that."

"Well, regardless, I just want to be up front about my plans."

"I can live with that."

Having someone I could trust was far more important than any longevity she could promise me. We'd deal with pregnancies as they happened.

"If we do wind up getting custody of the boys, I'll be in charge of them when Henrik's on the road, so even though they should be in school most of the day, I'll have to be home if they're sick or have doctors' appointments and such."

"Like I said, a lot of what you'll do can be done virtually. Not all of it, but the things I need you for in person, like meetings in New York with the league and things like that, we'll know in advance."

"Then I want to hear more." She smiled. "In fact, I want to hear *everything*."

We talked all through lunch and beyond. She was smart and interested in the details of what we would be doing, with the added bonus of having been both a college and professional hockey player herself. I'd known that but it had slipped my mind until it came up, making her almost perfect for the job. She was probably overqualified, but with her planning to start a family soon, it wouldn't make sense to give her an executive position. I had a few of those to fill, but I hadn't found the right people yet, and I didn't want to settle. It was easier to leave things the way they were and hire replacements as I found them.

"I do have to talk to Henrik about all of this," she said as we started to wind down. "But I'm sure he'll be excited for me. He knows how bored I've been."

"Have you been house hunting?" I asked.

"A little, but everything here is so expensive. We're a little shell-shocked at the pricing compared to Fort Lauderdale."

"I know. L.A. is a horrible real estate market. That's the only negative about living here. Everything else is so perfect, but housing costs can be a real deterrent."

"We're also planning a wedding for next summer and trying to get custody of the boys, so there's been a lot going on."

"Believe me, I understand."

"You sure you're okay?" She met my gaze curiously. "You look... sad."

"Oh." I guessed I wasn't as good of an actress as I'd hoped. "Well, Gabe and I had a fight. He's in Denver at his daughter's first softball tournament and I was supposed to go, but I had so much to do."

"And he was mad when you cancelled?"

"Yes, but it was more than that. We have a history of putting work before our relationship. That's part of the reason we divorced the first time. We were trying to do things differently this time around, but it's not like I work for the widget factory at some dead-end job. This is a huge deal, and I have so much to prove. I can't—"

"Why?" she asked.

"Excuse me?"

"Why do you have to prove anything to anyone? I understand that you inherited the team from your late husband, and you want to make him proud, so to speak, but beyond that, why do you care what anyone thinks?"

"Because I'm a woman in a male-dominated field and if I fail, they're going to say it's because I'm a woman. And I fucking hate that stigma."

"I get that. But at the end of the day, is the team's success more important than Gabe? If you wind up going all the way and winning the Stanley Cup this year, but you lose him in the process, will it be worth it? You don't have to answer me, but it's something you should probably think about."

"It's not so much about the team's success as my own," I admitted after a moment. "Edward's sons have done nothing but tell the whole world how I manipulated him into leaving me the team. How I don't deserve to be here and how inept I am. I need to prove them wrong. I just do. For myself and for Edward."

"But at what cost? There's only so much you can do. You know that, right? You could do everything perfectly, make all the best trades, the best business decisions, and have the most incredible team. And they could still be terrible. There are variables like injuries and family emergencies that could change everything, no matter how much you've planned. When it's all said and done, you could be the best team owner in the history of team owners and still have the worst season ever. Then what?"

"Well, I guess there's always next season."

"And the season after that. One day you'll wake up with a championship-winning team and nothing else. I don't know you that well, but I'm pretty confident in assuming that's not what you want. You want kids, a family, someone to share your life with."

"I do, but I guess the truth is—I want it all. I want the dream family but I also want the career. Lots of women have both, so why can't I?"

"I think you can, but there have to be limits. It can't be all work, all the time. There has to be work-work-work and then some play. Family time. A little of whatever it is that makes you happy outside of work."

"I tried. I told Gabe I would fly up for Saturday but he basically said that wasn't good enough. Then we went off on a tangent about the past and how leopards don't change their spots and—" I cut myself off, rubbing the bridge of my nose. "I don't even know what happened. One minute we were talking, the next we were... fighting." I couldn't bring myself to admit we'd broken up.

"So, he's in Denver now?"

"Yeah."

"Well, you can fly out and surprise him, or you can text and tell him you're not ready to give up on things and you want to talk when he gets home."

Those were both good options.

The problem was that I'd scheduled an all-day meeting for tomorrow with my heads of staff and had two million other things to do as well.

"I need a little time to think," I said aloud. "I have to figure out exactly what I want before I can talk to him about it."

"That's smart. But do it soon. Seems to me most people don't get a second chance with the love of their life."

"What makes you say he's the love of my life?" I asked curiously since I'd never told her that.

"It's all over your face every time you say his name."

28

———————

G *abe*

Being the coward I was, I didn't tell Tricia, Tricia's boyfriend Cole, or Brandy that Harper and I had broken up. I gave them exaggerated excuses for how busy she was, and that she was planning to send Brandy something special to make it up to her, and of course, Brandy was so excited at the prospect of a gift that I was going to have to reach out to Harper to make sure she sent something. Even if I had to pick it out and pay for it.

God, I was an asshole sometimes.

Luckily, the first game of the tournament started at nine o'clock Friday morning and they played another one at two in the afternoon, followed by a third at six-thirty. We were all wiped out by the time we got back to the hotel, and the festivities started all over again on Saturday at eight.

I'd played a lot of hockey tournaments as a kid, but I didn't remember them being this intense at this age. There was a ton of competition, and some of these kids were really, really talented.

Including Brandy. She had a hell of an arm for a nine-year-old, and she could hit too.

"She's fucking amazing," I murmured to Tricia during Saturday's second game.

"She really is. Athletics come so easily to her. Just like you."

I couldn't help but grin.

It was silly since we had no control over genetics, but I liked knowing she'd gotten her athleticism from me.

"Woohoo!" Cole was on his feet as Brandy smacked the ball over the left fielder's shoulder.

"That's my girl!" I jumped up too and we cheered as she rounded second base, heading for third. She paused, looked to her coach and then threw herself full speed at third, sliding in a fraction of a second before the third baseman caught the ball to tag her.

"Safe!" Tricia yelled, whistling louder than anyone I'd ever heard.

"Damn, when did you learn to do that?" I asked, laughing.

"When you have a kid who's an athlete, you learn to whistle."

I grinned, clapping along with everyone else.

This was so exciting, and for what had to be the tenth time, I wished Harper had been here with me.

Cole seemed like a good guy. He was some kind of computer programmer, with glasses and thinning hair, but he was tall and in good shape. He seemed to adore Tricia and was good with Brandy, so I didn't have anything negative to say. Not that who she dated was any of my business, but the whole point of this weekend had been for us to get to know each other.

"So, you want to tell me the real reason Harper didn't come," Tricia said as we walked to the concession stand to get some water.

"We had an argument," I said lightly. "She's busy and wanted to fly up just for the day, but I was annoyed and told her not to bother."

She grimaced. "Seriously? Why would you do that? She was obviously making an effort."

"You weren't married to her ten years ago," I muttered. "This is like history repeating itself. She always put her job ahead of our relationship and—"

"Because *you* never put your job ahead of a relationship?" she countered, eyeing me. "Look, you and I were never in love. I got pregnant and you did the right thing, so I won't compare our marriage to your others. But you put hockey before everything when we were together, so we never truly gave it a chance. I can't imagine it was much different in your first or third marriages either."

"Oh, I'm not blameless in the selfishness department, but there was never any question of what my life would be like. If you marry a professional athlete, that's how it has to be during the season."

"Of course, but why is she being held to a different standard? Your job has specific time constraints, and so does hers. She's probably busiest now, right before the season starts, while you'll be busier once it gets underway. It's unfortunate, but that's reality. Why are you upset about how busy she is when you're going to be equally busy starting very soon?"

I didn't have an answer for that.

"I don't know," I said finally. "I just know that we can't do the same shit we did a decade ago and expect different results. Something has to give. Someone has to be willing to change the narrative of the relationship."

"And that's going to be you, though, right?" She met my gaze head-on. "You're planning to retire in no more than a couple of years, so then you can stay home and be a support system while she works and follows her dream. Because you *already* followed yours. Or am I missing something?"

I stared at her in confusion.

Was that the way things were supposed to be?

Could it possibly be that simple?

I'd had my career—the best career in the world as far as I was concerned—but my body couldn't do it for much longer. I eventually had to retire no matter what I wanted, and the only question was whether it would be after this season or possibly one more. That didn't mean Harper had to retire, though. Hell, her career was just beginning, and there wasn't a single reason why she couldn't continue to work while I stayed home with the kids. Traveled to see Brandy. Spend time with friends. Maybe even found something I could do within the Phantoms' organization that wouldn't be full-time.

Why hadn't I considered this before now?

"You're a good guy, Gabe," Tricia said, gently squeezing my arm. "But you do tend to get a little wrapped up in yourself. If you want to make things work with Harper this time, you have to step out of your comfort zone. You're going to retire sooner in the near-ish future, and your entire life will change. Do you want her to be at your side for it or do you want to be alone?"

Well, wasn't that the fucking million-dollar question?

I had so much to think about.

~

BRANDY'S TEAM made it to the championship game on Sunday and we were back at the field at ten in the morning. It was a brutally hot day, and we'd been baking in the sun all weekend. We were tired and sunburned but also excited and ready to see Brandy's team win the whole thing. It really didn't amount to anything but bragging rights, but it was a big deal for the kids.

"So, are you looking forward to hockey season?" Cole asked me as we settled in the bleachers, waiting for the game to start. "Or is it old hat after so many years?"

That was an interesting question because it was both.

"That's hard to answer," I replied. "It's definitely old hat, and as a veteran in the league, I don't get overly excited about training camp anymore. The first few days are for the rookies anyway. The rest of us kind of hang out, working out and getting to know each other again. Watching the young guys is fun because you get to see their potential, who you might be playing with this season, stuff like that.

"On the flip side, the beginning of every season is a chance to start new. On day one you can dream about making the playoffs, winning the championship, stuff like that. The possibilities are endless and there's energy in the locker room that doesn't necessarily last all season. Every room is different, every season is different, but the first few weeks are always special."

"Even if you lose?" Cole asked. "I'm not an athlete so it's foreign to me. Like, what happens if you lose the first three games of the season? Does that diminish that energy?"

"To a degree, sure." I nodded. "But sometimes it just means the coaches are figuring out a new system, testing new lines. They try to do that in the pre-season, but they also let new guys have a shot in pre-season, so nothing is finalized. It's a little complicated to explain the dynamic."

"Yeah, but interesting. At least from the outside looking in."

"It's interesting on the inside too. A lot of that is happening now, as the coaching staff makes plans and comes up with the general strategy."

"Is Harper a part of that?" Tricia asked. "Like, how much of that does she do as the owner?"

"Right now, Harper is both owner and President of the organization. So she's a lot more involved than other owners are. She has input in almost everything, making her job harder than that of other owners."

"Did she do this intentionally?" Cole asked. "Or is it because she hasn't had time to hire the right people?"

"A little of both. She's trying to surround herself with people she trusts, who also share her vision for the team, and that takes time. Her late husband left her with a mess, and when you add in the fact that her former stepchildren are still trying to overturn the ruling on the will, it's been a bit of a nightmare."

"Sounds like she's kicking ass and taking names," Cole said, nodding. "Good for her."

His comment was like a punch in the face.

Why was I busy whining about how she didn't have time for me instead of showing her how proud I was of her? Because I was. I was annoyed at how little free time she had, but I was incredibly proud of what she was doing. She was showing her stepsons and the entire hockey world how dedicated she was to making the Phantoms a success. It was mostly happening behind the scenes right now, but once the season started, people would see how much she'd put into the team and the upcoming season.

And I was sitting here feeling sorry for myself because I wasn't getting my way.

"Let's go, Bluejays!" Tricia let out another one of her whistles and I forced myself to focus on the game.

For one more day, I needed to focus on my daughter. These were nine- and ten-year-old girls, but they were fast, talented, and exciting to watch. This tournament wasn't for the kids who played for fun. These girls were athletic and driven, the members of both teams determined to win.

"Damn, both teams are so good," I said at the bottom of the eighth inning when the score was tied.

"If this was pro baseball, they'd bring in a closer to finish them off," Cole muttered. "We could get out of this sun and go home."

"Right?" I chuckled.

"We may not have an official closer, but Brandy is going back out there next inning to kick their asses," Tricia said, eyeing both Cole and me. "No more complaining, you two!"

"Yes, ma'am." Cole nodded somberly before winking at me and we all laughed.

Once again, I wished Harper was here to be a part of this.

She would have fit right in, and I had a feeling she and Tricia would have gotten along well.

But Harper was at home doing what she needed to do.

For herself and for the Phantoms. If we were going to find a way to work through this, and I still wanted to, I had to give her the freedom to be who she was. Even if it meant things would be harder for me. Even if it meant having less time with her than I wanted.

Even though change was really fucking hard.

"Come on, baby, you got this!" Tricia clapped loudly when Brandy jogged out to take her turn at bat.

The pitcher from the other team wound up and sent the ball

careening toward Brandy's torso, and she jumped out of the way to avoid being hit.

Ball one.

The second pitch headed straight for Brandy's bat, but she swung and missed.

Strike one.

The pitcher wound up and then everything happened so quickly I almost missed it.

The ball was fast and hard, making contact with the side of Brandy's head.

She went down holding her face.

Even from here I could see the blood.

"Brandy!" Tricia screamed her name as I vaulted over the railing and onto the field, running toward my daughter.

29

———————

H*arper*

THE WEEKEND WAS BUSY, with me trying to accomplish a dozen different things. My goal was to get everything done so that tonight I could focus on something just as important as the Phantoms: Gabe. I planned to text him as soon as possible and tell him I wanted to talk, no matter how late it was when he got home. Then we would hash out whatever it was we had to hash out.

There was no perfect solution for us.

For us to even attempt to be together, there would have to be a great deal of compromise.

I needed one hockey season to get my feet under me, but the plan to propel the Phantoms forward wasn't going to change. Gabe would have to think about what he wanted in that regard. Could we take one year to put our heads down and give everything we had to our careers?

He wanted a championship.

It wasn't realistic to think we could make that happen this season, but both of us had things to prove.

I wanted to prove I was worthy of the legacy Edward had left me and continue overseeing the Phantoms for a long time. Eventually, I would hire a President of Hockey Operations to take over much of what I was doing, but until I found the perfect person to do it, it was all me.

Gabe wanted to go out on top, with either a championship or at least a stellar season that he could be proud of.

Beyond that, we had to think about our visions for the future, both individually and together. Whether or not we could find middle ground remained to be seen, but I didn't want to give up this easily. Not after all we'd been through and how good it had been over the summer.

I didn't know what was going to happen, or if he was even open to this discussion, but I had to try.

I loved him.

I always had.

As I kicked off my shoes and hung my purse on the stool by the island, I thought about what to say. I should have called him, but he was probably at the airport or maybe on the plane, so a text would be easier.

HARPER: Hey. I hope you had a great weekend. I've spent most of it thinking about you. About us. And I'm sorry I couldn't be there. Do you think we could talk? I really don't want to leave things as they are. There has to be a way to compromise so we can both have what we want. I've never stopped loving you and this doesn't feel like how it should end. I'll wait up. Love, Me.

I didn't normally sign texts, but this was different.

This was a kind of love letter.

A very basic one, but nonetheless, I hoped it meant as much to him as it did to me.

With that done, I went into the bathroom and ran a bath, pouring in drops of my favorite essential oils and putting my hair up in a bun. It had been a long few days and tomorrow was going to be stressful.

I planned to talk to the entire team, letting them know who I was and what my vision was for the Phantoms. How I wanted to earn their trust and respect but understood that it wouldn't happen overnight. And let them know that my door would always be open.

Maybe that was unconventional. I had no way of knowing what others did since the only other owners I knew well were Remy Knight and Gage Caldwell. They did have an open-door policy, but my understanding was that it wasn't that way for everyone. Some owners weren't involved at all; they were simply figureheads who handled some of the finances.

I planned to be much more.

For this season, anyway.

I sank into the water and closed my eyes.

My phone rang and I reached for it lazily.

Henrik.

Uh oh.

"Hey, what's up?" I asked answering on the second ring.

"I have a problem," he said, his voice subdued.

My chest tightened worriedly. "What's wrong? You okay?"

"Yeah, everyone is fine—well, not everyone." He paused. "My ex-wife, the boys' mother. Lydia. She's dead."

"Dead?" I asked in surprise. "Oh my god. What happened? She's your age, isn't she?"

"A couple of years younger, yeah. She was in Africa, doing a photo shoot. She was attacked and killed. By a lion."

"I'm sorry, what? Did you say a lion?"

"I don't have a lot of details yet. Her father just called me, and he was pretty shaken up. The boys are here with us because this photo shoot assignment came up last-minute. We've been trying to manage their schoolwork from here since we can't commute back and forth every day. Anyway, my understanding is that it was... brutal. And I have to figure out how to tell the boys... *fuck*. They're only eight, Harper. How the fuck do I tell them their mom was eaten by a goddamn lion without scarring them for life?"

"You don't," I said. "You tell them there was a car accident or something. You absolutely don't tell them about a lion."

"Right."

"Do you need to take tomorrow off?"

"I can't take tomorrow off," he replied in frustration. "It's the first day of training camp! I have to be there. I'm not going to tell the boys yet. Probably not until the weekend. I mean, there's never going to be a good time to tell them their mother is dead. Jesus fucking Christ. I really want to strangle her right now. How could this happen?"

"What can I do?" I asked. "Do you need anything?"

"No. I don't know. Maybe. I'm just afraid it might hit the news. She was working for National Geographic, so an incident like that will probably hit CNN or at least the Associated Press. We monitor their internet use, but we can't monitor what their friends and teachers see. And Lydia is well-known at the school, so people will recognize her name if it is on the news."

"But they're not at school, right? You're doing everything from home until you figure out the situation. Autumn can stay with them this week until everything is sorted out. I'll manage without her. Maybe Sloane can fly out to help me since she's been trying to slowly bring Autumn up to speed anyway."

"Okay. Yeah." He sounded flustered.

"It's going to be okay. I'm so sorry this happened, and the timing couldn't be worse, but don't worry about the team. Short-term, you have a great coaching staff in place, and Dom and Drake could literally jump in to help out while you're dealing with this."

"I appreciate you, Harper. More than you know."

"Whatever you need."

We talked for a few more minutes before disconnecting.

The universe was definitely trying to tell me something.

It was reminding me that family came first.

Life happened.

And work wasn't everything.

One of many things I would talk with Gabe about when he got home.

I WAS UP EARLY, showering and changing into a pinstripe pantsuit. I put on a simple button-down royal blue blouse that Gabe said matched my eyes, and simple black pumps. I wanted to look feminine but professional. I needed everyone to think of me as their boss, whether they found me attractive or not, but I refused to pretend to be someone I wasn't. I was a woman. Period. There was no reason to wear dowdy clothes or put my hair in a bun so that the male-dominated staff would be more comfortable. That wasn't my job.

I was disappointed Autumn wouldn't be there with me, but I'd already booked Sloane on a flight for this morning, so she'd arrive by midday.

I gazed across the patio at the guest house, wondering where Gabe was. He hadn't texted me back yesterday, and as far as I could tell, he hadn't come home either. It was possible his flight had been delayed or something, but there was no way he hadn't seen my text.

And for whatever reason, he'd chosen not to respond.

I couldn't worry about that right now, though.

Today was the day.

The first day of the season from my perspective.

The day I showed up as the boss to a staff that was ninety-percent male.

There were a few ladies in the sales and marketing departments, but none were managers. One of the staff photographers was a woman, and we had quite a few women on the janitorial crew, but that was it. Beyond that, the only women were Sloane and me. When Sloane officially left, it would be Autumn and me. The whole thing was a little daunting.

I got to the arena just after seven, smiling at the middle-aged security guard at the door leading in from the executive staff's parking lot.

"Good morning, Ms. Barrowman." He nodded.

"Morning, Bruce." I held out the basket of muffins in my hand. "Muffin?"

"Don't mind if I do." He plucked one from the basket and sniffed it. "This smells delicious."

"Enjoy!" I'd wanted to make them myself, but there had been no way for me to bake ten dozen muffins this morning. I'd hired Brianna to make them and she'd dropped them off at six o'clock this morning.

She was truly a lifesaver.

She was going to get a nice Christmas gift this year.

"Morning, Harper." Dom nodded in my direction. He and Drake were waiting for me as I rounded the corner to the hallway that led to the main conference room.

"What's wrong?" I asked automatically, taking in the looks on their faces.

"Eddie and Tim are here."

"Are you fucking kidding me?" I demanded.

"I wish I was." Dom met my gaze. "Tell us what you want us to do."

"I have to handle it," I said after a moment. "I can't let the team or the staff see that I'm intimidated by them. In the future, however, I want them banned from the arena. Take away their parking passes and all credentials allowing them access to the business offices or locker room area."

"I'll handle that," Drake said, nodding.

"And we've got your back today, no matter what. Just be prepared for what's waiting in the conference room. It's a party right now." He glanced down at my basket of muffins. "And they told the boys they provided breakfast."

I rolled my eyes. "Seriously? I have the receipts for the coffee and breakfast sandwiches I ordered."

"Yeah, well, they seem to think you won't embarrass yourself by bringing that up."

"Then they don't know me very well." I straightened my spine. "I need to lock my things in my office and then head down there. You have anything else on your mind?"

"I'm going to go keep an eye on things," Dom said.

"I'll walk with you, if you don't mind?" Drake said, falling into step beside me.

"Not at all. Have you talked to Henrik yet today?"

"Yeah, he told us about his ex." Drake shook his head as we stepped onto the elevator. "That's fucked up."

"Right?"

"How's Brandy? Do you know how surgery went?"

"What?" I looked up at him in confusion. "Brandy?"

He frowned. "Gabe's daughter. She was injured in her game yesterday. He called Henrik to get Doc Ritter's phone number." Dr. Ritter was the team's ophthalmologist.

"He... Dammit." Now it made sense that he hadn't responded to my text and hadn't come home last night, but it hurt that he hadn't felt like he could reach out to me in an emergency.

"You didn't know?"

"We had a fight," I admitted, putting away my things. "He went to Denver without me and we haven't talked since Wednesday night."

"Oh, shit. Sorry. I didn't mean to talk out of turn."

"No, it's fine. I would've heard anyway. Henrik probably spaced with the situation with his ex dying."

"Yeah." He paused. "I guess that's two."

"Two what?"

"Two bad things happening on the first day of the new season. I hope this doesn't mean there's one more. You know, how bad things happen in threes?"

"Actually, if Tim and Eddie are here, that's the third bad thing. So we should be in the clear once I give them the boot."

I locked my office and headed back to the elevators.

I was going to handle Eddie and Tim and then talk to my team. *My* team.

I'd find out what was going on with Brandy as soon as I spoke to Gabe, but everything else would have to wait.

30

———————

H*arper*

I WOULD HAVE BEEN a liar if I said I wasn't nervous as I walked toward the conference room. I could hear voices and laughter all the way down the hall, indicating we had a happy group and it pissed me off that Tim and Eddie had beat me to the punch this morning. That had been by design on their part. I had no doubt of that. If I'd gotten here at seven fifteen, they probably would have been here at six, even though none of the players would have been here yet.

With Drake behind me, I stepped into the room and took a look around.

Players milling about, many with coffee cups in their hands. Some had bottled water, others were on their phones, but no one seemed to be in any hurry to get started with the day. Tim and Eddie were holding court in the corner, laughing with Philippe Lilleberg. He'd been on my list of people to trade, but no one had been willing to make a decent offer, so I was stuck with him for now.

The players invited to camp technically didn't have to be here until eight, so I'd wait until eight to make any kind of announcement. However, I was going to deal with Tim and Eddie immediately.

I strode across the room toward them without making eye contact with anyone else.

"Tim. Eddie." I cocked my head. "What are you doing here?"

"This is still our team," Tim replied, fixing me with a condescending look.

"We've been running the team with Dad for most of our lives," Eddie added.

"What are you talking about?" I snapped. "You spent four years away at college and then five in Europe, working for the company your father got you a job with. You haven't spent any significant time here since you were in high school. And even during the short time when you did work here, you let Tim handle everything."

Eddie's face was a little red, and I knew people were watching, listening, but I had nothing to hide.

"But I have, and no one wants you here," Tim interjected, lifting his hand and motioning around the room. "Everyone knows you manipulated Dad into changing his will. And we're going back to court to prove it. It'll save you a lot of humiliation if you walk away now, Harper."

I chuckled. "You'd like that, wouldn't you? But there was no manipulation, and the judge already ruled that you don't have a case. If you'd like to spend your inheritance going back and forth to court, knock yourselves out. In the meantime, I need you to leave my arena because I have a team to run."

"It's not your arena!" Eddie protested, laughing.

But Dom had just come in flanked by two security guards, and the room fell silent.

"You're just embarrassing yourself," Tim hissed.

"I'm not embarrassed," I responded calmly. "I own the team and I work here. You, on the other hand, are both sad, pathetic excuses of bitter men who are behaving like toddlers who just lost their favorite toy. This is my company, my team, my conference room. And I want you out of it." I turned to look at everyone who seemed to be watching us intently. "Any of you who don't want to be here are welcome to leave. Contact your agents and/or attorneys and we can make a trade happen this week. I don't need you here if you don't want to be here. There are a dozen guys in the minors who would give their left nut for a chance to come to camp. And it's not too late to get them here." I turned to Dom. "Can you see these gentlemen out please? And make sure they can't come back."

I walked to the head of the long conference table and opened the basket of muffins.

"These were made by Brianna James, a gourmet chef and the wife of Declan James, from Nobody's Fool, for those of you who enjoy a little rock and roll. Please help yourself as we wait for everyone else to arrive. In the meantime, if you have questions or concerns, feel free to open a dialogue with me. That's partly why I'm here."

There was an uncomfortable silence as Eddie and Tim were escorted out by security, with Drake overseeing the process. Dom hovered near me, as if concerned someone might attack me or something, and Gerard seemed to be working the room. This wasn't how I'd envisioned the first day, but there was no help for that.

"Hey, Ms. B." Jensen Bang came over to me with a smile and plucked a muffin out of the basket. "I'm not going anywhere, and I think it's great to see a woman at the helm. I'm excited for the changes that are coming. It sure as shit wasn't working the way it was."

"Thank you." I smiled back at the six-foot-five-inch defenseman who made me feel tiny.

"And these are freakin' awesome!" He motioned to Shane Finnegan. "Dude, you gotta try one!"

A moment later, a few more players came over to the table and took muffins, giving me a smile or introducing themselves, and I slowly began to relax. Gabe had told me Jensen was called Big

Bang by his teammates both because of his size and because he was the world's biggest fan of the television show, "The Big Bang Theory."

Gabe.

I was so frustrated with our current situation and that he wasn't here.

I was also worried about Brandy, but since he hadn't reached out, I had no way of knowing what was going on. I was going to call him when I had a moment, but it was almost eight and more players and staff were wandering in.

"Welcome, everyone." I got everyone's attention right at eight. My nervousness seemed to be letting up now that Tim and Eddie were gone, and I looked around the room at both familiar faces and strangers. Hopefully, they would all be my friends—or at least friendly employees—by the end of the season.

"Thank you for coming and welcome to a new season of Phantoms hockey. I know you all probably have a lot of questions. You've heard the rumors, many of you were here to see Tim and Eddie trying to embarrass me earlier, and some of you remember my late husband, Edward Barrowman. I want you all to know how much he cared about you and this team. That's why he left it to me and not to his sons.

"He put Tim in charge when he got sick and I don't need to tell you how tough the last few years have been. The fact of the matter is, not everyone can run a hockey team. Or even a business. Edward loved his sons, but he also loved this team. So, I'm going to say this once, and then we're never going to talk about it again. He left *everything* to his sons. I'm talking hundreds of millions of dollars. Everything he had." I paused dramatically. "Everything except this team. Because he didn't trust them to fix what's been broken. He trusted *me.*

"If you believe I somehow coerced or manipulated him, then you haven't been paying attention. Why would I take this on? I have money. I have an MBA and am highly employable. I don't need the kind of bad publicity, drama, and stress this job is bringing me. But I'm doing it because in the years I was with

Edward, I came to love this team too. So you can join me in making the Phantoms a force to be reckoned with in the hockey world, or you can ask for a trade. It's that simple. Love me or hate me, we're going to be a contender this season, and I won't put up with any bullshit."

Now it was time to get real.

The mild-mannered, softspoken lady in me was momentarily stepping out.

The college-educated businesswoman who had something to prove was about to give everyone something to think about.

"You want to talk about my tits? Great. Go for it. If that's what it takes to get you scoring goals and winning games? Knock yourselves out. But you will not talk smack about me outside of the locker room. If I find out you are, your ass is gone. I don't care how much it costs. You don't have to like me, but you will treat me with respect. You will show up every day and do what your coaches tell you. You will work hard and give this team everything you've got, every fucking day.

"And you know what you get in return? A second family. Your hockey family. If you have an emergency, come to us. If you need something, ask. This is more than a job for me, and it should be for you too. We're going to be spending a lot of time together over the next seven or eight months—"

"Nine!" Jensen called out. "We're going all the way. Come on, boys, let's see some excitement in the room for a playoff run!"

A few guys laughed while others clapped and whistled.

"That's right." I smiled. "We're going to remind everyone that the Phantoms are contenders. That we're back. And we're back with a vengeance. We may not win the whole thing, but we will win back our dignity and respect within the league. And I want to hear every single one of you say you're in." I turned, pointing to Jensen. "You in, Big Bang?"

He chuckled. "I'm in, boss!"

I turned to Henrik. "What about you, Coach?"

"Fuck yeah." He nodded.

I went around the room, pointing out each and every player,

coach, and senior staff member. By the time I was done, I knew a lot of names and also had a pretty good idea who was going to get traded. The good news was that the majority of the team seemed excited. They might not have been thrilled with me, but my gut told me they were going to give me a chance. At least I hoped so.

"That went pretty well," Dom murmured to me as Henrik and the assistant coaches took over, giving the rookies an idea what was to come this week.

"I think so." I nodded. "Thanks for having my back."

"Absolutely."

"You think my speech was too much?"

"No. I think you showed them you're in charge and that you mean business. They'll either come around or they won't. And if they won't, well, like you said, they can leave."

"I'm going back to my office to take care of a few things, and then I was thinking we'd spend some time watching the rookies before lunch."

"Sounds like a plan. I have a few calls to make too, so ping me when you're ready to come back down."

"Will do."

I slipped out of the room and took my phone out of my pocket.

Still no word from Gabe.

And it hurt more than it should have.

I knew he was busy and distracted, but he should have let me know. If for no other reason than it was the first day of training camp and he wasn't here.

Yes, he'd reached out to Henrik.

He still should have told me.

I had to fix things between us.

If only I knew how.

31

G *abe*

IT HAD BEEN a brutal twenty-four hours. Brandy had needed emergency surgery to relieve pressure on her eye, not to mention fixing her dislocated jaw and broken nose. We'd also discovered that the pitcher who'd thrown the ball that hit her was playing illegally. This tournament was for nine- and ten-year-olds, and that girl was almost twelve. What that meant was beyond me.

I honestly hadn't paid much attention to the details since the only thing I cared about was Brandy, but it was supposedly a huge problem. There were also rumors that it had been done intentionally, because they knew Brandy was the better pitcher and they'd wanted to put her out of commission before the final inning. That kind of thing pissed me off, but short-term, all I wanted was to make sure my daughter was okay. I had no doubt Tricia would deal with whatever else was going on within the softball league once they got home.

When I'd gotten down to the field after the hit yesterday, I'd never been so scared in my life. There'd been so much fucking blood, and Brandy had been writhing on the ground holding her face. I'd seen tons of injuries in hockey, including a few of my own, but it was a totally different thing when it was your child. Especially one so young.

All things considered she was a tough kid. She didn't cry when she got vaccinations, didn't complain when she had to take medicine that tasted bad, and according to Tricia, she was pretty chill when she was sick. To see her lying there whimpering in agony had almost undone me and made me want to hurt people.

It had taken a lot of self-control not to grab the kid who'd done this to her and shake her.

Obviously, I'd never lay my hands on anyone, let alone a child, but in that moment, I'd wanted to.

On the other hand, I had to hand it to Cole.

He'd been calm, cool, and collected, keeping everyone except for us and the on-site paramedics away from Brandy. He'd handled giving the hospital staff Brandy's insurance information so Tricia and I wouldn't have to leave her side, and he'd made sure we had everything we needed during surgery.

I was glad Tricia had found someone like him.

As it was happening, I'd been pissed off at Harper all over again.

I'd needed her at my side, and she wasn't because she put her job before me.

As always.

Now that I'd slept a few hours and had mainlined enough coffee to fill a bathtub, I realized how ridiculous that was. None of us could have known this would happen or that I'd need her, and today was the first day of training camp. That wasn't something she could miss.

Of course, then I'd also woken up and read the text she'd sent yesterday that I hadn't had time to look at.

She wanted to talk.

She'd always loved me.

There had to be a way to compromise.

Those were words I'd been dying to hear from her.

But she'd sent that message at a time when I couldn't think about much of anything other than my daughter.

Now that I'd taken the time to read her message, I felt guilty that I hadn't looked at it yesterday, but I'd been too stressed to focus on anything other than what was going on with Brandy. I hadn't even told Harper what was going on, taking the easy way out and calling Henrik instead. Under normal circumstances, calling my coach was the right move, but the relationship Harper and I had, well, it wasn't what anyone would call normal.

"Dad?" Brandy's voice brought me out of my reverie, and I quickly got up, going over to take her hand.

"How are you feeling, kiddo?" I asked.

"Like I got hit by a soft-ball sized truck."

I chuckled. "You in pain? Do you need me to call the nurse?"

"No. I'm okay. Where's Mommy?" She only called us Mommy and Daddy when she wasn't feeling well, and my heart squeezed with worry all over again.

"She went to the hotel to take a shower. She'll be back in a little while. Do you need me to call her?"

"No." She reached up and touched her bandaged face. "Is it ugly?"

"Eh, you have a little swelling and a black eye, but otherwise, it's not bad."

She shook her head in exasperation. "Don't lie, Dad."

"I'm not." I smiled as I leaned over and gently kissed her forehead. She was going to give some lucky guy a run for his money someday. "You're very swollen and have a pretty impressive black eye, but I don't consider that *ugly*. It's just an injury. And trust me, I've had a lot of them, so I would know."

"That means it's ugly."

"Don't worry about that. When it heals, you'll be as beautiful as ever."

"Did she do it on purpose?" she asked after a moment. "The pitcher from the other team. I heard Mommy on the phone and... is that true?"

I sighed. "I don't know, honey. No one can read her mind."

"The other team was mad. They thought they'd be able to beat us, and then we were tougher than they were expecting."

"Yeah? Where did you hear that?"

"At the pool Saturday night. They were talking about how the team from Wisconsin was going to be so easy to beat."

The kids had gone swimming when we got back to the hotel Saturday night, but she hadn't said anything about overhearing talk about them.

"Well, all sports are competitive," I said carefully. "And most athletes hate to lose."

"Do you hate to lose?"

"Sure. But I'm not going to hit someone with a puck just because we lose a game."

"So... do *you* think she did it on purpose?"

"I honestly don't know. Is that what you believe?"

"My gut tells me yes."

I almost chuckled.

Sometimes I was amazed at the words that came out of her mouth. She was smart and sassy and such a brilliant combination of her mother and me. It was an honor watching her grow and turn into a young lady.

"Well," I said carefully. "It's good to pay attention to your gut, but you can't make accusations based on just that. We should wait and see what your coaches find out. See if there's any evidence."

"I guess." She eyed me, abruptly changing the subject. "Don't you have to be at training camp this week?"

"I'm supposed to be, but there's nothing for the starting goalie to do the first few days, so I asked my coach if I could stay here with you until I know you're going to be okay."

"I'll be fine. There are a million doctors here and you know Mom will yell at people if they don't take care of me. You should go home to Harper. She needs you more than I do."

"What makes you say that?" I asked in surprise.

"Don't you read the news?" she asked, rolling the one eye I could see. "Cole said *everybody* in hockey is talking about her, and

Mom said she wouldn't do Harper's job even if they gave her a zillion dollars."

"Her job *is* hard right now," I conceded, wondering what else Tricia and Cole had said about Harper. Or Harper and me. "But she has a great staff to help her."

"Shouldn't you be the one to help her? Mom said you're her boyfriend."

"Well, yes, but she's good at her job. She doesn't need me to help her."

"Even if the misfits in the locker room are mean to her?"

"The misfits in the locker room?" I had no idea what she was talking about.

She cocked her head. "Maybe that's not the right word. Mom said it. I think it means men who don't like women."

"You mean... misogynists?"

"That's it!"

I was impressed she remembered the definition.

"Harper's tough," I said gently. "She'll be fine."

"Mom said you were being stubborn, and you were going to get your heart broken." She paused. "But I don't know what that means."

I nearly rolled my eyes. "That's why you shouldn't be eavesdropping on grown-up conversations."

She shrugged. "I can't help it if they think I'm deaf."

I laughed.

If nothing else, I was fairly certain Brandy was on the mend.

I LEFT for L.A. that afternoon, once we knew Brandy would be released from the hospital within the next day or so. The Phantoms' team ophthalmologist had consulted with the surgeon in Denver over the phone and concurred with the other doctor's assessment. I felt a lot better about leaving, even though walking away from that hospital room had been hard as hell.

I probably could have gotten away with missing another day or two of camp, but I'd gone to L.A. promising to be a leader in the locker room and Harper needed me to do that. Maybe now more than ever. Ivan had texted me, updating me on the arrival of Eddie and Tim this morning, so I felt even worse about not being there.

I called her on the way to the airport, but it went straight to voicemail, so I left a message. "Hey, it's me. Sorry I've been out of touch, but you probably heard that Brandy got hit with a softball. She had something called a blowout fracture of her orbital bone that required surgery. She's okay now, but it was a crazy twenty-four hours. Anyway, I got your text. And I want to talk too. I've been thinking about you a lot. I'll be home in a few hours if you want to wait up. I'll see you soon, babe. And, by the way... I've never stopped loving you either."

32

____

H*arper*

I WAS at the arena all day.

I watched the rookies showing off their skills doing lunges and other workout routines I didn't even know the name of.

I ate lunch with the guys, talking and getting to know a handful.

There were meetings, phone calls, and a handful of fires to put out.

By the time Sloane arrived at three, I was a bundle of nervous energy, drinking too much coffee and bouncing from one place to another.

At five, I sat down with Henrik, Dom, Gerard, Drake, and Glen Danvers and Randy Dupont, Henrik's two assistant coaches. It had been a productive but exhausting day, and we needed to recap. For my sanity, if nothing else.

I invited the head of Media Relations, Bart Harris, to join us at the beginning, and the dour-faced man's attitude solidified my desire to replace him as soon as possible. He had zero personality and seemed completely inept.

"Lots of chatter on the socials," he said, not looking up from his phone. "Someone leaked the scene between you and the Barrowman boys, so it's out there already."

"What are you doing to mitigate that?" I asked him.

He glanced up. "What do you want me to do? It's not like it's a lie. It happened. Someone took a video and released it. We can't pretend it didn't happen."

I managed to not reach across the table and slap him even though my hand itched to do it.

"We don't have to pretend anything," I said through gritted teeth. "But we can flood the social media platforms with good news, videos of the guys working out, the camaraderie at lunch time, that sort of thing. That changes the narrative and gives people something else to focus on."

"Oh." He made a face. "I guess. But I don't know if we have anything like that ready."

Was this guy for real?

Did I have to do his job for him?

I was going to start interviewing people to replace him immediately.

"Ask Toby," I said, glancing at Sloane, who gave me a little nod. "We can have him and Teresa get together to come up with a few clips."

"I can—" Bart began, but I held up a hand to cut him off.

"You should have already done this. It's your job to make us look shiny and happy. Especially these first few days. I'd like to see us flooding social media with fun stuff, so you should get to work on *that*. We don't need you for anything else right now. Thanks."

He paled slightly, his Adam's apple bobbing up and down with his hard swallow.

I was probably being an asshole, but I didn't care. He'd totally dropped the ball and I didn't have time for that. Not now.

"Sloane, can you work with Bart and Teresa to get things

going? It looks like we're going to be hiring someone new to handle media relations?"

"Already on it." Sloane got to her feet. "Do you want me to oversee this or would you rather I stay here to take notes?"

"I can handle notes." I smiled at her. "I need you working on social media more."

"No problem." She slipped out, and Drake chuckled.

"You're going to be a ballbuster, eh, boss?"

"Someone has to," I muttered. "What the hell was he thinking? And has anyone seen what's on social media?"

"It's not pretty," Dom murmured, scrolling something on his phone. "The clip of Edward Barrowman's two sons being escorted out by security is fucking everywhere."

I huffed out a frustrated breath. "Fuckers. They knew I would kick them out, so they had someone film and release it."

"One of the staff?" I asked quietly.

"More likely a player," Henrik said. "You're going to get push-back, Harper. I'm already hearing rumblings."

Irrationally, that just made me mad at Gabe.

Fucking Gabe.

I didn't begrudge his being with Brandy, it was just the worst possible timing.

"Find out who," I said abruptly. I looked around the table. "Who has a techy person that can potentially track where the video originated?"

No one said anything at first, but finally Dom spoke up. "I know someone. You want his number? His name is Chains... er, Darryl Carruthers. He owns a firm that does cyber security and bodyguard services. He's out of Vegas."

"Yes, please." I nodded. "And whoever it was is going to get fired or traded. Are we in agreement?" I looked around the room. "I can't have people working here who are actively doing things against the Phantoms' organization. Or me. It's counterproductive."

"I concur," Gerard said. "We don't need that shit around here.

We've been dealing with negativity the last five years anyway. I'm ready for it to stop."

Everyone else nodded.

I felt a mild throbbing behind my eyes, the beginnings of a headache, and I longed to reach into my purse for something to help. I didn't want to show weakness in front of the men who worked for me, though, so I took a sip of water and continued with my brief agenda.

"Henrik, please let us know if you need anything and when your ex-wife's funeral is. I know many of us would like to support you, Autumn, and the boys, in whatever way possible."

"I appreciate that." He nodded. "It's not going to be until next week because they have to bring her remains back from Africa and it's a whole thing."

We talked for a few more minutes and finally everyone took their leave.

I wandered back to my office, wondering if I'd be able to sit in the tub again tonight.

Sloane was staying with me, so we'd probably get something to eat and chat a while.

Maybe we could go somewhere or pick up takeout, because I was too tired to cook.

A brief memory of Gabe standing at the grill preparing dinner for us made me smile. And miss him.

My stomach rumbled and I would have done anything for some of his grilled corn.

Hell, I would have done anything to have him waiting at the house when I got home. Just like he had all summer.

I wanted some version of that back but wasn't sure I'd be able to get it.

I DIDN'T SEE that he'd left me a voicemail until Sloane and I got home with the Chinese food we'd picked up. I listened to it as she set out our food and I couldn't help but smile.

"Good news?" she asked as we settled down to eat.

I let her listen to his voicemail since she knew everything that was going on between us.

"Aw. That's sweet. See? I told you everything would be okay."

I reached for the bottle of wine on the counter. It was my favorite cabernet and I'd opened the bottle last night, anticipating having a glass or two tonight. I'd only had half a glass last night, so it felt strangely light, and I glanced down at it curiously. Had I had more than I'd thought?

"You're killing me with that," Sloane moaned, watching me. "I liked it better before I knew I was pregnant and could eat and drink whatever I wanted."

I chuckled, pouring myself a glass. "I'll take it into the bath with me once we eat so you won't have to watch for long. But think of it this way—you're more than halfway through your pregnancy so wine and sushi are practically around the corner!"

"Four more months," she protested, wrinkling her nose. "I shouldn't complain, though. I really haven't had any issues. No morning sickness, moderate weight gain, and now that I'm in my second trimester, I've got tons of energy."

"Have you picked names yet?" I settled at the counter and dug into my moo goo gai pan.

"We think Jonas for a boy, an Americanized version of Johan's name, or Amelia for a girl. We're not sure though."

"Those are nice."

"What about you? Still have baby-making on hold?"

"Yeah. No matter what happens with Gabe, I can't think about getting pregnant until next year."

"Maybe it's happening this way for a reason," she suggested softly. "The universe is giving you and Gabe time to find your footing together."

"Maybe." I hoped she was right because no matter what my practical mind said, my heart was disappointed that I hadn't gotten pregnant that night we'd thrown caution to the wind. "The biggest issue is my age. I'm thirty-six. Thirty-seven by the time we would even think about trying. That means thirty-eight would be the earliest I could have a baby."

"Women are having babies well into their forties now. And you can afford the best care. It's going to be okay."

"I'm glad you're so optimistic."

"Someone has to be." She took a bite of chicken fried rice. "This is so good. The restaurants in Fort Lauderdale are okay, but man, I miss the food here."

"I can't imagine living anywhere else," I admitted. "This is home."

"Have you and Gabe talked about where you're going to live when he retires? Is he willing to stay here?"

"We haven't talked about any of that yet. I guess we have a lot to discuss when he gets home."

"I'm going to put on my headphones and go to bed. I don't need to hear any of what's going to happen in your bedroom tonight. Should I sleep out at his place?"

I laughed. "Don't worry. If things go well, we'll try to be quiet."

"Yeah, right." She laughed too. "Johan and I say that all the time. And we're never quiet. There's an entire neighborhood in the suburbs of Bratislava who knows exactly what I sound like when I come."

I met her eyes with a wide-eyed stare and then we both burst out laughing.

"Oh my god. How do you look everyone in the eye? I would die of embarrassment."

"After the first ten times it happened, I gave up trying to hide it and I think Johan secretly pounds his chest and shit."

"Okay, then. Well, I'm beat, so I'm going to take my wine and go sit in the tub. Will you turn out the lights before you go to bed?"

"Absolutely."

"See you in the morning. And remember Gabe will be here, so don't come to breakfast in your bra and panties!"

She giggled. "Good night."

I padded down the hall to my room and closed the door.

My phone buzzed in my pocket, and the text from Gabe made me sigh.

GABE: *Flight delayed. Probably won't be home until late. Don't wait up.*

HARPER: *Come say hi anyway. And don't forget—Sloane is here so don't scare her by parading through the house naked.*

GABE: *LOL Got it. See you later, beautiful.*

We hadn't decided anything—we hadn't even talked yet—but this felt good.

Like we were on the right track.

I really, really hoped so.

I set my glass on the edge of the tub and turned on the water.

In a way, I couldn't wait to get to sleep because I'd hopefully wake up to Gabe being next to me. Or inside of me.

I'd be happy with either.

33

———————

G *abe*

THE PLANE DIDN'T LAND at LAX until well after midnight due to staffing issues. Apparently, there hadn't been a pilot available, so we'd had to wait for his replacement. I was tired but anxious to get home to Harper. She would probably be asleep, but that was okay. I'd sleep next to her tonight and hopefully wake her up with an awesome orgasm that might put us both in a better mood for the conversation we had to have.

We had to be at work in the morning, which was only a few hours away at this point, but I'd gladly sacrifice sleep to spend more time with her. If we were going to compromise, this might be a good place to start.

Us finding a new normal would be tantamount to that.

We'd find a rhythm professionally that would hopefully mimic what we'd been building over the summer. There would be less free time, but we could maximize the time we did have. Lots of guys did it.

I drove home listening to a song by Nobody's Fool called "Wicked X." The lyrics made me chuckle and think of Harper.

She's my ex
My sexy wicked ex
We're always having sex
And she makes me start to flex

Come on sexy girl,
Show me how it's done
Let's have a little fun
Before I head into the sun

I DIDN'T KNOW where the guy in the song was heading out to, but I wasn't going anywhere. I'd been content in Fort Lauderdale, but I was genuinely *happy* here in L.A. And it was almost entirely because of Harper. She filled all the empty, broken parts of me with light and laughter and, most of all, love. We hadn't used those words this time around, not directly, but maybe that was a good thing because I felt it so much more acutely than I ever had before.

Whether it was time or maturity or some other intangible thing, the bond between us was stronger this time. I couldn't explain why, but it washed over me like a second skin, making me feel safe and wanted. That was a crazy thing to admit, and I'd most likely never say those words out loud, but that was how I felt, and I didn't want to be the guy who couldn't articulate his feelings. Not anymore.

We'd hit a bump in the road, but despite that last conversation before I left for Denver, that was all it was. A fucking bump. It wasn't a roadblock or any other damn thing—it was just a tiny little bump that I was now confident we could get past. Over. Around. It didn't matter how we did it, only that we would.

I stepped on the gas, more anxious than ever to get home.

Home.

How long had it been since I'd had a home?

I'd certainly had places to sleep that were mine.

Apartments and condos and such.

Places where I kept my things and could relax in.

But a home?

A place I couldn't wait to get to for more reasons than just a comfortable bed and big screen TV?

Not in a very long time.

Maybe not ever because Harper and I had been living in separate dorms when we first met, and we hadn't been able to officially live together because of my hockey scholarship, though we had sleepovers as often as possible. When I graduated and went to the minors, I lived in a rented apartment essentially by myself since she was still in grad school and could only come to visit. By the time Harper and I had moved in together, the marriage had been in the early stages of falling apart, so we'd never had a real home together. One that we were happy in. Not until now anyway.

Technically, it was her house, but it felt like our house.

The place where we would begin our lives again.

A strange glow greeted me as I turned onto our street, and I slowed down.

What the hell was that?

I approached the house at a crawl, squinting against the glare of the streetlights.

Orange.

Why was there orange light coming from behind the house?

It was weird.

Then it hit me.

Fire.

The thought seemed to pop into my head out of nowhere and I slammed on the brakes.

Was that fire coming from behind the house?

That was where the grill was.

And there was an extra full tank of propane in the garage.

Not to mention all the pool chemicals out in the pool house.

Shit!

I left my car on the street, grabbed my phone, and hit the button to open the gate as I bolted toward the house. I skirted around the side, heading for the patio since that was where the flames and smoke seemed to be coming from. I rounded the corner and froze, staring at the flames engulfing the guest house and inching toward the grill. It was the kind that was built into a cabinet of the outdoor kitchen area, so it wasn't something I could just roll to a safer location. And a key was needed to unlock the housing that protected the propane tank.

If the flames hit it, this was going to be dangerous.

Very, very dangerous.

And the Santa Ana winds were picking up tonight, which worried me. It was early in the season for Santa Anas but I'd read that we needed to be careful because of how dry it was right now. One stray ember could potentially light up the whole neighborhood, so I needed to get Harper and Sloane out of here.

I ran to the back door, but the sliding glass doors were locked, and I banged on them with my fist, calling out to Harper.

"Harper! Sloane! Wake up!" I banged again but didn't wait around for a response.

I yanked my phone out of my pocket and dialed 911 as I ran back to the front of the house. Harper had given me a key, but I fumbled and dropped it in my haste to get the door open while yelling out the address to the dispatcher.

"Dammit." I had the phone wedged between my ear and shoulder as I kept the 911 operator on the line.

"Harper! Sloane!" I yelled out their names as I raced down the hall.

Throwing open the door to the primary bedroom, I could see Harper's form under the blankets, but she wasn't moving.

And why the hell weren't the smoke alarms going off?

"Harper!" I ran toward her, shaking her a little rougher than I intended. "Babe! Wake up!"

She barely stirred, nestling deeper into the pillow and I shook her a little harder. "Harper, come on. Wake up!"

An explosion so loud it made my ears ring shook the house like an earthquake. I could hear glass shattering all around us and

I threw myself on top of Harper as the large bay window practically imploded around us.

"Fuck! Harper!"

She moaned, softly uttering my name.

"Babe, come on. You have to wake up." There was a faint burning sensation in my back but I didn't have time to worry about it as I got to my knees and yanked her free of the bedding. Harper was naked and her eyes were still closed, so I wrapped her in the blankets and lifted her in my arms.

A second explosion sent us toppling back onto the bed and I realized the fire had reached either the propane tank or the chemicals in the pool house, which meant the whole house could go up any minute now.

We had to get out of here.

Leaving Harper where she was for a second, I ran to the guest room, throwing open the door as I yelled Sloane's name. She was on the bed with headphones on, fast asleep, and I roughly shook her leg.

"Fire! Get up!"

To her credit, she came awake quickly and sat up, looking around wildly as she yanked the headphones off in confusion. "What the hell, Gabe?"

"Fire!" I repeated. "We have to go now! Get out of the house."

"Shit!" She grabbed her phone from the nightstand and slid her feet into a pair of sandals by the bed. "Where's Harper?"

"I can't wake her up," I panted, heading back toward the primary bedroom. "I'm going to carry her, but you go on and get out!"

I didn't hear whether or not she responded as I went back to Harper, who was still asleep.

There was an acrid smell in the air now, and I didn't hesitate to grab Harper and throw her over my shoulder. I winced as pain shot through my back, but I wasn't going to stop moving until we were safely outside.

"Gabe!" I heard Sloane calling my name and I moved faster,

my eyes starting to sting from the smoke that had begun to fill the house.

Flames were licking up the walls of the kitchen and panic filled me.

Everything had happened quickly, so the house could blow up and/or collapse at any time.

Sloane had left the front door open, and I launched myself through it just as another explosion rocked the night.

I went down to my knees, dropping Harper in the process.

Then I threw myself on top of her once again, protecting her body from falling debris and sending up a little prayer into the universe as sparks fell all around us.

Somewhere in the distance I heard the wail of sirens and there was a slight ringing in my ears, but I was more worried about Harper because she still hadn't woken up.

Why was she out cold and how had a fucking fire started and spread so quickly?

My gut told me this wasn't an accident, but I didn't have enough information to come up with any theories.

All I cared about right now was making sure we were safe and Harper got the help she needed.

"Gabe?" Sloane tugged at my shirt. "Come on. You're too close to the house."

I looked over my shoulder to see flames shooting up through the roof and behind the windows.

How the hell had it engulfed the house so quickly?

"Fuck." I managed to get to my feet and lifted Harper again, and the three of us moved to the gate just as the first firetruck pulled up.

34

H*arper*

HOW MUCH DID I drink last night?

The thought came and went pretty quickly as I came awake and shifted, wondering why I was so uncomfortable and why my head was pounding.

Had Gabe gotten home?

My eyes popped open, and I was momentarily confused.

Where the hell was I?

I started to sit up but a gentle hand on my chest kept me in place. "Easy. I'm right here." Gabe's soft voice and familiar smile warmed me, but I was still confused.

"Where am I? What's going on?"

"Do you remember anything about last night?" he asked, his eyes meeting mine.

"N-no." I looked around. "Are we in a hospital?"

"Yes. You were out cold when I got home last night. I couldn't wake you up and had to carry you out of the house."

None of this made sense. "You carried me out of the house? Why?"

He reached out and wrapped both of his hands around one of mine. "A lot happened last night, but before I tell you everything, I want you to know that no one was hurt. You and Sloane are both safe."

I narrowed my gaze as I stared at him. "Gabe?"

"There was an accident. Or something."

"Or something? Which was it, an accident or something else? Just tell me already!" For some reason, panic was setting in and my heart rate kicked into gear.

"I don't have a lot of details yet. They're doing an investigation, but there was a fire. And...your house burned down."

It took a few seconds for his words to sink in. "What?"

"I know it's jarring, but everything is going to be okay. Just breathe."

"My house burned down?" I repeated slowly.

"I'm sorry."

"Like, there was a small fire, or it burned to the ground?"

He hesitated. "I don't know how bad it is. I haven't left your side since we got here. From what I've heard, the damage is...substantial."

"I'm so confused," I whispered, staring at him. "I don't..."

"I got home late," he said, leaning closer to me, his gorgeous face inches from mine. "Around two thirty in the morning. I thought I saw flames, so I left my car on the street and walked around back. My place, the guest house, was on fire, and it was spreading fast. The pool house was next, and I figured there were chemicals and shit in there that might go off, so I ran into the house to find you and Sloane."

"You... ran into a burning building for me?" I wasn't sure why I was trying to be funny, but tears stung my eyelids as I imagined how many terrible things could have happened to him. To Sloane. To all of us.

"Well, to be fair, the house itself wasn't on fire when I went in," he replied. "And it wasn't just for you since I had to get Sloane out too."

"Gabe." I didn't even try to stop the tears that began streaming down my cheeks. "How could you... I mean, what if you'd..." I started crying harder and he scooted onto the bed to wrap his arms around me.

"I'm fine. I'm right here. You're safe. Sloane is safe. Everything is okay."

I sobbed against his shoulder, a torrent of emotion escaping me. I was overwhelmed and confused, but also warm and safe.

Safe with Gabe.

"Please don't leave," I whispered against his shirt.

"I'm right here," he said, stroking my hair.

"I mean, ever. I don't think I'll survive if you leave me again."

"Oh, baby, I'm not going anywhere. As long as you want me around, I'll be right here." He lifted my chin and gazed into my eyes. "I love you, Harper. I always have and I always will. I think we've grown up enough to know it's never going to be easy, but it'll be worth it."

"Promise?"

"Promise." He pressed his lips to mine just as someone knocked on the door.

"Hey, you two, sorry to interrupt but there are a lot of people here to see you. And I've held off the police as long as I could." Sloane stood in the doorway looking apologetic.

"Police?" I glanced at her worriedly.

She looked over her shoulder and then hurried over to the bed, lowering her voice. "It was definitely arson, and I'm sure they're going to investigate whether or not you did it for the insurance money or whatever bullshit they think."

"Seriously?" I stared at her.

"Don't worry. I've already called Madeline and that security guy Dom recommended, Darryl Carruthers, is here. He wants to talk to you before the police, if possible." Madeline Aronson was my attorney.

"Can't this wait?" Gabe asked irritably.

"Nope." Sloane shook her head. "They're foaming at the mouth to get in here, but the doctor wouldn't let them wake her."

"I'm fine, Gabe. And I don't have anything to hide. I have no idea what happened, but I want to find out as much as they do."

"Hang on, let me grab Darryl real quick." Sloane ducked back out and I looked at Gabe.

"You'll stay with me?"

"I already promised you I wasn't going anywhere."

"This is different."

"No, it's all the same. Whenever you need me, I'll be here. It's that simple."

How long had I waited to hear something like that?

Too long.

"I love you, Gabe."

"I love you too, babe."

He brushed my hair back from my face, letting his fingers linger on my skin.

God, that felt good.

"Ms. Barrowman." A tall, good-looking guy who looked about forty, with short-cropped blond hair and deep-set blue eyes came in. "I'm Darryl Carruthers. Dom said we should talk."

"Yes. Thank you for coming."

"The cops are on their way to talk to you, so we don't have much time. I just wanted to ask you if I have your permission to hack into your security system. Even if the mechanism itself was destroyed in the fire, it would have uploaded the images to the server before that happened."

"You don't have to hack anything," I said. "I can give you my logins—oh! I just realized everything was at the house. Did my computer and phone burn in the fire?"

"I didn't think to grab your phone with all the chaos," Gabe said. "Sorry about that, but Sloane was quick enough to pick up your purse and laptop on her way out of the house." He motioned to a laptop I hadn't noticed before on the counter by the sink, next to my favorite Coach bag.

"May I?" Darryl asked me, reaching for the laptop.

"Absolutely." I nodded.

"Look, I'm going to take this and get to work. Hopefully, my men can find something that will help with the investigation."

"Do I need to sign something?" I asked quickly. "Or give you a retainer?"

He grinned. "No worries. Dom and I go way back. You also got a glowing recommendation from Gage Caldwell, so that's good enough for me."

"Thank you." I'd have to remember to thank Gage as well.

Everything was happening so fast, but as he'd promised, Gabe was right by my side. He didn't leave when the police and arson investigators came to talk to me, and he gripped my hand tightly when the doctor came in.

"Hello, Ms. Barrowman. I'm Dr. Lange." The serious-looking doctor studied a chart in front of her. "Could we have some privacy?" She looked at Gabe.

"No," I said firmly. "I want him to stay."

She scowled but finally nodded. "All right. Do you remember anything from last night?"

"The police already asked me that," I responded. "The last thing I remember was feeling sleepy in the bathtub and going to bed."

"Well, it makes sense. There was a very high amount of Rohypnol in your system."

"She was roofied?" Gabe gripped my hand even tighter. "Are you sure?"

"I'm quite sure."

"But how..." My voice trailed. "I was at work all day and felt fine. My assistant and I picked up Chinese food on the way home, but we didn't decide that until we were almost to the restaurant, so unless Mr. and Mrs. Sun, who own the Golden Fortune Cookie are roofie'ing all their customers, it couldn't have been the food."

"And you didn't leave the house after that?"

"No. We ate and then I went in to take a bath. I only had two glasses of wine but—" I stopped abruptly, trying to remember something that was lurking at the edges of my memory banks.

"But?" Dr. Lange pressed.

"There was something weird about the wine. It's my favorite and I only opened the bottle the night before... I only had half a glass so it should have still been pretty full last night. When I picked it up, I remember thinking it was light, but Sloane and I were talking so I shrugged it off."

Gabe and the doctor both looked at me.

"No way," I said firmly. "She would never. And then, what? She went to bed so she could die in the fire?"

"The fire hadn't reached the house yet," Gabe said. "Maybe she was awake and waiting."

I stared at them, shaking my head.

There was no universe where I could believe that of Sloane.

Not in a million years.

And yet it fit.

It was convenient.

Almost too convenient.

"There's no way. The arson team is going to investigate, and Darryl is going to check the security footage. If there's something to see, they'll find it."

"Harper..." Gabe began.

But he didn't know Sloane like I did.

"Let's see what Darryl finds," I whispered finally.

"In the meantime, I'd like you to stay one more day for observation," Dr. Lange said. "The amount in your system was very high, so I want to make sure there aren't any lingering effects."

"I feel okay other than a headache," I admitted. "And I'm hungry."

"You don't have any restrictions, dietary or otherwise, this is just a precaution. Take it easy today and, assuming there are no issues, you'll be out of here tomorrow."

"Thank you, Doctor."

She left and I looked at Gabe. "I don't care what it looks like, it wasn't Sloane."

"I didn't say anything."

"But you're thinking it," I said, wagging a finger at him.

"Look, I don't know what happened, so for now I'll reserve judgement. Darryl comes highly recommended, and I'm sure the arson department is going to do a thorough investigation. If there's evidence, someone is going to find it."

"It's Eddie and Tim," I said softly. "I don't know how we're going to prove it, but me getting drugged wasn't an accident. That means someone didn't want me to wake up."

"And the smoke detectors weren't going off," he said. "Which means someone took the time to disarm them."

"Someone was in my house," I said, fear whipping through me. "Someone was in my fucking house. They drugged my wine, disarmed my smoke detectors, and poured accelerant everywhere, according to the cops. They were trying to kill me. Not just hurt me or take the team away from me, but they literally wanted me dead." I felt sick to my stomach saying the words.

"Well, they failed. And as long as I'm still breathing, they'll continue to fail. You can take that to the bank."

35

———

G *abe*

Harper had wanted me to go to a hotel and get some rest, but there was zero chance I was leaving her. She was putting up a brave front, but I could see the fear in her eyes and the tension on her face. She was scared and worried, which in turn scared and worried me. But I was also pissed.

Deep down, I knew she was right. Sloane hadn't been involved. This was all Eddie and Tim. We might not be able to prove it yet, but it was the only thing that made sense. Somehow, there had to be a way to get to the bottom of it and stop them before they tried again, but for now, we were settled in a suite at the Four Seasons in Beverly Hills.

I'd stayed with Harper all night and she'd been released this morning. Darryl, who insisted we called him Chains, met us there and escorted us here personally, making sure to get us settled while he introduced us to the security team he would be leaving behind. For the time being, Harper would have full-time security by a guy named Rage, and there would be guards working in shifts outside the door twenty-four-seven.

Meanwhile, I was anxious to put a little normalcy back into her life, so I'd run a bath for her and ordered dinner from room service. Sloane had thoughtfully done some shopping for us, running to a mall to buy us a few days' worth of underwear, shorts, and T-shirts, as well as sandals for Harper since she'd literally been naked when I took her out of the house.

The investigator told us the house was a total loss, although the fireproof safe in the primary bedroom closet had made it through, as well as some of Harper's cast iron cookware and a handful of other things. Everything else, for the most part, had been destroyed. Part of me was frustrated. I had memorabilia from my high school hockey days, along with mementos from when Brandy was a baby, but I could replace most of it.

The one thing I could never replace was Harper.

"Well, this is nice," she said as she came out of the bathroom in a fluffy white robe, her hair wrapped in a towel.

"I thought we deserved a little bit of nice after the last couple of days," I replied. "Plus, I thought we could talk."

"That sounds perfect." She slid into the chair across from me and put her napkin across her lap.

We ate in companionable silence for a few minutes until she looked up and cocked her head. "You want to start?"

"The conversation?" I chuckled. "I can if you want."

"Go ahead. I like listening to your voice."

"Well, to be honest, I had a bunch of things I wanted to say when I imagined this conversation in my head. But after everything that's happened, I barely remember it. All I know is, I love you and don't want to lose you."

"I love you too."

"When I saw the flames behind the house, all I could think about was getting to you, making sure you were okay. I didn't care about how many hours you work or who's going to have to sacrifice what for us to be together. Whatever you want, I'll do it. We have to make time for Brandy, but beyond that, I don't care. I'll do whatever it takes to make you happy."

"That sounds incredibly one-sided," she whispered, a soft smile on her face. "Right now, we're dealing with a trauma so we're—"

"No. Stop." I cut her off. "I mean, yes, we are dealing with the aftermath of a trauma, but this is just a much less eloquent way of saying what I was planning to say anyway. I want to play hockey for one more year. Maybe two. You know that. I need to spend time with Brandy, but nothing in that regard is going to change until I retire. For now, I'll fly out there when I can and bring her here when she's not in school. I don't have the details worked out and I assumed you'd be okay with it..." I paused, looking at her.

"Of course. She can come visit as often as possible. That will never be a problem."

"Then nothing else matters."

"What about when I'm working eighty-hour weeks? Are you going to start going to strip clubs and acting out?" There was a twinkle in her eyes but a hint of seriousness in her voice.

"There may be a bachelor party or two that take place at a strip club in my future," I replied honestly, "but there will never be another lap dance or my hands on another woman's body. Do you trust me, Harper? Can you live with that?"

"I can live with that." She dipped her head, as if hiding the faint smile playing on her lips. "And I do trust you."

"So... how long do you think you're going to be working these eighty-hour weeks?"

"The rest of this season," she said. "I need one season, Gabe. At the end of it, we'll reassess." She paused. "Unless I get pregnant in the interim. Then we'll reassess based on how I'm feeling and when I'm due."

"Okay, then the plan is for the next year we're going to put our noses to the grind and follow our dreams."

"Gabe." She reached across the table for my hands.

"Yeah, babe?"

"*You* are my dream. You're the thing I want most in life. I don't want to walk away from the team, but I will if you ask me to."

"Not a chance in hell. What kind of selfish prick would that make me?"

"I unconsciously put a job before you once before, so I won't do it again."

"I think you were protecting yourself," I said slowly. "You felt like you were losing me, so you kept yourself too busy to notice. We can't bury our heads in the sand, babe. This time around, when the going gets tough—and it inevitably will—we have to communicate. Make time for each other. Block out time on the calendar that's just for us. Before we know it, this season will be over and we'll be back to grilling by the pool and long, lazy nights in the tub."

"Are you sure?"

"Absolutely." I paused. "There's just one other thing I want. And I had a whole scenario planned, but it literally went up in flames. So..." I slid off my chair and onto one knee. "The ring I bought you is still at the house, and I don't know how it fared in the fire since we can't get in there for a while. But I don't want to wait to ask you to marry me again. So I made this." I held out the little circle I'd crafted from a piece of paper I'd found on the desk. It was crude and more oblong than round, but it made the point.

"Oh, Gabe." She dropped to her knees in front of me and slid the ring on her finger. "Yes. I will marry you again."

I pressed my lips to hers and she wrapped her arms around my neck.

"Take me to bed, Gabriel DeLugo."

"You're not finished with dinner..."

"I'm finished." She slowly got to her feet, and I stood with her.

She let her robe fall away, leaving me with the most glorious view of her naked body. She was still as slender and shapely as she'd been the first time I saw her naked and it never failed to amaze me that all I had to do was look at her to get turned on. There was nothing better than the two of us being naked together, so I made short work of my own clothes.

"Have I told you how beautiful you are lately?" I whispered, digging my fingers into the hair at the back of her neck.

"Yes. But you can tell me again."

I leaned in to kiss her, nipping at her lips. "You take my breath away. I can't stop looking at you. Touching you. Thinking about you. And it hasn't changed since we were teenagers."

She wrapped one arm around my neck and moved her other one down until she'd closed her fist around my cock. I sucked in a sharp breath, pleasure washing over me as I slid my tongue between her lips and feasted on her mouth. Kissing her was one of my favorite things. Not as much as being inside of her but—.

Shit.

I reluctantly broke away.

"Babe. Wait."

"What's wrong?" Her eyes met mine in surprise.

"I don't have a condom."

"Oh." She blinked, staring at me.

Then she smiled.

"I'm willing to live dangerously if you are."

"You think? I thought you wanted to wait?"

"I do. But I also want a baby. With you. If it happens, it happens. We can be careful sometimes, less careful other times. Does it really matter?"

"It doesn't matter to me, but I want you to be okay with it."

"As long as I have you, I'm okay with everything."

"I really like the sound of that."

"Make love to me, Gabe."

I lifted her in my arms and carried her to bed.

36

———

G *abe*

I GOT to training camp on Friday. It had been a long week, but it was time for me to do what I'd come to L.A. to do: manage the mood and climate in the locker room. From what Ivan had been telling me, I had my work cut out for me, but I was up to the task. Especially after what had happened at the house. We'd been allowed to visit, and while we couldn't go into the house, the cleanup team had been gracious enough to bring out her safe and a few things that had survived the fire. Ironically, she'd had a pair of running shoes in the garage that hadn't been touched, and though there was some smoke damage, her car was fine as well.

The firefighters had arrived in time to keep the fire from the garage, so she was happy about that. My car had been on the street, so we had vehicles, her laptop, and a couple of pairs of shoes. Between the Rohypnol in her system and accelerant all over the house, she'd been cleared of any wrongdoing, but it would be months before she saw insurance money. We hadn't even begun to think about whether or not she would rebuild or buy something new, but in my heart of hearts, I wanted a completely fresh start. We'd talk about it when she was ready, though.

She was still processing the whole thing, and having a body-guard was a constant reminder that someone—Tim, Eddie, or someone else—had tried to kill her. It made me crazy to think someone out there was after her, but there was no help for it. We were mitigating the situation as best we could, and since she was back at work today, I had to focus on my job as well. And I wasn't talking about keeping pucks from slipping between the pipes, either.

"It's about fucking time!" Jensen yelled out when I got to the locker room.

"Goalies think they are special," Ivan said with a grin. "You know how it is."

"My kid had surgery and then my house burned down," I said dryly. "How about a little support over here?"

"Seriously?" Shane stared at me.

"Dude, that's brutal." Someone else shook his head, though I couldn't remember the guy's name.

"Wait, didn't Ms. Barrowman's house burn down too?" A rookie named Connor Brooks asked, confusion on his face.

"He's bangin' her," Phil murmured in a stage whisper.

I'd been prepared for this so I didn't lose my temper.

Not yet anyway.

"Okay, everybody, listen up." I looked around until I had every-one's attention. "We're going to have a conversation about my love life. Just this once, so listen good. Ms. Barrowman and I were college sweethearts and were married a long time ago. We were young and stupid, so we got divorced. Now we're back together. We're getting remarried. The details are none of your fucking business, but the future is. I know a handful of you, and most of you probably know who I am. I'm at the end of my career, but the Phantoms brought me here to do what I do best—mind the net."

"Probably *a lot* of reasons she brought you here," Phil said, meeting my eyes.

"We got back together after she traded for me," I replied, "but that's not the point. The point is that you have two choices. The first is to bring drama and bullshit to the locker room because you want to talk shit about Harper and me. And since it's a free country and you're all adults, you can do that. But when it fucks up the chemistry on the team and we get to hit the golf course in April again, that's on you."

I took a moment to look around again, making eye contact with as many of them as I could.

"Your other option is to man the fuck up, act like the professionals you're supposed to be, and leave all the bullshit outside. We have the opportunity to start over. She's made a lot of changes, and I'm sure some of you are butt hurt over it, but don't pretend like she's the first and only owner to clean house. This isn't the first time most of you have been traded, and it probably won't be the last. So, let's move past the personal and make this all about hockey. We can be friends or we can be enemies, I don't really give a shit. But if your goal is golf in April, do what you've got to do. The only other thing I'll say is if I catch you talking shit about her in this room or anywhere outside of the privacy of your own home, we're going to have a problem. You don't have to like her, but you do have to treat her with a modicum of respect."

No one moved.

A few guys shifted restlessly.

Phil was trying to hide the fact that he was attempting to point the phone in my direction.

Son of a bitch.

He was recording this.

Which made me almost positive it was him who'd taken the video of Eddie and Tim being escorted from the building.

"Whatcha doin' over there, Phil?" I asked casually, approaching him before he could turn off whatever he was doing. I snatched it out of his hand and looked down. Sure enough, it was recording. Luckily, it didn't appear to be live.

"Hey! He reached for it, but I danced out of his way and Jensen put his massive body between us, a menacing look on his face.

"God dammit, Gabe." Phil wasn't stupid enough to put his hands on Jensen.

"You were recording me," I said, holding up the phone to show everyone. "So you're the fucking spy. Who do you work for, Phil? Eddie? Tim? Taking money from the press?"

Phil's ears turned red but he lifted his chin defiantly. "We don't want her here," he said. "No one does. She doesn't know shit about hockey and the only reason the old man left her the team is because she somehow forced him to."

I shook my head. "Even if that was true, you don't betray the sanctity of the locker room, man. This is private. What we say and do behind these doors is sacred. If we can't trust each other here, how can we trust each other on the ice?"

"What the fuck, man?" Jensen gave Phil a look. "Seriously?"

"This was a dick move," Ivan said quietly, shaking his head.

"I don't love the idea of a woman at the helm," Shane admitted, "but I would never betray my teammates. Good or bad, what we say in here is fucking private."

Most of the guys in the room murmured some version of agreement.

I hit the stop button and then deleted the video before tossing Phil his phone. "As far as I'm concerned, I don't want *you* here."

"And I suppose you're going to tell your *girlfriend*—" He said the word with a snarl. "—Oh, excuse me, *fiancée*, to trade me."

"That was already going to happen once she found out who leaked the last video, so you made your own bed, buddy."

"I'm not your fucking buddy."

"No, you're not." I met his gaze directly, not moving when he took another menacing step in my direction. Jensen started to get between us again, but I put a hand on his arm. "I'm good. Let him take his shot. I've been dying for somebody to."

Phil's jaw worked in irritation, but he seemed conflicted.

Pussy-assed motherfucker didn't even have the balls to come at me.

"You haven't been here," Phil finally hissed. "You haven't struggled with us the last few years. You haven't seen what this team has gone through while the old man was sick."

"While the old man was sick, *Tim and Eddie* were running things," I pointed out. "They're the reason you've had the issues you've had. Bad management trickles down, and that's the thing about Harper. She has an MBA so she knows business and, thanks to Edward coaching her the year before his death, she knows this team inside and out. Her plans are to make this team better and all of you shit-talking behind the scenes are keeping her from being able to do that."

"It can't be any worse," Jensen said after a moment. "We finished dead last the last two seasons. Last. Not in the bottom few, but last. Two years in a row. And I *have* been here, so I lived it. I also know that Harper is intelligent, articulate, and determined. You can see it in her eyes when she talks, and the energy in any room she walks into is almost palpable—that means you can almost feel it, for the slow boys in the back."

Some of the guys chuckled while Ivan flipped him off.

"I don't know what's coming," Linc said, "but like Big Bang said, it can't be worse than last season. We need to give her a chance. Like it or not, she's our boss. Technically, she hasn't done anything wrong, despite the rumors floating around. So why not go into this with open minds? If it turns out to be another shit show of a season, then we'll probably have to make personal decisions about our careers, but what do we have to lose by giving her a shot to prove us wrong?"

"I'm with Linc," Jensen said. "I'm down with the changes Ms. B made. Those of us who've been here for a few years know how bad it's been, and now that you say it, Gabe, it started when Tim took over for Mr. B."

"I just got here," Connor spoke up. "And this is my first year in the league, but all I care about is playing at this level. Everything else is background noise. I wouldn't know the difference if the owner is Ms. Barrowman or Frosty the Snowman. It's not our job to worry about business. Our job is hockey. Again, I know I've been here, like, five minutes, but you guys do what you want. Me? I'm going to play my ass off."

"Out of the mouths of babes," I murmured, clapping him on the shoulder. "You've got a good attitude, kid. It'll take you far."

"Thanks." He grinned at me.

"All right, I think we've done enough talking for today." Henrik had been lurking by the door, listening but not adding to the conversation. "Everyone ready to get on the ice?"

"Let's do it," I called out.

Everyone was still in various stages of undress, so we all scattered to finish putting on gear, lacing up skates, or just screwing around. Phil was in a hushed but obviously heated conversation with Henrik, and I took a minute to text Harper before locking up my things.

GABE: Phil is the one who released that video—trade his ass. He's going to be a troublemaker. I can't get into it now, but we'll talk tonight.

I put my stuff away and turned to see a handful of my teammates standing there.

Uh oh.

This could go very, very wrong.

"I just wanted to say," a big defenseman named Mason Harrington said, "I'm glad you spoke up. I don't have a problem with Ms. Barrowman, but there's been so much negativity, I wasn't sure if it was smart to piss everyone off by voicing my opinion on that."

"Same with me." Evan Laurenz was another D-man, with a gap-toothed smile and a firm handshake. "And I've been watching you play since I was a kid, so it's kind of cool to be out there with you."

I chuckled. "Thanks. I think."

"I'm ready to play. I don't really care what's going on up in the executive offices," Marty Nadeau added.

"To be honest, I never liked..." Teague Landry dropped his voice as he glanced around. "Phil. He's always been kind of a dick. So yeah, I'm more than willing to give Ms. B a chance." He paused. "Is she going to be Mrs. *D* going forward?"

There was a momentary pause as Marty laughed into his hand and Mason tried to cough over a chuckle.

Calling Harper Mrs. *D* might be problematic, depending on how dirty your mind was, but it was still funny.

"Okay, let's make sure she never hears us calling her Mrs. D," I said after a moment.

We all laughed.

"All right, let's get this party started."

The group dissipated and Ivan and Jensen approached me.

"Looks like we got over a big hurdle today," Ivan said.

"Yeah. And I appreciate your support. Both of you."

Jensen nodded. "That's what we're here for."

"One of you should wear the C this year," I said, referring to the letter the team captain wore on his jersey.

"You can have it," Ivan said to Jensen. "Mostly, I want to punch the refs in the face."

"I may not be very popular after taking a stand today," Jensen said. "But whatever the guys want is fine with me."

"You might be a lot more popular than you think," I told him.

"One day at a time," he said. "New season, new team, new opportunities. I'm here for it."

"Amen to that."

EPILOGUE

H*arper*
One year later...

I RUBBED my hand over my protruding stomach and said a prayer I didn't go into labor on opening night. I'd actually been due yesterday but so far, I felt fine. Other than the usual pregnancy issues, like a sore back and not being able to see my ankles anymore. I'd worked through my entire pregnancy, for the most part, and other than a little fatigue at the beginning, it hadn't slowed me down at all.

Gabe and I had impulsively eloped in Las Vegas during the All-Star break last winter and found out we were pregnant a few weeks later. It was all working out nicely, despite my hoping to wait until summer to start trying.

We'd bought a new house and moved in over the summer, bringing Brandy out to spend a month with us. We'd let her choose and decorate a bedroom, as well as give us suggestions for the nursery. We wanted her to feel like she was at least a little bit part of everything going on, and she'd seemed excited. Even Tricia had started texting me daily, offering suggestions and asking how I was feeling.

In general, my life was better than anything I could have imagined.

Gabe and I were happy, I'd come a long way with the Phantoms—both on and off the ice—and things had fallen into place nicely.

The only negative was that the arson case was still ongoing, with the insurance refused to pay until some sort of resolution was found. Luckily, I wasn't worried about money.

I kept my finances under wraps because they were none of anyone's business, but the truth was, Edward had more than taken care of me. Due to our age difference, he'd always assumed he would die first, and because his sons didn't like me, he'd started planning for my future the moment we'd gotten married. I had more stocks and bonds than I could keep track of, and I could live an extremely comfortable lifestyle even without my salary from the Phantoms.

I also had investment properties that brought in money, as well as jewelry that was worth a fortune in a safe deposit box that hadn't been impacted by the fire. Edward had realized Eddie and Tim would most likely make my life difficult when he died, so he'd wanted to make sure I never had to worry about money. He hadn't anticipated them making nuisances of themselves with regard to the Phantoms, but I was handling that.

So far, every case they'd brought against me had been thrown out.

They'd been quiet for a while, and I hoped that continued because I really didn't want to think about them once the baby came.

Gabe and I were having a little boy, and I'd asked him if we could make the baby's middle name Edward. I'd wanted to honor my late husband in some way and Gabe had been incredibly gracious about it. Our baby boy would be named Gabriel Edward DeLugo, and we agreed it had a nice ring to it.

"Hey, Mama Phantom." Jensen came over and put one of his

big hands on my stomach. "Baby Phantom still not interested in making an appearance?"

The guys on the team had started calling my bump Baby Phantom last season during the playoffs and it had stuck.

I grinned. "Not yet. Any day now."

"Still no Baby Phantom?" Connor came over and lightly tapped my stomach.

This had also become a thing during the playoffs so it made sense that they would pick up the routine again on opening night of the season. Of course, we'd hoped Baby Phantom would be here by now, but no such luck.

"You ready to come out yet?" Ivan asked, leaning over and talking directly to my stomach. "Uncle Ivan is waiting."

"Would you guys stop touching my wife?" Gabe grumbled, glaring at them.

He wasn't really mad, though.

I chuckled, reaching up to kiss him. "Baby Phantom is going to have a lot of uncles."

"He is." He smiled down at me.

During the playoffs, I'd stood in the hallway just outside the locker room and each player had lightly tapped my stomach before heading down the tunnel toward the ice. It had been the good luck charm that got us to the second round, so Gabe understood the guys were just excited.

Besides, this would be the first baby born to the Phantoms since I'd taken over.

Autumn was also pregnant, but she was only four months along, so my baby would be the first.

Assuming he ever got here.

"All right, boys, let's go." Henrik looked at me. "You ready, Harper?"

I looked at the team. "You boys want to continue our tradition with the belly tapping?" I asked them. "I won't be offended if you say no."

"Until the baby comes, belly tapping continues," Jensen said. He looked to Gabe. "Lead the way, Daddy Phantom."

Gabe grinned as I positioned myself outside the door.

He didn't tap my belly like the others. Instead, he leaned over and kissed it.

"Play good," I whispered, touching his hair.

"I love you," he whispered back.

"Love you too."

He headed down the tunnel with the rest of the team behind him, each one pausing to lightly tap my stomach.

Life was good.

Thank you for reading Power Play. If you could leave a review at the platform of your choice, I'd be eternally grateful. It's so helpful.

Want the scoop about Jensen and Bailey? Turn the page for more information about them, as well as book two, FOUL PLAY!

HIT 'EM HARD (BANG BROTHERS HOCKEY, BOOK 3)

The limo pulled to a stop in front of the theater, and I smoothed my hands down the front of my skintight gown. It was a one-of-a-kind Alexa Humboldt design in a light color that matched my skin tone. If not for the lack of nipples and body hair, I almost appeared nude at a quick glance.

Alexa had designed it specifically for me, at my request, for the shock value.

My fiancé, Dirk Reynolds, hated it from the moment I put it on.

But that was too bad.

I wasn't about to let a guy tell me what to wear on the red carpet or anywhere else.

"You ready, Ms. Walker?" The driver called out as he slowed to a stop.

The paparazzi was out in full force, surrounding the area around the red carpet where the attendees of tonight's award ceremony would be entering the building.

My recent engagement had been big news the last month, so I was sure they were waiting to bombard us with questions even though this was only the entrance to the building. The official red-carpet event, where interviews and photographs happened, would be in a different area inside the complex.

"I'm ready, Hans." I nodded in the direction of the chauffeur, who was my regular driver. I preferred to have him with me when I went to big events like this because he was experienced, the safest driver I knew, and I trusted him to be discreet about anything he might see or hear in the limo.

Dirk and I had been arguing since I'd put the dress on, so I was already stressed and not looking forward to spending the evening with him. The last thing I needed was word to leak that we were on the outs. Even though we were.

I'd heard stories about how guys changed once you got married, but I'd never heard them about it happening once you got engaged. It was like someone had flipped a switch. He suddenly had something to say about everything in my life. What movie projects I took on, how much time I spent playing video games, or what I wore to an awards ceremony.

It wasn't like this was new.

I'd been a gamer for as long as we'd known each other.

Wearing provocative clothes out in public was part of my persona.

And the roles I accepted were none of his fucking business.

I was already considering ending the engagement, but I planned to talk to him first.

The limo slowed to a stop, and I saw the paparazzi move closer expectantly. They didn't know who was inside each limo, but they knew everyone showing up tonight was Hollywood royalty.

"Are you going to let me get out first?" Dirk asked wryly.

I managed not to roll my eyes.

The last time we'd done an event like this, he'd been drunk and hadn't wanted to get out at all, so I'd exited the limo without him. Then, when he'd stumbled out after me, it had been a whole thing in the media about how ungentlemanly he'd behaved.

That had been the night I'd started to question our relationship.

"Go ahead," I said politely, not wanting to fight with him anymore.

He stepped out when Hans opened the door, taking a moment to wave to the crowd.

Of course, he was more interested in his ten seconds of solo attention than offering a hand to me.

I really needed to rethink all my life choices.

Finally, Dirk turned, proffering a hand, and I took it, slowly sliding out of the limo.

And of course, the press started firing questions at me faster than I could have answered, even if I'd wanted to.

"Bailey, have you set a date yet?"

"Bailey, are you getting married in L.A.?"

"Who designed your gown, Bailey?"

"Bailey, are you taking the Scorsese project?"

Scorsese project? There was no offer on the table from the legendary producer. At least, as far as I knew. I'd have my agent doublecheck, but I would have known if Martin Scorsese had reached out to my team.

I smiled and waved, letting Dirk hold my hand as we walked toward the entrance of the building.

"Scorsese?" he hissed in my ear. "You didn't tell me about a Scorsese script!"

"Because there isn't one!" I snapped back. "Jesus, don't you know fishing when you hear it?"

"You don't have to get snippy!" he muttered.

I ignored him, heading for the entrance as I pasted on my most professional smile and answered questions about my dress, hedged on questions about the wedding, and finally made my way into the ballroom.

"Bailey!" My best friend and fellow actress, Sage Reynolds, waved as she came over to say hello.

We hugged and air kissed, since we didn't want to mess up our makeup, and she grinned at me.

"You look fantastic. Alexa Humboldt breaks the red carpet once again."

Alexa and I had a habit of coming up with designs that had everyone talking. Conversation about the dress would keep me in the headlines for weeks, and since I was currently between projects, that was a good thing. Even if they hated the dress. But I didn't think that was the case this time.

"Hey, beautiful!" Manny Collette, my co-star in the last movie I'd done, blew me a kiss as he walked by with his wife, and a few other actors I knew waved or said hello.

"Why didn't you talk to Manny?" Dirk demanded in my ear. "Find out what he's working on."

"Because he's with his wife and busy with friends," I retorted.

Was it too much to ask to simply want to have a good time tonight?

I didn't need to network twenty-four-seven.

Maybe the break-up talk needed to happen now.

Tonight.

I turned to tell him we needed to talk but he'd already moved off with a director I recognized.

Well, the break-up would have to wait, but it was happening tonight.

***

I didn't win the award for Best Actress I'd been nominated for, but that was okay. I'd lost to a legendary actress named Judith Winslow, and she deserved it. I'd always looked up to her, so I didn't feel bad losing to her. Besides, I'd won the award for best supporting actress last year, and I was only twenty-five, so I had plenty of time to win the big ones.

"That was bullshit," Dirk said as we filed out at the end of the ceremony. "You deserved that award more than that old hag, Judy Winslow."

I scowled at him. "She's a legend," I said quietly. "And keep your voice down."

"I don't give a fuck who hears me!"

"Well, I do. Judy is a friend."

"I'm your fiancé."

It was on the tip of my tongue to tell him he wouldn't be after tonight, but I refrained. I'd wait until we were back in the limo heading home. I wasn't heading to any after parties because I wanted to get this over with.

We made our way out to the loading area where the limos were waiting, and I tapped my foot impatiently.

I suddenly couldn't wait to give him back his ring.

"Hey, girl!" Sage waved as she breezed past me. "Stay strong," she breathed against my ear. "And call me tomorrow!"

We'd talked earlier in the evening, so she knew what the plan was.

I waved at her before getting into the limo.

Did I want to wait until we got home or should I do it in the car?

He'd just moved into my house in Marina del Rey, so we had a long drive, and I didn't want to have to think about it the whole time.

"I think we need to take a break," I said quietly, biting the bullet.

"A break?" He looked up from whatever he was doing on his phone in confusion. "What are you talking about?"

"I'm not sure I'm ready to get married," I said. "And we've been fighting a lot since you moved in. Maybe we rushed things." We'd only been together nine months.

"Rushed things?" He stared at me. "I gave up my apartment to move in with you!"

"And you don't pay any bills," I said quietly. "You should have been able to save up."

"Save up? What the fuck, Bailey?" His expressive dark eyes turned almost black. "This isn't funny."

"I'm not laughing." I glanced down at the ring on my finger, itching to remove it.

"What did I do?" he demanded, his voice softening as if he'd just now realized I was serious. "Are you mad about the Madalina thing?"

Madalina was my housekeeper and he'd yelled at her the other morning for folding his socks incorrectly. He'd raised his voice and berated her to the point he'd made her cry, and I'd been furious. I'd warned him not to ever speak to her that way again, and he'd apologized, but I'd been terrified she would quit.

"That was one of many red flags in the last couple of months," I admitted. "There have just been a some things that make me uncomfortable."

"I'm sorry." He scooted closer to me on the seat, reaching for me. "I'll do better. What if we go away to Coronado for the weekend and—"

"Dirk. Stop." I slid a little way away from him. "I want to give us a little time apart so we can think. Like I said, a break."

"I don't have anywhere to go," he said, his jaw working in obvious irritation. "You know I'm out of work right now so I can't even get a new apartment."

"You can go to your mom's," I pointed out.

His face tightened. "You want me to move in with my mom like I'm some kind of kid? Are you serious right now?"

"I don't know what you want me to say," I said quietly. "I'll be happy to give you enough money for the security deposit or whatever you'll need to get an apartment, but you're going to have to figure out the rest. You promised you were going to get a regular job if none of those auditions last month panned out, yet you've been dragging your feet. Even if we weren't taking a break, you need to work, Dirk."

"You selfish little bitch." He glared at me. "Who put this shit in your head? Was it Sage? Or that cunt of an agent of yours? Huh? Who was it?" He snaked out a hand, gripping me by the throat.

"Dirk!" I squealed in surprise. "Stop it!"

"You can't just toss me away like yesterday's trash!" he yelled.

He had my throat in a death grip and I couldn't breathe.

He'd never laid a hand on me before, so this caught me by surprise, but I'd been in Hollywood for seven years at this point, and I'd learned a trick or two. Besides, Han was up front. All I had to do was get his attention.

"Dirk!" I gasped out his name, wiggling to try and get away from him. "Please!"

When he refused to let go and squeezed even harder, I knew I had limited time. I reached down and grabbed one of the Manolo Blahnik stilettos off my feet. I threw it toward the privacy screen, nearly crying in relief as it thudded against it.

"Ms. Walker?" Hans lowered the screen and looked back at us. "Hey! You need to let her go!"

"Cunt!" Dirk growled, shoving me away from him.

The back of my head bounced off the glass of one of the windows, making everything in my field of vision blur.

"Ms. Walker!" Hans was calling my name.

"Shut up, you fat fuck!" Dirk picked up a water bottle and hurled it in his direction.

I tried to talk but nothing came out, my throat burning from the assault.

The car swerved as Dirk yelled insults and continued throwing things.

"Fuck!" I thought I heard Hans yell but then the car jolted violently, throwing me across the back and slamming me into another window.

There was the sound of breaking glass and someone screamed.

It might have been me.

Then there was nothing.

Find links to Hit 'em Hard and all of my books here.

FOUL PLAY (L.A. PHANTOMS, BOOK TWO)

When one of the most beautiful women in the world friend zones you, what's a determined hockey player supposed to do?
Change her mind.

Get more information about Ivan and Cheyenne's story here. And turn the page for links to all of my books!

ALSO BY KAT MIZERA

Lauderdale Knights:

Knight Before Christmas (A Garland Grove/Lauderdale Knights holiday novel)

Slap Shot

Big Shot

Long Shot

Hot Shot

Sure Shot

Rough Shot

Cheap Shot

Holiday Shot (A Lauderdale Knights holiday novella)

L.A. Phantoms:

Hit 'em Hard (A Bang Brothers Hockey/LA Phantoms prequel)

Power Play

Foul Play

Rock Hard:

Play

Pause

Rewind

Fast Forward

Rock Harder:

Rock Bottom

Rock God

Rock Steady

Rock On

Las Vegas Sidewinders:
Dominic

Cody's Christmas Surprise

Drake

Karl

Anatoli

Zakk

Toli & Tessa

Brock

Vladimir

Royce

Nate

Sidewinders: Ever After

Jared

Dmitri's Christmas Angel

Ian

Dax *(A Royal Protectors/Sidewinders crossover novel)*

Suze's Diary (A Sidewinders Companion Novella)

Sidewinders: Generations:
Zaan

Tore

Anton

Van

Decker

Alaska Blizzard:
Defending Dani

Holding Hailey

Winning Whitney

Losing Laurel

Saving Sara

Chasing Charli

A Very Blizzard Christmas

Tending Tara

Calling Cassie

Playing Peyton

Catching Lana (An Alaska Blizzard Companion Novel)

St. Louis Mavericks (with Brenda Rothert)

Hard Fall

Hard Limit

Hard Pass

Hard Luck

Hard Hit

The Royal Trilogy:

Nowhere Left to Fall

Nowhere Left to Run

Nowhere Left to Hide

Royal Protectors:

Sandor

Cocky Protector (book 1.5, part of the Cocky Heroes Club series)

Xander

Axel

Dax *(A Royal Protectors/Sidewinders crossover novel)*

Inferno:

Salvation's Inferno

Temptation's Inferno

Redemption's Inferno

Tropical Inferno (formerly "Tropical Ice")

Romancing Europe:

Adonis in Athens

Smitten in Santorini

Lucky in Lugano

View Kat's entire collection of books at www.KatMizera.com

ABOUT THE AUTHOR

USA Today Bestselling author Kat Mizera was born in Miami Beach with a healthy dose of wanderlust. She's lived from coast to coast, and everywhere in between, but home is wherever her family is.

A devoted mom and wife to her wonderful and supportive husband (Kevin) and two amazing boys (Nick and Max), Kat loves to travel the globe with her adventurous, hockey loving family. Greece is at the top of that list. She hopes to one day retire there, spending her days writing books on the beach.

Kat is former freelance sports writer who now writes steamy hockey romance about her favorite fictional teams, the Las Vegas Sidewinders and the Alaska Blizzard. The library of novels she's penned also include sexy contemporary stories about baseball stars, alpha sex club owners, special forces heroes, rock stars and royalty. Regardless of genre, her books about bad boys with hearts of gold will steal your breath, rock your world and melt your heart.

WHERE TO FOLLOW KAT:

WEBSITE
FACEBOOK
TWITTER
INSTAGRAM
BOOKBUB
KAT'S PRIVATE FACEBOOK GROUP